1212

1212

YEAR OF THE JOURNEY

by Kathleen McDonnell

Second
Story
Press

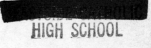

Library and Archives Canada Cataloguing in Publication

McDonnell, Kathleen, 1947-
1212: year of the journey / by Kathleen McDonnell.
ISBN 1-897187-11-4

1. Children's Crusade, 1212--Juvenile fiction. I. Title.
II. Title: Twelve twelve.

PS8575.D669T84 2006   jC813'.54   C2006-903493-1

Edited by Anne Millyard
Cover illustration © Colin Mayne
Maps by P. Rutter
Design by Melissa Kaita

Printed and bound in Canada
First published in the USA in 2007

Second Story Press gratefully acknowledges the support of the Ontario Arts Council and the Canada Council for the Arts for our publishing program. We acknowledge the financial support of the Government of Canada through the Book Publishing Industry Development Program.

Published by
SECOND STORY PRESS
20 Maud Street, Suite 401
Toronto, Ontario, Canada
M5V 2M5

www.secondstorypress.ca
Author's website: www.kathleenmcdonnell.com

For my brothers and sisters

PROLOGUE
April 1233

I HAVE JOURNEYED LONG AND FAR to arrive here at the foot of Montségur — the well-named Safe Mountain, for it is indeed a long and rugged climb to the fortress atop. It is many years since my feet have touched the soil of my homeland, many years since that tumultuous summer of 1212 when thousands walked in a great mass through the fields and towns of Europe, in fevered search of a new world, the world to come.

Now I walk alone, following the way of that great pilgrimage on my return to the place of my childhood. For the moment, I pause here in my journey, propelled by the dream that will not loosen its grip on my soul.

Is this the mountain of my dream? Will it be the face of the one I hope to see as I round the final bend in the path? Her figure appearing above the juniper bushes? I will not know until I make my way to the summit. Now, as I begin my ascent, the memories of that time come flooding back into my mind, as clearly as if they happened yesterday …

CHAPTER 1

The False Knight on the Road
July 1209

As she bit into the plump, golden pear, it felt to Blanche as though the wet sweetness of the entire Languedoc harvest was exploding in her mouth.

Just moments earlier she had been walking through the market with Perrine when she spied a basket of the rose-tinged fruit. She tugged the maidservant's skirt excitedly.

"Perrine, look! The *rousselots* have come in!"

Perrine was busy haggling over the price of a chicken with a man at one of the poultry stalls. She didn't bother looking in the direction Blanche was pointing.

"Don't try to fool old Perrine," she said, rapping the child lightly on the top of the head. "It's far too early for *rousselots.*"

"They are *rousselots!*" Blanche insisted, pulling her toward the fruit stall and pointing to the lush, shiny skins. "See?"

"So they are," Perrine agreed, picking up one of the pears.

"Can we take a basket home?" Blanche asked. "Mama would want us to if she knew they were in already."

3

"Perhaps," Perrine said, shooting a look toward the fruitmonger. "If we can be sure they haven't been picked too early."

"Not a chance, old girl," said the man, holding out one of the pears to Blanche. "Here, let the young one try it. She'll tell you they're at their peak."

Blanche nodded eagerly as the sweet juice cascaded through her mouth.

"He's right, Perrine. It's delicious!"

Now the stallkeeper held out a pear to the maidservant.

"See for yourself," he said with a grin. "Two *deniers* a basket."

Perrine took the fruit warily. She prided herself on her bargaining skills and hated being taken for a too-easy sale. But as soon as she tasted the fruit, Blanche could see the maid's annoyance evaporate. Clearly there was no use in haggling over price. The pear was superbly ripe and such early, wonderful fruit would be quickly snatched up at any price.

They walked away, Perrine carrying the basket, Blanche sucking on the core of her pear till the juice covered her chin.

"I love *rousselot* pears!" she said to Perrine. "I think they're my favorite thing in the whole world."

"That's what you said the other day about cassoulet," the maid replied tartly.

"I love cassoulet too!" Blanche cried.

While Perrine went to look at bunches of white turnips, Blanche wondered how it was that anyone could willingly give up eating the flesh of animals — especially the tasty pork

4

sausages and rich duck confit in cassoulet. She especially loved the smells wafting from the kitchen when Perrine was preparing the duck — rubbing the legs and breast with salt and garlic, then putting them in the big pot of shivering fat to simmer for hours.

Blanche knew, of course, that like all Good Christians she would eventually take the *consolamentum* and renounce the world, including the eating of meat. She had secretly decided to wait until she was an old woman so that she could go on eating cassoulet as long as possible. At the dinner table her parents often stressed that Blanche and her sisters should not enjoy the things of this world too much. It was coming up to harvest time, and Blanche knew that though they dutifully spoke the words of renunciation, her mother and father would bite into the *rousselots* with as much relish as she did.

When she and Perrine arrived home from the market, Blanche was disappointed to find that no one showed much interest in her bounty. Her uncle Guilhabert was at the house, and he and Blanche's father were deep in animated conversation about the town meeting earlier that day.

"Raymond Roger says the papal forces are less than a day's march away," Guilhabert was saying. "He saw them with his own eyes. Thousands bivouaced just outside Montpellier."

Blanche sighed inwardly when she heard the name of the viscount, Raymond Roger Trencavel. It meant that yet again the grown-ups were talking about the soldiers coming down

5

from the north. For weeks, it seemed to Blanche, people in Béziers had talked of nothing else.

"Thousands?" said her father. "Where did the pope get all those troops?"

"The Capetian king, of course," replied Guilhabert, speaking of the current sovereign from that French royal house. "Philip Augustus was all too eager to help out, the better to get his dirty paws on our rich southern lands!"

"I heard the bishop demanded that all the Perfects be turned over to Amaury, his legate," her father said. "Along with the Jews."

Guilhabert threw back his head with a vigorous laugh.

"Oh, yes!" he bellowed. "Turn over the heretics and the Jews! Their own neighbors, and the most illustrious citizens of Béziers. The town council all but laughed in his face!"

Blanche had been hearing the word *heretic* more and more lately. She wanted to break in to ask what it meant, but the men went on talking animatedly.

"If the pope thinks we're about to knuckle under to those northern bumpkins, he's in for a surprise," said her father. "The town is well fortified. We can hold out for a month — longer if we have to."

"By then the fools will have dropped their swords and run home to their fields," Guilhabert added. "They won't so much as stick a toe in to cross the river."

"As usual, Amaury's threats carry about as much weight as a peeled apple!" said her father, and both men broke into hearty laughter again.

The mention of apples prompted Blanche to tell them about the *rousselots*, when a voice broke in from behind her.

"If you ask me, it's you two who are the fools!"

Blanche whirled around and saw her mother standing in the doorway. Her father glowered.

"Who are you calling a fool, woman?"

"You, husband," said her mother, stepping forward forcefully. "And you too, brother, and the rest of the men of Béziers. Look at you all, strutting around like peacocks itching for a fight."

"Dear sister," said Guilhabert, softly touching her shoulder. "I know this talk of siege is frightening, but that's what it is, talk. The bluster of Amaury and the bishops. Nothing will come of it..."

Blanche's mother pulled away sharply.

"Don't patronize me, brother," she snapped. "You don't have any idea what they're capable of. Which is why you are a fool."

The vehemence in her mother's voice shook Blanche. Both her parents had been on edge these past few weeks. Blanche had shrugged it off as the usual railing against the pope and the Church of Rome.

She'd never heard anyone use the term in Béziers, of course, but Blanche was aware that outsiders referred to her family and other Good Christians as *Cathars*, a term that in their eyes perpetuated the slander that they kissed the behinds of cats in their rituals. It was the Good Christians of Languedoc who held fast to the purity of the original faith. The Church of Rome, as Blanche's parents had told her and

7

her sisters since they were babies, had become corrupted by the world, fat and overblown like the cathedrals that were springing up all over Europe with their massive columns and *arc-boutants*. God never intended for His church to come to this — an institution indistinguishable from earthly kingdoms, obsessed with wealth and power, peopled by hypocrite priests and bishops who took women into their beds even as they preached the Fourth Commandment.

But recently, the tone of her parents' talk had changed, with all the focus on what they called the "crusade." Only a few nights ago she'd walked in on a heated discussion between them.

"The Jews have been expelled throughout the north, and in England too," she heard her mother say. "Who's to say it's not going to be our turn next?"

Blanche knew that *expel* meant "drive out," and she couldn't fathom what her mother was talking about. Jews were among the most prosperous people in Béziers. Her father did business with Jewish merchants, many of whom had been fed and entertained in Blanche's own house. Why, Bertrand Aton was Jewish, and he was the viscount's *bayle*, one of the most powerful and respected men in Béziers.

Blanche had been about to ask her mother what she meant, but at the sight of her, both parents clammed up. She pretended she hadn't heard anything, even though her head was more filled with questions than ever. Why would the northerners send Jews away? Where did they go? Would her family get sent away too?

Blanche could see that now was another of those times when she should hold her tongue. And yet she was so excited about the *rousselots* that she couldn't restrain herself any longer. She went to her mother.

"Look, Mama!"

Blanche held up the basket to show her the beautiful rose-tinged pears. Her mother only stared at them, as if they were alien objects she had never laid eyes on before.

"*Rousselots*, Mama. They've come in early this year!"

To Blanche's astonishment, her mother burst into tears.

∾

That night Blanche slept fitfully. One time she woke up and looked around. Both her sisters were sleeping soundly on either side of her, but when she turned toward her parents' bed she saw her mother on her knees beside the bed, her hands cupped over her face in prayer.

Just before dawn, Blanche finally fell into a deep sleep. When she finally awoke. the sun was high in the sky, streaming in through the window, and she was the only one in the room. She was surprised to have slept in so late. It was usually her job to help Perrine with the morning marketing.

When she went out into the big room, Perrine was still there. The maid and Blanche's mother were packing a basket with bread, a large round of cheese, some jugs of beer, turnips and the *rousselot* pears. They were whipping around the room at such a hectic pace that the woodcocks hanging in the corner were swaying back and forth.

"Mama? Perrine? What about the marketing?"

Her mother shook her head impatiently.

"No market today, Blanchette. We're getting ready to go to the cathedral."

The cathedral? Of course, Blanche thought. Today was the feast day of Saint Mary Magdalene! One of the few days of the year her family and the other Good Christians of Béziers deigned to set foot inside the great church. Much as they disapproved of the popes' penchant for naming so many "saints" — to the point that they were becoming indistinguishable from a panoply of pagan gods — to the Good Christians Mary Magdalene was different: she was the most exalted among the apostles, outranking even Peter and his successors. According to the old legends, Mary Magdalene was the beloved of Jesus himself, the one to whom he first appeared after discarding his earthly body. So every year on the twenty-second of July, the Good Christians joined with their more orthodox brethren to attend the mass in her honor, though of course at the Communion they declined to take the wafer in their mouths.

But why were Perrine and Mama packing all this food? And where was Papa?

"Your father is at the ramparts, with the rest of the men," said her mother.

"What's he doing there?"

"There's no time to explain now, Blanchette. Go and pack some things to wear. We may be gone a few days."

"Gone?" Blanche objected. "I thought you said we were going to the cathedral."

Perrine stepped forward and rapped her on the head, not at all playfully as she had the day before.

"Shut your mouth and do as your mother says!"

Blanche ran quickly into the bedroom, stung and humiliated by Perrine's harsh tone. As she went through her clothes, she fought back tears. What was Papa doing at the ramparts? Why were Perrine and Mama so irritable? Why wouldn't anyone tell her what was going on?

She heard a commotion and looked out the window. Clusters of people — mostly women and children — were streaming up the street, carrying bundles of clothing and baskets of food. Blanche realized they were all making their way up the hill, toward the cathedral.

A shiver ran down her spine. Hurriedly she went back to her packing.

They all left the house, Perrine going on ahead with the two younger girls. Blanche watched as her mother lowered the heavy latch on the door, then turned to catch up with Perrine. A hand grabbed her shoulder and she whirled around.

Her mother was looking at her with a strange ferocity and terror that Blanche had never seen before.

"Remember, Blanchette," she said, squeezing her daughter's shoulder even harder. "You are named for Blanche de Laurac, a great holy woman and staunch defender of the faith. You must never, ever forget that!"

"I won't, Mama," Blanche murmured, but by now she was terrified beyond words at her mother's erratic behavior. Why would she say such a strange thing at a time like this?

As they joined the throng streaming up the hill, her mother was hailed by her cousin Philippa, carrying her baby of only a few months and with two young children gripping her skirt.

"Philippa!" Her mother called out.

"Alazais!" Philippa exclaimed. "Have you heard news from the ramparts?"

A voice called out from behind them.

"The enemy has broken through the gates! They've begun crossing the bridge and they're not far behind."

They turned to see a sentry racing up from behind them. His words brought shouts of consternation from the crowd.

"God help us!"

"How could that happen?"

"Some boys went out to heckle the crusaders and left the gate down when they scrambled back in," the sentry called back as he continued up the hill.

Philippa clutched her baby tightly to her chest. Blanche saw her mother put a hand on her cousin's shoulder.

"Don't worry, Philippa. Bernard and the men will beat them back down the river. Even if some have managed to enter the city, we will be safe in the cathedral."

Blanche felt reassured by her mother's words. And things were starting to make sense now. The pope's crusading army had arrived at the city gates, as her parents and uncle had been speculating all these weeks. So while the men fought them off, the women and children would take refuge for a few days in the churches of Béziers, for no soldier would commit sacrilege by bringing arms into the house of God.

Blanche wondered about her father. Surely the men would be safe on the battlements surrounding the city. She looked down toward the river, hoping to see something, but there was nothing but the distant zing! of mangonels and trebuchets, followed by a barrage of shouts.

She turned back and resumed walking up the hill. She was surrounded by people, but her mother and Perrine were nowhere to be seen. They had to be farther ahead, she decided, and scrambled to catch up. After running a way up the hill, she stopped to catch her breath. Still no sign of her mother, Perrine and her sisters. Perhaps she was mistaken about having fallen behind herself. Maybe her mother was back in the crowd below, still talking with cousin Philippa and the other women.

She spied a woman carrying a baby. Philippa! Her mother had to be nearby.

"Aunt Philippa! Do you know where my —?"

The woman turned toward her, and Blanche saw it wasn't Philippa at all. Then she surveyed the crowd: not a single familiar face among them. She realized that as small as her own world seemed, Béziers was in truth a large city, with many people she did not know.

"Mama! Mama, where are you?"

Blanche ran back down the hill, a growing sense of panic gripping her. The crowd was thinning out now. Most of the women and children had mounted the hill and turned toward the cathedral.

She was about to turn and race back up the hill after them. Then she spied the soldiers.

She was high up enough to look down on the river Orb, and as they scrambled across the ancient strong bridge she could see they wore tunics with the figure of the cross roughly stitched onto the front. Many were brandishing swords high over their heads.

"What in heaven's name are you doing out here alone?"

She whirled around and looked into the face of a man, one she thought looked familiar.

"Why aren't you in the cathedral with the others?"

Blanche sniffed fearfully.

"I'm looking for my mother. I don't know where she is."

She realized now that the man was someone her father did business with. She couldn't remember his name, but she recognized him as one of the Jewish wool merchants.

"I know you," he said. "You're Bernard D'Alayrac's daughter."

Blanche nodded, but the man was looking away from her, toward the lower town and the bridge. Hundreds of soldiers were streaming across it, and it was clear from the commotion that they'd gotten through the gate and were making their way into the heart of the town.

"There's no time to get to the cathedral," he told her. "The soldiers will be here soon."

"What should I do?"

"Come with me," said the man.

He led her around a corner to his shop. Out front sat a wagon piled high with bales of wool just arrived from the countryside. The man slit open one of the bales and pulled out several large balls of wool.

"Here," he said, pointing to the open space inside the bale. "You can fit in there. Climb in."

"Inside the wool?" said Blanche, uncertain whether that was what he really meant.

The man nodded and shoved her quickly into the bale, pulling the sack down to cover the opening he'd made.

"There. Now stay here and don't come out until I or one of your parents comes to get you."

"Here?" Blanche said. "Why can't I hide in your shop?"

The man shook his head firmly.

"The soldiers will be searching everywhere. Except here. Now be quiet. Don't stir. Don't even peek out. I'll be back for you when I can."

The man closed the flap over the bale, and Blanche was almost completely enclosed in the soft wool. She expected that it would be hot inside the bale, but the wool had recently been washed and was still damp and cool.

Was the merchant going to the cathedral with the others? If so, why didn't he take her with him? Everything had happened so fast that she hadn't thought to ask him. She called out after him, but her voice was smothered by the growing clamor of the advancing soldiers.

Had they come to "expel" her family and the other Good Christians? The thought chilled her. What if they forced her mother and sisters to leave right away? Where would they go? How would she find them?

And what about her father? Blanche knew he was down on the battlements, fighting to keep the crusaders from entering the town. What was he doing now? Had they taken him prisoner?

The thundering of feet pounding up the hill grew louder and louder. Blanche heard shouts and the clang of metal. The soldiers were not far from where she lay ensconced in the wool bale. There was a narrow crack where the man had slit the bale, and despite what he'd told her, Blanche couldn't keep herself from peeking through it.

A cluster of foot soldiers surrounded a horse. Astride it was a man in gray metal armor. In one hand he carried a long spear, in the other a shield bearing a crest of what looked like a lion with a forked tail. The visor of his helmet almost completely covered the upper part of his face, except for a narrow slit for his eyes.

Blanche had never seen a knight in armor before, and the sight of him was unsettling. Encased in all that metal, he looked like some alien, not-quite-human being. As she watched him, Blanche recalled the melody of a popular riddle song about a boy who meets the devil disguised as a knight:

> "Has your mother more than you?" said the False Knight on the road.
> "None of them's for you," said the child and he stood.

"The men are wondering what to do, sire," she heard one of the soldiers say. "The people have all taken sanctuary in the cathedral."

"No sanctuary for heretics," said the man astride the horse. "Their very presence in the house of God is an abomination."

"But, sire, there are hundreds packed in there, heretic and faithful alike. How will we tell them apart?"

"No point in trying," said the knight offhandedly. "They'll protect one another anyway. Kill them all. God will know His own."

The soldiers looked at one another, unbelieving.

"All?"

"But, sire ..."

"You have your orders," said the knight brusquely. "Now go."

As the soldiers hurried off, there was a commotion. Blanche looked over to see another group of soldiers leading a man toward the knight. He walked slowly, with an air of defiance, despite the fact that his hands were bound behind his back. Blanche recognized him instantly as Aimery Golairan, one of the Perfects, a holy man of the Good Christians

"See this prize we got!" one of the men was shouting. "One of the leaders!"

"He came out of the cathedral," said another. "Offered his life if we'd spare the ones inside."

"That's noble of you, heathen," said the knight.

Aimery Golairan stiffened.

"Nobility has nothing to do with it," he said calmly. "I have no fear of death."

"Why?" said the knight. "Because you've taken your blasphemous version of last rites?"

"You ought to be afraid!" said one of the soldiers. "Because you're going to burn in hell for all eternity!"

The holy man didn't blink an eye.

"Your corrupt doctrines twist the truth beyond all recognition. I am not going to hell, I am leaving it. Hell is here, on this earthly plane, created by Satan himself. Eternity is the creation of the God of Pure Love. You do me a kindness to dispatch me there."

"A kindness we won't bestow," said the commander. "Until you've been made to see the error of your ways."

Blanche saw the knight bend down from his mount and gesture to one of the soldiers. The soldier nodded in return, then took a knife from the sheath on his belt and raised it close to Aimery Golairan's head. Then, with a great flourish, the knight on the horse lifted the metal helmet off his head and threw it on the ground beside him.

"Here, heretic!" he cried, leaning down and putting his face close to Aimery's "Behold the face of God's avenging angel!"

Blanche watched the scene in terror, scarcely daring to breathe.

"I think I hear a bell," said the False Knight on the road.
"It's ringing you to hell," said the child and he stood.

In that instant, the knight's face burned itself onto Blanche's memory. She felt herself gripped by waves of fear and nausea.

"Take him to Carcassonne!" the knight ordered, still looking down at Aimery, "where he can bid his fellow believers heed the words of the Gospel of Saint Matthew, chapter eighteen, verse nine."

The last thing Blanche heard as she lost consciousness was the pounding of horse's hooves as the knight's voice rang out:

"If thine eye offend thee, pluck it out!"

༒

She was being carried in a pouch, something like the sling her mother used to tote her and her sisters when they were babies. It was dark and warm and safe. Then on one side of the pouch she noticed a long slit in the fabric. Through the slit she thought she could make out a pair of eyes, looking at her. She turned away, not wanting to look back at them. Outside the pouch there was a low growling sound, as if a small animal was trying to gnaw its way through the fabric. She had the sense that there was something terrible out there on the other side of the pouch, something she didn't want to see.

Blanche started awake, still encased in damp wool. How long had she been asleep, she wondered. Minutes? Hours?

She lifted the flap of the bale with one finger and peeked out. The sun had passed behind the cathedral spire. It was well on into the afternoon. Carefully she poked her head out of the bale and looked around. No sign of any living thing. An eerie silence seemed to envelop the whole city.

There was a faint smell of something burning in the distance. She craned her neck and looked up the hill. Curls of black smoke wafted up into the air. What was going on? Where was everyone? Would the merchant come back for her? Had he found her mother and told her where Blanche was hiding?

She wriggled out of the bale and climbed down from the cart. She had been hunched up in the bale for so long, her limbs felt like jelly, and her legs almost buckled underneath her.

Suddenly she heard the clatter of horses' hooves. Soldiers! Frantically, she tried to clamber back onto the cart but only managed to overturn it completely.

"Halt!"

The bale tumbled open and spilled out bundles of soft wool, covering her face. She couldn't see who spoke or tell which direction the voice came from. Blanche put her head down and prayed silently, keeping utterly still as the pounding of the hooves drew nearer and nearer to the overturned cart. Then, abruptly, they stopped.

She felt the wool on top of her being pulled away.

"What in the name of heaven …?"

Blanche looked up. A young knight was standing over her. He wore a hood and hauberk of chain mail, covered partly by a loose cloth tunic stained with patches of blood.

"What are you doing here?"

She was too frightened to speak. All she could do was shake her head helplessly.

"You've been hiding here all this time, little Bitteroise?"

The young knight didn't wait for an answer. He looked up the street. More horses were coming. To Blanche's astonishment, he threw the wool over her again and laid the bale wrap on top of the pile.

"Stay there," he hissed at her. "Don't move!"

The pounding of the horses' hooves came to a halt. Blanche heard a man's voice.

"Looks as if the knight from Lyon has found himself some nice Languedoc wool!"

Several other men's voices joined in, with jocular laughter.

"Some loot you got there."

"You'll do much better in the upper town, my friend."

"Their wool is already spun!"

Blanche heard the young knight shout over to the men.

"I have no interest in the wool. I just wanted to see what knocked this cart over."

"Don't be a fool," one of the men called back. "There's lots of good stuff in the upper town. Go on, help yourself."

"I thought we came to rid this city of heresy, not rob the Bitterois of their possessions."

"What do you care? Or does your sympathy for fellow southerners carry more weight than your allegiance to the Holy Father and the king?"

"My actions today have shown clearly enough where my allegiance lies," the knight responded sharply. "I don't have to answer to the likes of you."

"Fine, Lyon," the soldier called back. "Suit yourself. But

where these wretched Bitterois have gone, they won't have any use for their possessions."

Blanche heard more laughter from the men as they rode off. So it was true. Her mother and sisters and all the Bitterois had been driven out by the crusaders. But why was this young knight hiding her from the others? Surely they intended to send her away to join her family. Blanche hoped it wasn't too far, wherever it was.

The gallop of the horses died away, and Blanche felt the wool being lifted off her again. She looked up at the young knight.

"Do you know where all the people have gone?"

A strange, contorted look came over the knight's face. It almost seemed to Blanche that he was stifling sobs. He quickly turned his face away and murmured something.

"Father, forgive us, for we know not what we do."

Without warning, he lifted the empty bale bag, whipped it around Blanche and carried her over to his horse.

"Now do as I tell you. Keep your head down, be quiet and try not to move around."

He hoisted her onto the horse's back, then mounted behind her. He pulled the reins as the horse began to trot, then dug in his heels to make the animal go faster.

Blanche turned her head slightly and whispered, "Are we going to where my mother and sisters are?"

"No." His voice sounded strained.

If he wasn't taking her to where her family and the others were, where were they going? What was he going to do with her?

As they rode through the city gates, Blanche felt ripples of anxiety through her body. She turned back. Billows of dark smoke were rising everywhere along the top of the wall.

The city of Béziers was in flames.

৵

CHAPTER 2
The First Night of Pesach
April 1210

As Abel made his way down from rue des Carreaux, he saw crowds of people streaming out of the church of Saint Frobert carrying what looked like slender green banners. Adults, children, even babies in their mothers' arms were clutching them. As he moved closer, Abel could see they were olive and palm branches, and he watched in fascination as the people moved aside to form a passageway for a donkey with a roughly carved wooden figure on its back. Behind the donkey a man in dark robes carried a cross mounted on a long pole. There was a figure hanging from the cross, which was garlanded with flowers and more palm fronds.

He recalled what his father had said earlier about today being a Christian feast day. Abel had had little to do with the Christians of Troyes. All he knew was what he had learned from the rabbi at the yeshiva — that they worshipped a prophet called Jesus who had lived more than a thousand years ago. They believed that this man Jesus was the Messiah, which Abel knew was preposterous, because of course the world still awaited the coming of the Messiah at *Olam Ha-Ba*, the world to come. Abel thought it likely that the suffering figure on the cross was Jesus. These Christians were an odd people, with their statues and palm fronds and garlands.

The crowd continued to spill out onto the street, and Abel soon found himself surrounded. He tried to blend into the throng as best he could, but he was carrying no branch, and with the black cap on his head he stood out anyway. For a few moments he was frightened, overwhelmed by the size of the crowd and his own sense of strangeness in it. He soon realized with relief that his size worked to his advantage, since only the children in the crowd seemed to notice him. As he took in their curious stares, it occurred to him that they had likely never laid eyes on a Jewish child before. Grown-ups had occasion to leave the Broce-aux-Juifs, the Jewish district, often enough — the men to do business in the rue du Chaperon, the women to shop at the markets. But young people like Abel rarely ventured out into the city proper. The yeshiva, the synagogue, his relatives, all the parts of his entire world were contained within a few steps of his home in the Broce-aux-Juifs.

Today he had been sent out on a special errand. His father was treating a patient with a high fever, and needed a special preparation of mandrake and gentian root to try to bring it down. Normally Abel's mother would go to the apothecary to fetch it, but she was busy with the preparations for the Seder that night. His father decided Abel should go, over his mother's protestations.

"That's all the way over to the Grande Rue," she said.

"He's nearly eleven years old. And it's a quiet day in the city. The streets are empty. The Christians are all in their churches."

Abel hurried on through the crowd. As he passed the church, he stole a quick look above the main entrance. His father had told him that hidden behind the statue of Saint Frobert was a Star of David. Some years before Abel was born, when the Christians had seized the synagogue on the rue de vieille Rome, they had expunged all signs of its Jewish character, but as the Star of David was chiseled right into the stone archway, the best they could do was cover it up. Abel thought he could make out the outlines of the sacred symbol behind the statue.

He was glad to put distance between himself and the Christian crowd. As he went on, he approached the stone wall surrounding the old city, so old that it dated back to the days of the Roman emperors. As he passed through the Artaud gate, he took a deep breath. This was the very first time in his life that he had ventured beyond the wall on his own, and he felt a strange mixture of anticipation and dread.

৵

"Who would like to comment on why Rashi does not refer to the Midrash in this passage?"

The rabbi posed the question to the class of boys studying the writings of Solomon ben Isaac, whose name — in its shortened form of Rashi — was revered in Jewish communities from England to the Rhineland to faraway Baghdad, more than a hundred years after his death. The Jews of Troyes were especially proud of their native son, and his commentary on the Torah was studied with great reverence in the yeshiva.

Abel was having trouble keeping his mind on what the rabbi was saying. His thoughts kept wandering back to his experiences in the city that morning. His head was a jumble of images and sensations: the vast halls of the cloth merchants in the rue du Chaperon, the knights casually chatting in their impressive garments on the steps of the Commandery of the Templars, the tilted buildings of Cat's Alley, a street so narrow that the houses leaned against one another over it. Things that Abel had only heard of, that had taken on an oversized, fantastical quality in his mind, he was now seeing.

He passed the Abbey of Notre-Dame-aux-Nonnains and saw, by the canal, the ruins of the great fire that had destroyed so much of the city years before Abel was born. The sight of it made real the terrible times his parents had often spoken of, when within just a few years Troyes had suffered a flood, a severe famine and the great fire. At the time, some people had blamed the Jews, claiming that the presence of so many nonbelievers had brought God's wrath on the city. Abel's parents and the rest of the Jews of Troyes had watched helplessly as the city authorities stripped the synagogues of their sacred Hebrew symbols and remade them into churches for the Christians.

"That's all in the past," his father was always careful to emphasize. "Now are the good times. Here in Troyes we are showing the rest of the world that Christians and Jews can live side by side in peace."

The rabbi's voice broke in on Abel's musings.

"Master ben Meir? Perhaps as the namesake of one of the subjects at hand, you have something to add?"

"Add? To what, sir?" Abel stammered.

"To our discussion of Rashi's commentary on the passage about the brothers Cain and Abel. A discussion to which you, apparently, have not been listening."

"I was distracted, Rabbi. I am sorry."

The rabbi turned to the class.

"Master ben Meir apparently has the same cavalier attitude as his father toward the work of our great patriarch Rashi."

Abel's face burned with embarrassment. He was all too aware of what the rabbi was talking about. His father's views had always been the subject of much discussion at the synagogue, but lately even more so. He had been championing the writings of a newer talmudic scholar, Moses ben Maimon, known as Maimonides, which the rabbis of Troyes regarded as a slight to Rashi's life and work. What was worse, some Jews considered Maimonides a heretic and dismissed his views because he had lived among the Muslims in Egypt.

All this bothered Abel's father no end.

"I intend no disrespect to our great ancestor Rashi," he insisted. "Rashi himself regarded the Talmud as a living document, to be questioned and pondered, not carved in stone for all time.

"We have much to learn from the Muslims," he said to anyone who would listen. "Look at their advances in science, their innovations in numbers and mathematics. Even the Christians have great poets and thinkers, like Abelard of Nantes. We Jews cannot afford to build walls enclosing ourselves. There are wonderful new currents of thought all around us. We are on the cusp of the new age, the time foretold by the prophet Isaiah, in which the religions will not fear one another but learn from one another."

Much as he admired his father's independence of mind, Abel sometimes wished he wouldn't be so vocal in expressing his views.

He turned back to the passage from Rashi, resolving to be a good student and make up for his father's unconventional beliefs.

ൟ

When he arrived home from the yeshiva, the house was filled with the aroma of roasting shank of lamb. His mother, aunt and sisters were bustling around the room, carrying sheets of matzo to the table and doing the final preparations on other Seder delicacies. They were about to begin the celebration of the first night of Pesach, Passover, the eight holy days commemorating how God instructed the Angel of Death to spare the first-born of Israel, and how the great prophet Moses led the people out of the land of Egypt. As they began to assemble around the table, his father bent down and gave him a warm embrace, and Abel felt all his earlier embarrassment and ambivalence melt away. Unlike many of the men he knew, his father was rarely harsh or demanding toward his children, and freely showed his tender feelings for them. Now, as he felt himself wrapped in his father's strong arms, Abel's mind wandered back to the day, indelibly etched in his memory, when his father had carried him to the yeshiva on his fifth birthday. There, before the rabbi and the elders, Abel dutifully recited what he had been memorizing for weeks: the Hebrew alphabet and the sacred incantation against forgetfulness. Then his father scooped him up in his arms again and carried him all the way down to the bank of the river Seine.

"Now begins your study of the Torah," he had told Abel with great solemnity. "It is a task that, like this great rushing river, will never end."

Abel's eyes ran over the table now before him. On the Seder plate were foods which symbolized the struggle of his ancestors as slaves in ancient Egypt. There was *moror*, the bitter herb which represented the suffering the Jews had endured, and *charoset*, a mixture of nuts, chopped apples and wine, red-brown in color like the clay from which the the Jews were forced to make bricks. On the table Abel also saw three pieces of flat bread called *matzos*, which he knew had a special meaning as well. When the Jews were finally escaping from their bondage they didn't have time to allow the baking bread to leaven, and so had to eat it flat, just as they were doing now at the Seder in commemoration.

Looking around at the faces of his parents, his sisters, his aunt and uncle and aged grandmother, all bathed in the warm, flickering glow of the candles, Abel felt a transporting happiness. His sortie into the world outside the Broce-aux-Juifs had been exciting but a bit scary, and now he was glad to be back in the safe, loving bosom of his family.

He'd been waiting with anticipation for the moment when he, as the youngest at the table, would ask the timeless question of the first night of Pesach. Now he looked over at his father, who nodded at him to begin.

"Ma nishtanah halailah hazeh mikol halailot?" *Why is this night different from all others?*

❧

CHAPTER 3
The Feast of Fools
December 1211

Orientis Partibus, adventavit asinus
Pulcher et fortissimus, Sarcinis aptissimus

As THE CONGREGATION SANG, Étienne watched the
small children run up and down the aisles of the Abbey of
the Trinity, laughing, banging on pots, screeching and making animal noises. All around him he saw people in various
outlandish costumes — masks, homemade donkey head-
dresses, jesters' hoods with dangling bells. A few men were
decked out in women's gowns and headcoverings, and some
even hiked up their skirts in mock lasciviousness. On the
altar a priest presided over the service, but his vestments
were in complete disarray — the chasuble was turned inside
out, the amice was tied around his waist and a cincture was
wrapped around his head and left dangling from his nose.

Suddenly the doors of the cathedral swung open, and a
clutch of altar boys, in dirty, tattered garments led a donkey
into the church, which set off a chorus of loud, spirited braying throughout the congregation.

From the east the donkey came,
fed on barley and rough hay

Ears like wings and eyes like flame,
Donkey, pull our sins away!
Wrap him now in cloth of gold;
All rejoice who see him pass
Mirth inhabit young and old,
on this feast day of the Ass!

After the donkey had been led all around the church, the priest stepped forward and called for decorum, angrily denouncing the congregation's rowdy behavior. Of course Étienne knew, as did everyone around him, that the priest wasn't serious, that the mock scolding was just part of the festivities, which were now building up to the main event. He watched the procession make its way up the centre aisle of the cathedral. A youth about his own age, wearing a mitre and carrying a bishop's staff, approached the altar. The choirboys began reciting the Magnificat, a psalm of praise. When they got to the words "He has brought down the powerful from their thrones, and lifted up the lowly," the priest stepped forward again and dumped a large pail of water over the boy's head.

"All hail the Boy Bishop!"

The entire congregation exploded in laughter and cheers.

Every year a boy in the parish was chosen to serve as Boy Bishop for the month leading up to the Feast of the Holy Innocents at the end of December. His investiture always took place on the Feast of Saint Nicholas, in recognition of the young age at which Saint Nicholas himself had become a bishop. It was considered a great honor to be chosen Boy Bishop, one that wasn't limited to children of the nobility. At the Abbey of the Trinity, as in many parishes, the choirboys held an election to choose one of their number, which meant that boys of any station — town or country, rich or poor — were eligible to be Boy Bishop. There had been a time when Étienne himself had hoped that he might one day be chosen to wear the mitre and backward vestments and lead the congregation in the raucous responses to the "Song of the Ass." But now that he had to work for his keep, he no longer had time to serve in the choir.

So on this crisp December night, Étienne was just one of the crowd in the torchlight parade winding its way through the streets of Vendôme. At various points on the processional route, the Boy Bishop stopped to bestow a blessing on the townspeople in exchange for money and gifts, and jugglers and musicians entertained the crowd from atop wagons. Finally the parade arrived in the village square, where a line of carts was already set up in a semicircle for the performance of the three short plays depicting well-known incidents drawn from the life of Saint Nicholas. The first told of how Saint Nicholas restored treasure stolen by three thieves named Click, Pinchdice and Razor, villains whom the crowd jeered with gusto. The second told the tale of how Saint Nicholas rescued three mariners caught in a raging storm at sea. The players used a large sheet of cloth for the sea, flapping it up and down to suggest the rolling waves.

Once the seas were calmed and the cloth put back out of sight, the men playing the mariners quickly changed costume, transforming themselves into young girls with high-pitched voices, much to the delight and hilarity of the crowd. This last play was the best known of all the tales about Saint Nicholas, about three sisters who despaired of ever finding suitors because their family was too poor to afford dowries for them. When he heard of the sisters' plight, Saint Nicholas climbed on the roof of their house and dropped the three bags loaded with gold coins down the chimney. Thus the sisters were able to marry, and the play ended with a triple wedding.

It was getting late, Étienne realized. It would take him much of the night to walk back to Cloyes. As he began to make his way toward the city gate, he noticed a crowd of people gathered around one of the wagons. On top of the wagon was a slight man in a rough brown robe, his head shaved bald on the top in a tonsure.

"Today is the day we throw off our sorrows and cares and play with one another, as little children do. For I say to you that this is the true message of the Boy Bishop: that we are never closer to God than when we are joyous and high-spirited as children, when we sing His praises as the birds of the air, when we run free as the beasts of the field."

Étienne walked over to get a better look at the speaker. He'd never seen one of these holy beggars, called mendicants, before. He had heard about them, and especially about their spiritual leader, Francis of Assisi, who had given up all his wealth to live a life of holy poverty. Francis, it was said, spoke to the birds and animals, the lowliest of God's creatures, and by the power of his words alone had tamed the man-eating wolves of Gubbio. The followers of Francis were becoming more and more numerous, spreading his teachings far beyond his home in Umbria into the towns and villages of France.

"We are all the beloved children of God," the brown-robed man went on. "All the creatures of the earth are equal in His eyes and in His love — not just on this day, but every day! And the poorest of the poor, who have nowhere to lay their heads, are the most blessed among men. For Christ our Lord has said 'the Last shall be First,' and on the last day He shall bring down the powerful from their thrones and lift up the lowly."

A few in the crowd snickered, thinking no one could take seriously the ravings of a beggar. But the mendicant's stirring words made a deep impression on Étienne. Rich and poor, children and elders — all equal in the eyes of God. That was the way it should be, he thought to himself — in this world as well as the next.

He couldn't stay to listen to any more of the man's preaching. Not unless he wanted to risk getting a licking from his uncle Gaston.

৯

As Étienne tended his small cooking fire on the hillside outside Cloyes, one of the lambs kept inching toward him. He recognized it as a runt, perpetually crowded out from the mother's teat by its larger, bolder siblings. As often happened with runts, this one had been constantly coming up to him, begging for food. He tried to shoo it away, but it was persistent, sniffing the ground around Étienne for crumbs of bread.

After waving it away several times, he started to lose patience. He picked up a stick and gave the runt a good sharp whack on the backside. The lamb shrank away, turning to see if he was going to do it again.

Étienne recalled what the follower of Francis had said about God's love for all creatures and immediately felt ashamed of what he had done. At that moment he realized he'd gotten so caught up in the festivities in Vendôme that he'd gone a whole day without thinking about his mother. Now sorrow flooded back into his heart with renewed force, the pain as sharp as the day he'd watched her walk down the road that led out of Cloyes.

In some ways it was almost a relief when his mother decided to join the Beguine community. The strain of living with her the past few years had become exhausting, with her unrelenting stream of visions — of the Cross, the bleeding wounds of Jesus, the blinding light of the Eucharist. She had been like that for as long as he could remember. Then came the terrible time when he was a small boy, a time that Étienne tried his best to put out of his mind, when the wave of plague swept through the Orléanais and claimed the lives of his father and baby brother within days of each other.

After that, his mother's visions became more frequent and intense. Some in the village thought she was a saint. Others said she was mad or possessed by the devil. In time she learned about the Beguines, a community of women who lived only for prayer and good works, and who welcomed women of any station, even peasants like herself. She became convinced that her calling lay with them. Étienne remembered clearly the day she'd told him of her intentions. God was calling her, she said. It was His will that she renounce all worldly ties and join the Beguine community so that she could live in closer union with Him.

Étienne was stunned. After all the sorrows that had befallen them, after all they'd been through together, how could she contemplate such a thing? She was all he had in the world.

"I not some worldly tie," he cried. "I am your son!"

She just gazed at him with a faraway look and said he must not be angry with her, for she was only doing God's will. The Beguine community was in Liège, only a couple of days' walk from Cloyes, she told him. He could come visit her from time to time. She would leave Étienne in the care of her brother, his uncle Gaston.

"Gaston will take good care of you until you're of an age to make your own way."

The very day his mother had left for Liège, Gaston announced that he'd hired Étienne out to one of the local sheep farmers. Since he wouldn't have time to go back and forth to Vendôme anymore, he'd have to drop out of the choir.

"This way you can work longer hours. You'll earn more."

"But, Uncle, my mother wouldn't want me to leave the choir," Étienne objected. "I have been a member since I was old enough to sing."

"Too bad." Gaston shrugged. "You're under my roof now. You're almost a man, and a man has to earn his keep."

Étienne was devastated. He thought of defying Gaston outright. But what if his uncle turned him out of his house? Then he'd be forced to resort to begging. He didn't want to become one of those pathetic young men roaming the streets of Vendôme with their hands perpetually outstretched.

He realized there was no way around it. He was dependent on Gaston. He asked for permission to go to the abbey for one more practice so that he could tell Brother Ignace that he was withdrawing from the choir, and why.

"Otherwise he'll think I'm just lazy and disobedient."

Gaston grudgingly agreed.

"Fine. You can go this one last time."

The next morning Étienne made his way across the fields to Vendôme, trying not to think about the fact that this would be his last time singing with the choir. When he arrived at the abbey, they were already in the midst of practicing hymns to the Blessed Virgin for Whitsunday.

Brother Ignace motioned to Étienne to take his place.

Regina coeli, laetare, Alleluia!

As Étienne opened his mouth to sing, he felt a tightening in his throat. Only the faintest sound came out. He looked around and was relieved to see that neither Brother Ignace nor the other boys seemed to notice anything. He took a deep breath and tried to ignore the strange sensation.

Quia quem meruisti portare.
Alleluia! Alleluia!

To his relief, the tightness seemed to be letting up as the hymn progressed. But something happened when he got to the last line.

Ora, ora, ora pro nobis Deum

As his lips encircled the long *O*'s, his voice suddenly broke into a great, choking sob. The singing came to an abrupt halt, as the boys all turned and looked at Étienne in shock.

He bolted from the gallery, racing down the stairway, his face burning with shame.

He heard Brother Ignace's voice behind him. He wanted to run all the way back to Cloyes so he wouldn't have to face him or the other boys. He was sure Brother Ignace would be furious with him. But when the friar called his name, his voice was unexpectedly gentle.

"What is it, my son?"

In a great rush of words and tears, Étienne told him about his uncle's decision. Brother Ignace listened, softly putting his hand on the boy's shoulder.

"I am so sorry to hear this, Étienne. The Lord will miss hearing that beautiful voice of yours singing His praises. But the Fourth Commandment says, 'Honor thy father and thy mother,' and your uncle has taken the place of your departed father on this earth. His wishes must be obeyed."

Father, not my will but thine be done.

Étienne tried to remind himself that his sorrows were as nothing compared with the suffering of Jesus Christ on the cross. But the thought only deepened his feeling of despair. The prospect of redemption, of being truly loved and embraced in the arms of God — all seemed impossibly remote to him now.

"Hail, friend!"

He was startled by the sound of a voice coming out of the darkness. Not that it was unusual to find people walking the relatively short distances between villages in the Orléanais at night, especially when the weather was mild. But the sight of a traveler emerging out of the mist unnerved Étienne.

"Hail!" he called out. "Who goes there?"

"A friend," the stranger replied. "I'm making my way to Picardy, and I saw your fire."

The man was short, with a grizzled face of indeterminate age. He wore a tattered cloak that clearly had seen better days. It almost looked to Étienne like a knight's cape, but of course a knight would have been traveling on horseback, not tromping through the hills of the Orléanais in the middle of the night.

"Mind if I stop and rest awhile?"

"Join me," said Étienne, clearing brush away from a spot near the fire. "I was cooking up a small hare. I'm sorry I have none of it left to offer you. I wanted to be sure to finish it before midnight."

"Of course," said the man. "No Christian may eat animal flesh on Friday."

"I do have a bit of bread left," said Étienne, immediately wishing he'd kept his mouth shut. The small end of the loaf was all he would have to eat between now and Saturday morning.

"Thank you, I will have some," said the stranger.

Étienne took the knob of bread out of his satchel and handed it to the man, who took it and began gnawing on it. They sat without speaking for what seemed to Étienne ages. The man seemed to be savoring the bread as if it were the last meal he would have for a long time.

He finished it and abruptly stood up.

"I'll be on my way, then."

"So soon?" Étienne asked. "You're welcome to stay by the fire a bit longer."

"Many thanks," said the stranger, "but I must get to Picardy by morning. I have important business there."

"Oh?" said Étienne. "What's your trade?"

"I deal in sacred relics," replied the man. "Would you like to see some of my wares?"

Étienne nodded eagerly. It was rare for a peasant like himself to get a chance to see holy relics up close.

The man opened his satchel, took out a reliquary and displayed the contents to Étienne.

"Here," he said, pointing to a small sack. "This contains the toenail clippings of Saint Wilgefortis, and here is a piece of wood from the true cross."

Étienne was aware that since the crusades to the Holy Land began over a century earlier, there were countless peddlers tromping across Europe claiming to have brought back relics of the true cross. They certainly couldn't all be telling the truth.

"Here's something that should appeal to a young person like yourself," the man was saying.

"What is it?"

"One of the bones of Saint Nicholas, the patron saint of children."

"Saint Nicholas is my favorite saint!" Étienne exclaimed. "I pray to him every night. But is it truly —"

He stopped himself and looked at the man.

"You're wondering if it's real?" the peddler said. "I assure you it is. You can tell by the aroma — the *manna di Santa Nicola*. It's unmistakable."

Étienne held the bone up to his nostril.

"See?" said the man. "You can smell it, can't you?"

Étienne nodded, having no idea whether this faint, nondescript odor was that he was supposed to smell.

"Where did you get it?" he asked the peddler.

"From a knight who was in Myra when it was sacked by the Saracens. He and the other crusaders risked their lives to smuggle these bones out."

"I wish I could go on a crusade," said Étienne.

"Maybe you will someday," said the man, as he began to close the reliquary.

Étienne shook his head.

"Shepherds don't go on crusades."

"How can you know what God has in store for you? Didn't Jesus Christ Himself say 'the last shall be first'?"

Étienne almost snapped at the man for mocking him but restrained himself, not wanting to seem rude. He watched as the man put the reliquary back in his satchel.

"Wait, don't forget this one," said Étienne, holding out the bone.

The man shook his head.

"No, friend. You are the Good Shepherd. Keep it as payment for sharing your meal with me."

Before Étienne could say any more, the stranger was gone, his ragged cape disappearing into the mist.

He looked at the bone. He had no idea if it really was a true relic of Saint Nicholas. He felt oddly comforted by it all the same.

A wave of great fatigue came over him. He lay down on the earth and pulled his woolen cloak over him. As he lay watching the glowing embers of the fire, he heard a low grunt. It was the runt again, sidling up beside him.

Étienne fell asleep with the lamb cradled in his arms.

He heard a voice calling his name.

"Étienne! Étienne!"

When he looked up, he saw a white-haired figure hovering in the air over him, wearing a tall bishop's mitre and a bright red tunic with the symbol of the Chi-Rho, signifying the name of Christ in Greek. In one hand he held a green bejeweled Bible embossed with a cross; in the other he carried three glistening golden balls.

Étienne fell to his knees, overcome with emotion.

"Blessed Saint Nicholas!"

He wanted to tell Saint Nicholas how much he longed to serve God. But the saint read his thoughts, and spoke to him.

"Thou art called to a great task, my son. God has chosen thee to lead a crusade of children to free the Holy Land from the Infidels."

"Children? But, blessed Saint Nicholas, what good would children be on a crusade?"

"This crusade will be unlike any that have gone before. It will conquer not by the sword but by the power of faith. The Saracens will be blinded by the pure hearts and simple faith of the children, and they will fall on their knees and beg to be baptized in the Holy Spirit. The crusader children will be as the Holy Innocents, giving themselves over to the glory of God. For our Lord Himself has said, 'Unless thou becomest like little children thou cannot enter the kingdom of Heaven.' "

"But how will we get to the Holy Land? Where will we find ships to take us there?"

"God has promised me, as the patron saint of children and of mariners, that He will make the waters divide before thee, as He parted the Red Sea for Moses and the Israelites."

"How can I lead a crusade, Saint Nicholas? Where will I find all these children?"

"Go to the king. Give him the precious relic. Let him smell the manna di Santa Nicola."

"But the king won't listen to a poor shepherd boy!"

"Thou art made in the image of the Good Shepherd Himself, who said, 'The last shall be first.' Farewell, my son."

"But, Saint Nicholas …"

The blazing figure vanished, though Étienne had barely begun to ask all the questions in his heart.

He awoke with a jolt. For a few moments, he forgot completely where he was, even *who* he was. The dream had felt so vivid, so real, more real than the ground beneath him, the hillside around him still enveloped in thick darkness.

It was only when he was fully awake, looking down at the bone resting in his hand, that Étienne remembered that in his dream, the face of Saint Nicholas was the same as that of the relic peddler, the stranger who had emerged earlier that night out of the darkness.

Had he been truly visited by Saint Nicholas himself? Was it Saint Nicholas with whom he had shared his last bit of bread, Saint Nicholas who had given him the relic of his own sacred bone? As the full weight of this realization began to sink in, he felt a quaking and trembling all through his body, and a great fear gripped his soul.

He knew from that moment that his life would never be the same again. He had been chosen. The command had been given. He knew what he had to do.

For there was no turning away from the call of God.

ॐ

CHAPTER 4
The Trade Fair
March 1212

"Idleness is the devil's friend."

The sound of Sister Saint Delphin's voice made Blanche grit her teeth in fury.

She knew just what was coming. The nun would berate her for taking too long a break from spinning, and when she objected that she needed to rest her fingers, she'd once again have to listen to Sister Saint Delphin's familiar litany of martyrs. "So you think you have a hard life, missy?" she'd say. "Be grateful you have fingers at all! Think of Saint Lucy, who plucked out her own eyes when a pagan suitor admired her beauty, saying she did not want to look on any lover but Jesus Christ himself!"

The stories made Blanche squirm, though Sister Saint Delphin seemed almost to relish the gory details. But to her surprise and relief, there was no martyr story this time. Sister Saint Delphin just breezed by her and sat down to gossip with the two novices who were learning to spin.

It was Sister Saint Delphin who'd looked Blanche up and down that first morning in the Cistercian convent and hissed in her face, "Your mother and father are right now burning in hell with their fellow heretics." The old nun's words stung her like a slap in the face. She could still feel, as if it was yesterday, the overwhelming despair that had gripped her at that moment, an agony unlike anything she'd yet experienced in her young life.

Why had he left her there? For a long time she fancied he would come back for her — the young knight who had scooped her up onto his horse that day and ridden off through the gates of Béziers. She dimly remembered arriving at the door of the convent in the middle of the night, the murmurs and muffled voices of the knight and the woman she would come to know as the abbess. She remembered him begging the abbess to take her in, to teach her the ways of the true faith and save her immortal soul. He broke into great heaving sobs, crying "Sister, there is blood on my hands." Blanche remembered looking at his hands and plainly seeing that they were clean and free of blood. But she was just a child then. Now she understood that it was a turn of phrase, a way of talking about his own guilt. She knew, though she tried not to think about it, of all the blood that had been spilled that terrible day at Béziers.

Sometimes at night she had dreams of being encased again in the soft wool, of the Good Knight finding her in there. She was flooded with a feeling of warmth and safety as he picked her up, still swaddled in the wool like a newborn babe. No, she couldn't believe he had taken part in the slaughter. She owed her life to him. He was her Good Knight.

Sister Saint Delphin noticed that she was lost in thought. "Get back to work, missy!" she barked at Blanche.

"Yes, Sister."

Blanche felt like digging her nails into the old nun's face.

The other sisters treated her well enough. There were a few who went out of their way to be kind to her, like the novice Sister Saint Jerome, who worked in the kitchen and sometimes slipped Blanche extra slabs of bread and cheese. She was aware that some of the nuns called her "little heathen" behind her back, and expressed surprise that she ate meat, which only betrayed their ignorance about Good Christians. Sometimes at dinner she ate more meat than she really wanted, just to further confound them.

But for Sister Saint Delphin she felt a deep, abiding hatred. She was completely at the mercy of this sour old woman, who exulted in her terrible misfortune and continually reminded Blanche that her only value was her prodigious ability to spin large amounts of wool in a short time.

Soon after she'd arrived at the convent, the nuns had put her to work. At first she found it comforting to do something familiar, an activity that reminded her of her mother and her life in Béziers. Over time she came to realize that her work had become an important source of income to the convent, which she greatly resented. But she couldn't refuse to spin — she had no choice. Her survival depended on the nuns.

She was alone in the world. There was not a single person who really knew her, who cared about her.

෨

As she looked around the crowded stalls of Chalon-sur-Saône, Blanche could hardly believe her luck. She was nearly overwhelmed by the sheer size and intoxicating sensations of the trade fair. She reveled in the smells of the fragrant spices from Arabia and Egypt and ran her fingers over the brilliantly dyed linens and silks from Lombardy. It was the first time she'd been away from the convent since the Good Knight had first brought her there. Sister Saint Delphin, of course, had strenuously opposed her being allowed to go. To the old nun's annoyance, Blanche managed to convince the abbess that her knowledge of the various woolens would help the nuns gain a good price for their cloth.

So she had accompanied Sister Saint Gérard to Chalon-sur-Saône, where they stayed at the local Cistercian abbey. The trade fair would run for several days, and Blanche hoped they wouldn't complete their business too quickly. But on their second day in Chalon-sur-Saône, Sister Saint Gerard announced that most of the cloth had been sold the day before, and that they would be leaving the next morning. What was worse, the nun told her she needn't come to the Hall of Woolens that day.

"I can handle the pricing. You'd just be sitting around idly. After mass you should go back to the abbey. The sisters there will find some work for you to do."

Blanche nodded dutifully, but she was heartsick. Only one more day, and she'd barely had a chance to see the fairgrounds, much less the rest of the town! When Sister Saint Gérard bade her goodbye as they came out of the cathedral, she started in the direction of the abbey, then turned back to make sure the nun was out of sight. Sister Saint Gérard would be busy at the Hall of Woolens all day. As long as Blanche stayed away from that area of the fairgrounds, she could spend the next few hours exploring. The nun would be none the wiser.

She headed toward the heart of town and soon found herself at the edge of the large, open square. The trade fair was a major event that brought hundreds of people into Chalon-sur-Saône. For those few days the atmosphere in the town was like one big festival, and even in the cool March weather the square was filled with clusters of people chatting, listening to troubadours and watching the performances of various troupes of traveling players.

Blanche made her way to an area of the square where a crowd was gathered around a troubadour from Bretagne, singing and accompanying himself on the lute. She recognized his song as one that she used to love when she was a little girl — about Renard, the rascally fox who always managed to outsmart Ysegrin the wolf. At the end of the song, he put down his lute and took out what looked like an oblong wooden box dotted with carved holes and a handle on one end. As he began turning the handle, Blanche was astonished to hear a droning sound rise up from the box. So this was some kind of music box!

She watched closely as the troubadour pressed down on the buttons lining one side of the box, plucking out a melody on a set of strings inside. All the while he kept turning the crank, which seemed to be the source of the characteristic drone. He proceeded to play a series of carols and *estampies*, to the delight of the crowd. People clapped to the spirited rhythms, and some began to dance. After the dance tunes, the troubadour asked for requests from the crowd.

"A *lai*!" someone called out.

"Yes — *Chèvrefoil*!" said another voice.

He launched into the familiar haunting ballad about the fabled lovers Tristan and Isolde.

Like the sweet honeysuckle twined around the hazel tree
When one is severed, the other dies.

Blanche had heard this *lai* before when she was a little girl in Béziers. But now the story of the doomed lovers stirred something deep and unfamiliar in her soul. She felt a rush of longing to experience the same kind of all-encompassing passion as Isolde felt for Tristan. As the afternoon wore on, she was lost in reverie, listening to more well-known *lais* about love between knights and high-born ladies.

It was only when the troubadour from Bretagne began to pack up his instruments that Blanche noticed just how low the sun had sunk in the sky. She rushed out of the square, barely managing to get back to the abbey before Sister Saint Gérard.

After mass the next morning, the nun told Blanche to go to the Hall of Woolens by herself.

"I want to visit and pray with the sisters for a while. Take the wagon, pack up the remainders and wait for me outside the Hall of Woolens."

Blanche rushed to the fairgrounds and quickly packed up what was left at the stall. She thought if she hurried, she could go to the square to hear the troubadour one last time. When she arrived at the square there was no sign of him. Disappointed, she turned to leave when she spied the wooden music box sitting forlornly on the ground by the edge of the square.

She went over to give it a closer look. Yes, it was just like the one she'd heard the day before.

"Do you know where the troubadour from Bretagne is?" she asked one of the players loading a cart nearby.

"He left this morning for the fair at Provins," came the reply.

"Isn't this his?"

The fellow shrugged.

"The *vielle-à-roux*? He must've forgotten it."

So that's what the strange-looking music box was called.

"Won't he come back for it?" she asked.

"Doubt it. He's well on his way to Provins by now. You want it?"

Blanche was taken aback.

"Me? I don't know how to play it."

"Neither does anybody in our troupe," he said. "Go on, take it before all these carts start rolling over it."

Instantly Blanche made a decision. She picked up the music box and walked quickly back to the place just outside the Hall of Woolens where she'd parked the loaded donkey cart. She reached under the stacks of cloth, lifted the rough goat-hair mat that lined the bottom of the cart and tucked the instrument underneath. Then she piled up the cloth to disguise the bulge made by the music box. If she was careful and made sure that it was she and not Sister Saint Gérard tending the cart, she could take it back to the convent without the nuns knowing.

She knew they would never allow her to keep such a thing. The songs of the troubadours celebrated earthly, carnal love over the love of God. In the eyes of the sisters, the *vielle* was sinful, an instrument of the devil himself.

૭

CHAPTER 5
Sheepstinker
April 1212

"Let's go find him!"

For the past week it seemed to Abel that his fellow students had talked of little else but the country boy. It was the class joke that everyone wanted to be in on. They streamed along the banks of the Seine in clusters of three or four, looking out for him as he hovered near the palace gate. They laughed and threw stones at him and vied with one another to come up with nicknames for him. The one that stuck was "Sheepstinker," because the boy bore the strong odor of the countryside.

Abel tried to ignore their antics and concentrate on his studies. After a couple of months in Paris, he was only now beginning to get used to the city, which had at first overwhelmed him with its massive cathedrals, its huge public buildings, its cobblestone-paved streets teeming with peddlers, beggars and women offering their bodies for a price.

He felt more at home in the Latin Quarter, where most of the students had their lodgings. The other boys complained about having to get up in the early morning, but

Abel couldn't wait to don his clerical gown and head for the Street of the Straw, as the lecture halls with their straw-covered floors were known. He was gripped by the excitement of ideas and philosophies he had never encountered before — Plato's *Republic*, Aristotle's treatises on metaphysics and natural history. He looked forward to reading the other ancients like Ptolemy, Euclid and Archimedes on astronomy and mathematics, and the writings of the Arab scholar Averroes, works that were only now being translated into Latin.

Abel felt like one of the cave dwellers in Plato's great allegory, blinded by the bright surface of the world around him, groping to understand the deepest mysteries of existence itself. He was thrilled to be living in a time when the old familiar ideas were being challenged, when everything was open to question. Ever since that day two years earlier, when he'd first stepped outside the walls of the old city, Abel longed to see more of the world beyond the Broce-aux-Juifs. He was hungry for knowledge, for experience of life's richness and variety, and he set his sights on attending the university in the great city of Paris.

At first it was difficult to persuade his family to allow him to go.

"What is there to be afraid of?" he challenged his father. "You yourself were educated among gentiles. You studied the texts of the Arab Avicenna, whom you call the greatest of all physicians."

Abel was his parents' only son, their cherished youngest child, and in time his spirited arguments brought them around. His father still faced the task of convincing the Elders that going to live among non-Jews wouldn't corrupt the boy's mind.

"I received my medical training at Montpellier, a school run by gentiles," he told them. "And the Jews of Troyes have benefited greatly from the knowledge I gained there. True education never corrupts the mind but enriches it."

One of the rabbis raised fears for Abel's safety, pointing out that the Church of Rome was currently engaged in a bloody crusade against heresy. The very word *crusade* struck terror in their hearts, as they remembered the slaughter of so many Jews a century earlier during the first crusade of 1096.

"It never bodes well for Jews when Christians go after unbelievers, even among their own."

"Not all Christians are blind followers of the bishops," Abel's father responded. "At the universities there are many Christians who are exploring new ideas, engaging in the kind of study and debate that Jewish scholars have always favored. The prophet Isaiah tells us *Olam Ha-Ba* will be a time of peace, when hatred, intolerance and war will cease. We Jews are the ones who must lead the way in bringing about the world to come. Even now, three hundred rabbis and their families are embarking on a great journey to the land of Israel, paving the way for the coming of the Messiah. Those of us who stay behind must do our part to honor their courage and steadfast faith."

As a child, Abel had sometimes felt embarrassed by his father's unconventional views. Now, as he listened to his passionate eloquence, he felt deeply grateful that, in truth, his father was among the very wisest of men.

In the end the Elders agreed, instructing Abel to keep Shabbat quietly, on his own, and stressing that he should do as little as possible to call attention to the fact that he was a Jew. This Abel had done faithfully, lighting candles, dipping his bread in salt and singing the "Shalom Aleichem" to himself.

But today was Sunday, the Christian Sabbath, and there were no classes. So when word spread among the students that Sheepstinker had moved from his accustomed spot by the palace gate to the cathedral, Abel decided to go along with them to check it out. He was a couple of years younger than most of them, and he knew they thought he was a bit strange, studying all the time. He wanted to do something to show he was one of them.

"Where is he?" he asked Frédérique, one of the ringleaders.

"Over there. In the ratty old cloak. See? Doesn't he look just like a sheep?"

Abel looked in the direction Frédérique was pointing. What he saw surprised him. With all the talk about Sheepstinker, he'd expected to see a craven, pathetic figure. But this country boy was tall, muscular, with a dignified bearing that belied his rough clothes and the odd picture he presented in the midst of this Paris crowd.

"Hey, Sheepstinker!"

The country boy looked in their direction, then turned away quickly, trying to give the impression he hadn't heard.

Abel caught the look of wounded dignity on his face. He had skin almost as ruddy as a southerner's, the look of someone who spends most of his time outdoors. What struck Abel even more were his large, soulful eyes that seemed to suggest he knew and felt far more than he had words to speak.

There was a commotion of horses, followed by a fanfare. An impressive-looking coach was arriving in the square. The country boy turned and walked toward it with a fierce, determined stride, like a proud animal.

"Let's go!" Frédérique called to the others. "He's heading toward the king's coach. This should be good!"

෨

The great pillars of Notre Dame cathedral loomed over Étienne like towers reaching to the sky.

He felt light-headed, almost faint. All the days he'd waited at the palace gate he'd had little to eat and hardly any sleep. Of course the palace guards had laughed at him. He'd expected that. But he had believed, naively, that one of them would eventually let him in, struck by the power of his faith. And once he was inside, once word had been brought to the king of the young shepherd from Cloyes who'd come bearing a message from Saint Nicholas himself, then Étienne was sure that all the difficulties he had endured would be worth it. But he'd been waiting for six days now, and he could feel the terrible gnawing cycle of doubts starting all over again.

For many weeks after that night on the hillside he had agonized over what to do. It seemed preposterous, the very idea of a shepherd boy being the bearer of a divine message to the king. Had he really been visited by Saint Nicholas? Had it been a true vision? At times he even feared that he might be possessed by the Devil, as many in Cloyes had said his mother had been. The turmoil in his own mind gave him a new sympathy with what she must have gone through.

He decided he must, through sheer force of will, banish all doubt. Like his mother, he would not shrink from what he'd been called to do. He would be strong and steadfast, wily and persistent.

He left his flock in the care of another shepherd, saying he was going to visit his mother in Liège and would return in a few days. Then he set out on his own for Paris.

On the morning of the seventh day after he'd arrived in the city, a thought struck him: the king would be attending Sunday mass at the cathedral! If he, Étienne, were to approach the monarch there, on the steps of the house of God, King Philip Augustus surely would not turn him away.

At dawn on Sunday, Étienne made his way to the square of Notre Dame. He'd only been there a short time when he heard shouts and laughter behind him. It was the gang of boys who'd been taunting him for days. He thought he'd managed to escape them, but now they'd followed him all the way to the cathedral.

He turned away, determined to ignore them, as he always did, when he heard a commotion. A fanfare sounded. A coach escorted by several mounted guards entered the square.

Étienne's heart leaped. The king had arrived!

The coach pulled to a stop in front of the cathedral steps. Two attendants hopped out and placed a stool on the ground for the king to step on. Philip Augustus emerged from the coach, easily recognizable not only by his royal robes but by the cloudy appearance of his left eye, in which he was completely blind. Étienne boldly stepped forward. As he expected, the guards immediately started to drag him away. But one of the king's aides smiled and whispered in Philip Augustus's ear. The king nodded and held up his hand.

"Stop!" the aide called out. "Let him be."

The guards let go of Étienne, and he fell to his knees in front of the king.

"Your Majesty, I am Étienne of Cloyes. I come bearing a message from Saint Nicholas."

"Ah, yes, I have heard about you. You're the boy who's been making a fuss outside the palace."

"Forgive me, Your Majesty, but Saint Nicholas appeared to me and bade me come to you."

"Saint Nicholas of Myra appeared to you, eh? And where did this remarkable encounter take place?"

"In the fields outside my village, Your Majesty. Where I was attending my flock."

"Did he march right through your braying lambs with his Chi-Rho and golden balls?" said Philip Augustus.

Étienne could see several of the king's aides stifling their laughter, but he ignored them.

"No, Your Majesty. He appeared in the guise of an ordinary traveler. I shared bread with him. It was only later, in a dream, that he revealed himself in all his saintly glory."

"I see," said the king. "And what did Saint Nicholas say to you in this dream?"

"He told me that God has chosen me to carry out a great work. He wants me to lead a crusade of children."

"A crusade of children?!"

By now a crowd had gathered in the square, and Étienne heard ripples of laughter behind him.

"Yes, Your Majesty," he replied. "It is to be called the Crusade of the New Innocents, in honor of the children slaughtered by Herod on the night of Christ's birth. He said we must march to the Holy Land and free it from the Infidels."

"So, according to Saint Nicholas," said Philip Augustus, "a bunch of children are going to accomplish what the great nobles and knights of Europe haven't been able to bring about in a hundred years and four crusades?"

"I know it must sound strange, Your Majesty, but Saint Nicholas assured me that the Crusade of the New Innocents will be like no other. He said we will conquer by the power of faith alone. The Saracens will be blinded by the light of the Holy Spirit and embrace the gospel."

"Really? Well, that would be good news, wouldn't it? What did you say your name was, boy?"

"Étienne, sire."

"Étienne. And what do you suppose moved Saint Nicholas to choose a shepherd boy from the Orléanais for this great task?"

"I don't know, Your Majesty. I am certainly not worthy of such an honor. He told me to come to Paris and tell you of God's desire for a new crusade, and here I am. And, look. He gave me this as a sign …"

As Étienne held out the relic, one of the king's aides intervened quickly and took it from him. The king eyed it with curiosity.

"And this is …?"

"A bone of Saint Nicholas, Your Majesty. You can tell by the *manna di Santa Nicola*."

The aide held up the bone to the king's nose.

"Hmm. I'll admit it does have a certain … aroma. But you know, Étienne," the king said, turning toward the crowd with a flourish, "if I lined up all the bones of Saint Nicholas that have turned up in Europe over the years, they'd reach all the way to Constantinople."

The crowd exploded into raucous laughter.

"No, to Jerusalem!" someone in the crowd yelled.

"Nicholas of Myra must have had very long arms!" one of the king's aides called out.

Étienne pulled himself up with steely dignity.

"Forgive me, Your Majesty. I am only trying to do God's will …"

"Let me tell you something about God's will, Étienne. It is God's will that knights should fight, kings rule, parents command and children obey. If I allow a mere boy to lead a crusade, the entire natural order of things is overturned. That can't be God's will, now can it?"

"But —"

King Philip Augustus cut him off with a sharp wave of his hand.

"I'm afraid it wasn't Saint Nicholas who visited you, my boy. It was Satan himself. He is a wily creature. He set a trap for you and you fell right into it. Now go back to your village, tend your flock and cease all this blasphemous talk."

჻

On the way back from the cathedral, Frédérique and the other boys laughed till their sides ached. Sheepstinker's encounter with the king was the best show they'd seen in ages. It would be the talk of the Street of the Straw for days to come.

After walking with them a way, Abel said he had to go back to his studies.

"It's Sunday!" they told him mockingly. "Only a fool studies on the Sabbath!"

"The Sabbath is for resting the body," said Abel. "But Saint Augustine says that the mind can no more stop working than the river can stop flowing."

They were so impressed with his learned reference to Augustine that Abel was pretty sure they had no idea he'd just made it up on the spot. What he wanted to say to them was "Today may be your Sabbath but it is not my Shabbat." But he didn't.

Of course, there were many Jews living in Paris. Philip Augustus had allowed them back into the city after expelling them and confiscating their wealth nearly twenty years earlier. He also slapped a series of heavy taxes on them, and they were forbidden to work in any profession other than lending money to people who were too poor to borrow from the bankers. There was bitter resentment, Abel knew, at the high rates of interest charged by the Jewish moneylenders, but when so many of their clients were considered bad risks, what choice did they have? How else were they going to eke out a living?

These days life for Jews everywhere was difficult, but at least the Jews of Troyes still had their dignity. Here in Paris, they were regarded with contempt. No, he couldn't afford to be open with his classmates. Perhaps once he was better established and had made some friends who could be trusted — perhaps then he could take them into his confidence. For now, it was best to keep his faith to himself.

Right now, he especially felt the need to get away from them all, to be alone and try to sort out the confused jumble of emotions he was feeling. He didn't really understand his reaction to the incident in the square. All Abel knew was that while Frédérique and the others stood laughing at Sheepstinker, he himself felt a strong sympathy for the unfortunate young man. He wanted to yell at the others to stop, then to go to the country boy and stroke his head comfortingly. He thought about what courage it had taken for Sheepstinker to approach the king and was filled with shame at his own cowardice.

He was too restless and agitated to go back to his room and study. He decided to walk over to Les Halles, the new market district. Though selling on Sundays was frowned upon by the church authorities, many of the vendors simply ignored the priests and set up their stalls once mass was over, knowing that as long as there were goods to sell, there would be customers to buy them. Since he'd come to Paris, Les Halles was one of Abel's favorite places to walk. It seemed to throb with life, to harness all the energy and ferment of the great city.

He arrived at the wall separating the open-air market from the old cemetery, where the Parisians used to bury their dead. On the other side were stalls in haphazard rows, piled with baskets of fruits and vegetables from the countryside. Wagons were everywhere, and pigs roamed freely, sniffing out scraps of garbage despite the constant efforts of city authorities to make vendors keep them penned up. Abel looked at the far edge of the market area, where, his father had told him, an entire Jewish quarter had once stood, demolished after they were banished decades earlier.

Then he saw him.

The country boy was huddled against the wall on the side where the old graveyard had been, convulsed with sobs. All the effort he'd made to hold on to his dignity in the face of the king's dismissal had given way to utter desolation.

Abel resolved to make up for his earlier cowardice. He approached the boy.

"Can I help you, friend?"

The country boy didn't even look up.

"Go away."

"Something's clearly troubling you," said Abel.

"I said go away! Leave me alone!"

"I only want to help."

"I know who you are. You and your friends. You want to have more fun at my expense."

"I'm sorry about that."

"Are you?"

"Let me make it up to you. At least let me let me get you something to eat. You look as if you haven't had a bite in days."

For a moment, the boy looked up at Abel, and then turned away.

"Stop being so proud. God wants you to accept my charity. You can hardly be the messenger of His word on an empty stomach. Come on."

୶

Later, as they sat outside one of the stalls, the country boy made his way through a large sausage, having already devoured two loaves. The sausage was made of pork, which of course Jews did not eat. Abel could see how famished the country boy was and how badly he wanted it, so he bought the pork, though he felt strange doing so.

Abel didn't want the boy to see how distasteful he found the sausage, so he made yet another attempt at conversation, though so far the boy had remained largely silent.

"What's your name?"

Abel was surprised to hear him finally respond.

"Étienne."

"Glad to meet you, Étienne. My name is Abel. I'm a student at the university."

The boy looked at him oddly.

"Abel? That's not a saint's name."

"No, it isn't. In the countryside people always name their children after saints but here in the city, things are more —"

Abel stopped himself, groping for a word that wouldn't sound condescending. Étienne merely shrugged.

"Abel was the good son of Adam and Eve," he said thoughtfully. "So I guess it's all right."

He fell silent again. Abel could see that Étienne was still embarrassed by his ravenous appetite and ashamed of needing charity. He searched around for something else to say, something casual that would make Étienne feel as if they were on an equal footing.

"Where do you come from, Étienne?"

"A village in the Orléanais. You wouldn't know of it," he replied, finally finishing off of the sausage.

"Try me," Abel urged. "It must have a name."

"Cloyes," said Étienne. "See, I told you you wouldn't have heard of it."

"You're right, I haven't," said Abel. "But it's very close to the name of Troyes, where I come from. Cloyes, Troyes. See? We're practically related."

Étienne looked at him quizzically. Abel immediately felt foolish that his attempt at wit had fallen so flat.

After a few more moments of silence, the country boy stood up.

"Farewell, Abel. Thank you for everything."

"Why?" said Abel. "Where are you going?"

"Home to Cloyes and my flock."

"What about your message to the king?"

A tense look crossed Étienne's face.

"You're making fun of me again."

"No, no, Étienne," Abel insisted. "I'm not, I swear it. I think it took real courage to do what you did, to go right up to the king and profess your beliefs. I admire you for that."

Étienne eyed him warily. Clearly, he couldn't fathom how a boy of privilege like Abel could possibly admire a peasant like him.

"Well, thank you for saying that," he replied. "But I was a fool to think that the king would listen to someone like me. I am not educated, like you. I don't know how to say things properly."

"That's not true," Abel shot back. "You express yourself very well. Education isn't everything. What about Peter the Hermit? He wasn't an educated man."

Étienne's eyes lit up.

"That's true. Peter the Hermit wasn't a priest or a noble, and he had thousands of followers."

In truth, Abel himself knew little about Peter the Hermit, leader of the fabled Peasants' Crusade more than a hundred years earlier. But he knew from listening to his fellow students that Christians held the charismatic preacher in high esteem. And he could see that the very mention of Peter the Hermit brought an immediate shift in Étienne's frame of mind.

"And there's Francis of Assisi, who teaches that all creatures are equal in the eyes of God, that He has a special love for the poor and downtrodden. The king spoke of God's will, but it was he who was not following God's will, turning me away like that."

"He should have treated you with the same respect as any nobleman," Abel agreed. "People act like kings are above the rest of us. But they're human. They make mistakes all the time."

Abel said this with a tinge of bitterness, thinking of the injustices Philip Augustus had inflicted on the Jews of his kingdom.

"Yes!" Étienne replied excitedly. "The king is only an earthly ruler. Even his decrees are subject to God's will."

Suddenly he turned to Abel and grabbed him by the shoulder.

"Now I understand!"

"What?" asked Abel, taken aback by the sudden shift in his mood.

"The king's rejection. It's another of God's tests!"

"Tests?"

"That's why Saint Nicholas bade me to go and see him. He knew that the king would turn me away! It all makes sense now! God is testing my resolve. He means for me to go and bring His message directly to the people! But how? How can I do that?"

Abel was at a loss to come up with a reply but quickly realized that the question wasn't meant for him. He watched as Étienne paced back and forth in an agitated state of mind, muttering what sounded like urgent, fevered prayers under his breath.

Suddenly, as if snapping out of a trance, the shepherd turned to Abel.

"Do you know the place called Saint Denis?"

"Saint Denis? Of course. It's just north of here."

"Is it far?"

"No, only a few hours' walk, I think. Why?"

"I must go there. I've heard that anyone can preach in the square in front of the shrine of Saint Denis. All kinds of people — tradesmen, peasants, even beggars — can stand up and be heard there, not just priests and bishops. Yes! Now I see what I must do. God has sent you to open my eyes. Thank you! Thank you!"

"Oh, but I didn't do anything …" Abel began, but barely got the words out before Étienne gripped his shoulders again, this time with even greater urgency.

"Will you go with me?"

"What?"

"Go with me to Saint Denis! God has sent you to me. You can help me find the right words to speak to people."

"I … I can't go to Saint Denis."

"Why not?"

"I have my studies, my classes …"

Abel's voice trailed off, and he saw a look of utter desolation cloud over Étienne's face. Without another word, the shepherd turned and began to walk away.

"Wait," Abel found himself blurting out. "I suppose I could come with you. For a day or so."

Étienne turned back toward him uncertainly.

"I don't want to trouble you."

"It's no trouble," said Abel. "The other students skip classes all the time, but I never do. I can afford to miss a few."

As before, there was an abrupt change in Étienne's mood. He rushed over to Abel with a look of elation.

"Thank you, my friend. God will bless you, I promise you. Let's get started."

"What? You want to start out for Saint Denis right now?" said Abel.

Étienne shrugged.

"Why not?"

"It's too late in the day."

"Late in the day?" Étienne let out a hearty laugh. "I stay out on the hillsides all night with my flock!"

Abel didn't want to admit that he was frightened of being out in the countryside at night.

"I have to pass on a book to another student," he said, quickly thinking of an excuse. "We have to share them, you see. Why don't I meet you here in the market tomorrow morning and we'll set out then?"

"Fine."

It occurred to Abel that unlike the peasant boy from Cloyes, he had lodgings to go to. He almost invited Étienne to share his room for the night, then thought better of it. Étienne, he knew, would be too proud to accept. He'd rather sleep on the street.

As he walked away Abel felt a strange mixture of fear and excitement, much as the time when, as a boy, he'd first ventured out beyond the walls of the Broce-aux-Juifs.

∾

He awoke in the gray dawn the next morning wondering what he'd gotten himself into. He had studying to do. What would his father say if he knew he was missing lectures to tramp through the countryside with a Christian boy he hardly knew?

He'd made a promise, and now he had to keep it.

When he spied Étienne waiting in the same corner of the market, Abel could see that he, too, was feeling awkward about the whole undertaking. The sellers were just setting up their stalls, and they said little as Abel bought some bread and fruit. Once they set out, Abel made a few attempts at conversation, but the country boy made little response. As the sun got higher in the sky, the silence between them persisted, and Abel was starting to deeply regret the whole undertaking. They'd probably have to spend at least one night in Saint Denis, wasting money that his family had so carefully saved for his education. He started to rack his brain for some excuse to turn back. Nothing came to him, and the farther they got from Paris the harder it became.

They'd been walking nearly an hour and stopped at a stream to have a drink. Abel took out one of the loaves and lopped off a thick slice with his knife. He held it out to Étienne, who stared at it for a moment, not moving. Abel wondered if his pride at having to accept charity was returning, when Étienne reached out, took the bread and bit into it. Still he continued to stare, until Abel realized it was the knife in his hand that held Étienne's interest. No ordinary knife, it had a fine, gleaming blade and a mother-of-pearl handle, intricately carved.

"Where did you get that?" he finally said between bites of the bread.

"It was given to me by my mother when I left for the university," Abel replied. "For good luck and protection. It was the same knife she used to hide under my pillow when I was a baby."

Étienne looked at him curiously.

"Why would your mother put a knife under your pillow?"

Abel was on the verge of explaining the Jewish custom of placing a knife under the pillow of a newborn to guard against the curse of Lilith, the first wife of Adam, who hovered around women in childbirth. But he remembered that Lilith was not mentioned in the Christian scriptures and stopped himself.

"To keep evil spirits at bay," he replied simply, holding the knife out for Étienne to look at.

"It's beautiful," he said, running his fingers along the blade. "If only my brother had had one of these under his pillow …"

"You had a brother who died?"

Étienne nodded.

"But he was baptized, so he is in heaven, alongside my father."

"I'm sorry," said Abel. "Do you have other family back in Cloyes?"

"No, there is only my mother and she …" Étienne paused, a look of pained confusion on his face. "She lives far away."

Abel wondered what had happened to his mother, but it was clear Étienne wanted to say no more on the subject.

"I always wanted to have a brother," he said, breaking the awkward silence. "Back home in Troyes I am surrounded by five sisters."

He immediately regretted his remark, fearing that it would be painful for someone who clearly had no family to speak of. Instead, Étienne looked at him in wide-eyed amazement.

"You have *five* sisters! I'll bet they boss you around no end!"

Abel nodded ruefully.

"You have no idea how much."

Étienne laughed, richly amused at the thought of growing up beleaguered by all those females. They resumed walking, and the words began to flow more easily between them. After a while, Étienne began recounting the visit from the relic peddler and the dream that revealed that his visitor had been Saint Nicholas himself. As he spoke, Abel noticed that the shepherd seemed to come alive in a whole different way. Étienne gave a vivid, dramatic description of the mysterious stranger emerging out of the dark night, then proceeded to act out the entire dream, playing the parts of Saint Nicholas and himself.

When he finished, Étienne looked at Abel with a wary expression, as though he feared that Abel might mock him.

"Forgive me for going on so long."

"You didn't. In truth, you told the story so well I could almost see it happening before my eyes."

"Really?" Étienne's eyes were wide with gratitude. "Of course, I don't speak as well as an educated person like you."

"You speak in a way that makes a person want to listen, which is more than I can say for some of my professors," Abel replied with a laugh. "Anyway, there are many things that cannot be learned from books."

He was beginning to see this country boy in a whole different light. Despite the gap that existed between their stations, he realized that in many ways he felt more at ease with Étienne than he did with his fellow students.

As they walked, Étienne told him about the follower of Francis of Assisi, whose words had made such a deep impression on him back in Vendôme. Abel had not heard of this man Francis and his group of holy beggars, who had spread out from Umbria to preach the message of peace and love for all God's creatures. As Étienne spoke, Abel was struck by how much Francis's teachings seemed to echo the beliefs of his own father, who often spoke of *Olam Ha-Ba*, the time of understanding among all peoples foretold by the prophet Isaiah.

He pondered whether to say anything to Étienne about the fact that he was a Jew. Maybe it would be wiser to wait awhile, until they knew each other better. Still, what risk could there be, with a Christian inspired by such ideas as Étienne? He was on the verge of saying something when Étienne stopped and pointed up ahead.

"Look."

The great spire of the shrine of Saint Denis was visible over the next hill.

The angelus bells were ringing for the end of midday prayers as they approached the city gates. They entered and headed straight for the centre of town. In the large public square in front of the shrine they saw a large crowd dotted with *jongleurs*, troupes of musicians, relic peddlers hawking their wares. Everywhere they looked, there were individual preachers who stood on raised carts, vying for people's attention and shouting to be heard over the din.

The scene reminded Abel of Les Halles, where the vendors competed to entice customers to come to their stalls, but even the marketplace back in Paris was tame compared with the spectacle here in Saint Denis. As they entered the square, he listened as one of the preachers, a blind man, exhorted the crowd around him.

"Bartimaeus called out to the Lord to heal his blindness, and Jesus said, 'Go, your faith has healed you.' So has God given me the gift of blindness so that through my faith I can heal others!"

They passed a group clustered around another cart, on top of which stood an elderly woman. She was hunched over, clutching a thick staff and chanting in a language unfamiliar to Abel.

"See? None of these people are priests," said Étienne. "No one is mocking them or making them feel they shouldn't speak."

They looked at each other, daunted by the swirl of activity around them, unsure what to do next.

"Let's go inside and pray," Étienne finally said.

As they entered the cathedral, they looked up at the famous rose window over the entrance. The shrine of Saint Denis was known all over Europe for its stained glass. Abel thought of Christian churches as gloomy and dark, like Notre Dame cathedral, which he had been in a few times with his fellow students. The rich and brilliant colors of the windows in Saint Denis let in so much light that the cathedral took on some of the welcoming warmth of a synagogue.

Étienne dropped to his knees and bowed his head in prayer. Abel did the same, giving the impression that he, too, was praying. As he silently waited for Étienne to finish, he pondered the many things about this Christian faith that struck him as strange and exotic — the hectic scene out in the square, the panoply of saints with their numerous feast days, the different ways Christians had of addressing God, whose very name Jews were forbidden to speak aloud.

After a few minutes, Étienne opened his eyes.

"I am ready now."

They came out of the cathedral and stood on the steps overlooking the square. Étienne looked hesitantly at Abel, then turned toward the square and began calling out for attention from the clusters of people nearby. A few looked in his direction, then drifted over, followed by others. A newcomer seemed, at least temporarily, to arouse people's curiosity.

"People of France, I come bearing a message from Saint Nicholas himself."

Abel expected to hear him begin the story that had he'd found so appealing on their walk to Saint Denis. But Étienne seemed self-conscious, unsure, and instead began to ramble on about the great works of Saint Nicholas, stories about his rescue of the mariners at sea, his dropping gold coins down the chimney of the three poor sisters.

Abel could see the crowd was growing restless.

"We've heard all those stories," someone finally called out. "What's this message you say you bring from him?"

"Saint Nicholas told me that God wants a new crusade to go and free the Holy Land."

A ripple of laughter went through the assembly.

"A crusade!"

"Led by a shepherd boy!"

"That's a good one."

Now the jocularity had taken hold of the whole crowd. In desperation, Étienne took the relic out of his pouch.

"He gave me a sign … this, his sacred bone."

"That's your proof? I can trade a sack of flour at the market for one of those!"

Now the crowd exploded in laughter. Étienne stood, unable to say a thing. People began to drift away. Étienne began to walk away, his face tight with humiliation. Abel ran after him.

"Wait, Étienne."

"You heard them. It's no use."

"No, Étienne. They'll listen, really they will. But it was as if you were giving a sermon, as if you were trying to be a priest in the pulpit. That's not what people come here for.

They're looking for something they don't get from the priests. They want to be moved, the way I was moved when you told me about the relic peddler and your dream. *That's* what you have to talk to them about, not a sermon about Saint Nicholas. You have a beautiful fire in you, Étienne. I saw it when you told me that story. These people will see it, too, if you let them."

Abel went after the people who had drifted away.

"Come back and hear my friend. You'll be moved and amazed by his story, I promise you."

Étienne looked at him hesitantly.

"Go on. Tell them story, just as you told it to me."

He began haltingly, beginning once again by telling of sitting by a small fire on the hillside outside Cloyes, and of the mysterious stranger who emerged out of the dark night. Little by little he grew more sure of himself and began to speak more fluidly.

"Even though he said little, I thought the stranger must be hungry. As I took out my last bit of bread to share with him, one of the lambs, a runt that had been rejected by its mother, came over and started begging for a morsel. To my surprise the stranger held out the bread to it. 'You must be hungry from your long journey,' I told him, 'and that scrawny lamb hasn't long to live anyway.' The stranger shook his head and said, 'Did not our Lord say, 'Feed my lambs' and 'As long as you do it for the least of my brethren, you do it for me'? Instantly I felt ashamed of my selfishness and held out my own morsel for the lamb. All of a sudden, a blazing light surrounded the stranger, and his tattered cloak was transformed into a rich silken robe emblazoned with a Chi-Rho. He raised one hand in a blessing and the other held three golden balls. Immediately I fell on my knees crying, 'Blessed Saint Nicholas!' Then he reached down under the skin on his arm. With no effort or pain at all he pulled out a small piece of bone and held it out to me, saying, 'For the unbelievers, show this as a sign of my coming.'"

Abel was taken aback. Had he heard right? Earlier Étienne had said that Saint Nicholas appeared to him in a dream. Now he seemed to be saying that the saint himself had appeared out of the darkness, pulled a bone right out of his own arm and given it to Étienne as a relic. He didn't want to contradict his friend. And he had to admit that this wild tale made an even better story, for the crowd grew more and more attentive as he spoke.

"Saint Nicholas told me I had been chosen by the Lord," Étienne went on, "to carry out a great task, to lead a new kind of crusade. A crusade of children!"

"Children!" A woman called out. "Saint Nicholas wants children to go on a crusade?"

"Yes," said Étienne with great earnestness. "*Dieu le veut!* God wills it."

"Fine," the woman said. "Take my boy. He never does a lick of work anyway."

"Mine, too," another voice called out. "One less mouth to feed."

Ripples of laughter began to spread through the crowd again.

"Why do you laugh?" Étienne chastised them.

"That's a ridiculous idea. Children can't go on a crusade."

"But Our Lord Himself said, 'Unless you become like little children you cannot enter the kingdom of heaven!'"

Étienne was faltering. Abel saw that he was in danger of losing the crowd, that people in this square could be very fickle. Only moments ago, they had been riveted by him, taking in every word, but now some were starting to drift away.

Eager to hold their attention, Abel spoke up.

"What my friend means to say is that the crusade is not only for children but for those who are pure of heart, as children are. Isn't that so?" he said, nodding in Étienne's direction.

"Yes! This crusade is open to all — just like the one led by Peter the Hermit. Anyone can join us — young, old, rich, poor, man or woman," said Étienne, recovering his confidence. "Why shouldn't it be this way? Haven't we stood by long enough as kings and knights march to the Holy Land, only to fail time and again to recapture our Savior's tomb? Shouldn't ordinary people have a chance to show what we can do?"

The effect of Étienne's words was explosive. Suddenly there was a volley of passionate outbursts from the crowd.

"It's about time!"

"Why should crusades be only for nobles and knights?"

"That's right! We're just as good as they are."

"Yes!" Étienne burst out. "We are all equal in the eyes of God. A new day is dawning, when the Lord will bring down the powerful from their thrones, and lift up the lowly. For did not Jesus Christ Himself say, 'The last shall be first'?"

The crowd cheered as he made his way down the steps of the cathedral, waving triumphantly.

"You were wonderful. You had them hanging on your every word," Abel told him as they headed away from the square. "They especially loved the part about Saint Nicholas pulling the bone right out of his own arm. You didn't tell me that."

"I didn't?" said Étienne. "When I was speaking to the crowd, it was almost as if I was back in the dream myself. I could see all the details so vividly in my mind. After that, I could feel their attention waning. Thank goodness you spoke up when you did. Do you think I should have gone on longer?"

"No," said Abel. "You stopped at just the right time. You left them wanting to hear more."

He decided to say nothing more about the dream, for Étienne seemed truly unaware of having altered it for the crowd. And it was, after all, only a dream.

"I don't know if I can do it again," said Étienne.

"Sure you can. We'll come back again tomorrow."

"What if no one comes to hear me?"

"Don't worry, they'll come," said Abel. "Word will get around. I'll bet you'll have an even bigger crowd."

They spent the rest of the day rambling through the town, stopping to play a raucous game of nine pins with some local boys. Later, famished, they stopped at a tavern where Abel bought them some stew and ale. Toward nightfall, they lay down under a large oak on the green beside the tavern and fell into an exhausted slumber.

Sometime after midnight, Abel found himself half-awake, looking up into the sky awash with stars, listening to the steady breathing of Étienne, lying nearby. He had never slept in the open air before, but instead of anxiety he felt a deep contentment. He felt as though he'd experienced more in the past day than in his whole life up until that point.

And in Étienne, he'd found a friend. Only now did it come home to him just how lonely and isolated he'd been feeling all those months in Paris.

ॐ

Abel's prediction turned out to be more accurate than either of them could have anticipated.

When they approached the shrine the next morning, they saw a large crowd gathered in the centre of the square. At first Abel thought it must be one of the saints' days that Christians were always celebrating.

Suddenly a woman's voice rose out of the crowd.

"That's him!"

Heads turned to look in their direction.

"The boy preacher! The one Saint Nicholas appeared to."

They both watched, terrified, as a flood of people surged toward them. Finally Étienne climbed the steps of the shrine and nervously faced the crowd.

"Go on," Abel tried to reassure him. "Remember yesterday. Tell them about Saint Nicholas."

Once again he began to recount the story of the stranger emerging out of the darkness who revealed himself in a blaze of light to be Saint Nicholas, this time adding more new details.

"At the moment that Saint Nicholas revealed himself to me, the hungry lamb to whom he had offered the last crust of bread fell to his knees and bowed his little head down to the earth. And one by one the entire flock of sheep came from all over the hillsides and they, too, fell to their knees and bowed down. And Saint Nicholas said, 'They kneel to the Lamb of God and to thee, Good Shepherd, whom God has chosen to lead the crusader children to the Holy Land.'"

Once again Abel was taken by surprise by Étienne's embellishments, and expected the crowd to dissolve into laughter at the description of the sheep bowing down to worship him. To Abel's amazement, they took the story completely seriously, listening to every word in rapt fascination. He realized that Étienne, the unschooled country boy, seemed to know instinctively what people longed to hear, that a story about a miracle would touch them far more deeply than an account of a mere dream.

"Saint Nicholas told me that I have been chosen to form a different kind of crusade," Étienne went on. "He said that God has become impatient with the pathetic efforts of kings and knights, that the time has come for a new kind of army — an army of the young, the weak, the poor — to wrest the

Holy Sepulchre once and for all from the clutches of the Infidel!"

A voice came booming from out of the crowd.

"The Mohammedans are barbarians who preach the gospel of Satan!"

"Their feet defile our Lord's sacred ground!" someone else shouted.

Others began to cry out similar denunciations, creating a babble that abated only when Étienne resumed speaking.

"We will carry no weapon but the cross. We will wear no armor but our pilgrim's robes. The power of our faith will overwhelm the Mohammedans. They will bow down before the cross and beg to be baptized in the Holy Spirit. So to all who doubt and dismiss us, I say, Stand back! Let us pass! We will show you what an army of children can do!"

The crowd responded with a deafening roar. The growing intensity of Étienne's words, combined with the shouts from the audience, roused them to a near-fever pitch, which Abel found unsettling. This Christian hatred of Muslims was mystifying to him. It was the Muslims, after all, who had welcomed the Jews back into Jerusalem after they had taken the city from Christian control nearly twenty years ago. And, far from being barbarians, people in the Arab world had a higher level of culture and learning than Europeans.

Where, he wondered, did Christians get these strange, distorted ideas? How could they talk of winning the hearts of Muslims and converting them to the Christian faith, while in the same breath speak of them as if they were monsters? How could they be so unshakably convinced of their own righteousness, when few of them had ever laid eyes on a living, breathing Muslim?

Suddenly he heard the Elder's voice in his head.

It never bodes well for Jews when Christians go after unbelievers.

Anxiety rippled up his spine, but he dismissed it. As unschooled and unacquainted with the larger world as Étienne was, he couldn't possibly share those ignorant beliefs, for they were so completely at odds with Francis's message of peace and love.

Abel resolved to talk to Étienne about all this. For the moment, at any rate, he couldn't even get close to Étienne, who was surrounded by a crush of people asking for his blessing and begging to be allowed to touch the bone of Saint Nicholas.

∾

Several days passed, and Abel still had not returned to Paris. He was beginning to worry about catching up on his studies, but he couldn't tear himself away from the remarkable events that were taking place, events that he himself helped to bring about.

For the phenomenon of the boy preacher was growing. People flocked to Saint Denis, at first from the surrounding villages, then from as far away as Picardy and Rouen. Every day hundreds more came to the square, so many that the other preachers were being squeezed out. It was Étienne, and only Étienne, whom people wanted to hear.

Not everyone regarded the boy preacher with the same devotion. On the Sunday after their arrival, the bishop of Saint Denis took to the pulpit to dismiss the whole notion of the crusade. Étienne, he told the congregation, was nothing but a misguided youth.

"God does not make His will known through shepherd boys, but through His representative on earth, Holy Mother Church."

Instead of discouraging people from flocking to Étienne, the bishop's sermon only increased their fervor, for the next day brought the largest crowds yet to the square. Abel began to see that the atmosphere at Saint Denis resulted from much more than simple faith; it was part of the general mood of rebellion against the clergy. People were enraged to see priests and bishops living in luxury while they had to scramble just to feed their families. More and more they sought out new spiritual leaders, like Francis of Assisi, who lived in true imitation of Christ and sought nothing for themselves. Even Francis himself had come from a wealthy family and had voluntarily chosen to live a life of poverty. The pilgrims of Saint Denis were eager to believe that God was speaking directly through one of their own, and so they embraced the shepherd boy from the Orléanais as a home-grown prophet.

Still, despite the enthusiasm of the burgeoning crowds, Abel was taken aback when, a fortnight after their arrival in Saint Denis, Étienne announced it was time for them to leave.

"Leave? Where are we going?"

"To the Holy Land, silly one," said Étienne, playfully tugging at his hair.

"But ... why now?" Abel sputtered.

"You can see for yourself. People are getting restless. They don't want to talk about crusading anymore. They want to do it."

The day after tomorrow they would set out for Marseille, Étienne said, the Mediterranean port from where the great Richard Coeur-de-Lion had embarked when he led the crusade twenty years earlier.

"King Richard needed ships to ferry his soldiers to the Holy Land, but we will get there by the power of our own feet."

"It will take weeks for all these people to walk all the way to Marseille," Abel objected. "How will we feed them all? Where will we stay?"

"Listen to you, worrying about such things. God will provide! We'll be mendicants, like Francis and his followers, owning nothing but the clothes on our backs. We'll live off the land and the charity of the people."

Abel was in a quandary. Until then, he'd just gone along with events day by day. Now he had to make a choice one way or the other. Should he return to Paris? Or set out for with Etienne and his followers?

He knew what he ought to do. He'd already missed a fortnight of classes, without his parents even knowing he was gone. So much had happened since that morning he'd first laid eyes on Étienne in the square at Notre Dame cathedral.

They'd been through so much together. How could he abandon his friend now?

After all, he told himself, the whole phenomenon couldn't last much longer. How could such a large group make it all the way to Marseille, on foot and without any provisions?

No, he couldn't bear to leave now. He had to see for himself how things would unfold.

๛

Abel wondered if they'd made a great mistake. Despite the huge crowds who had flocked to hear Étienne preach, when the time came to embark on the pilgrimage, there were only few dozen boys gathered at the edge of the square. A couple of them wore roughly sewn crosses on their tunics. One had tied a ragged red cloth to a long stick and carried it aloft as a banner. The *gonfanon* was split into two waving tails, in imitation of the famous *oriflamme* of Saint Denis, which according to legend, had once belonged to the great king Charlemagne himself.

Seeing the assembled group, Étienne was crestfallen.

"Is that all?"

He quickly shook off his disappointment and called them together. Bowing his head, he led them in reciting the *Pater Noster*, then sang one of the hymns he knew from his time in the choir at Vendôme, *Veni, Creator Spiritus*. At the end of the hymn, he signaled to the boy carrying the banner to raise it up, then turned and began to lead them in procession out of the square.

As the motley group made its way to the gates of Saint Denis, Abel realized they had been naive to expect that many would actually take up the call to go on a crusade. There were crops to be tended, families to look after. The boys who showed up were mostly orphans and penniless youth who had no work, no obligations and nothing to lose. For them, the prospect of taking to the road as holy pilgrims was more appealing than the treatment they received as ordinary beggars. A few of the boys were simply tagging along with older siblings, while some wanted to escape the endless drudgery of work in the fields. Whatever their motives, Abel thought they were probably fortunate to have even these few followers. He certainly didn't expect any more to join them.

As they approached a small farm a few miles outside of Saint Denis, they saw a boy pulling a plow through the field. He stopped and pointed to the makeshift banner with a curious look on his face.

"I heard about you," he called out. "You're the ones following the boy preacher."

"Yes!" one of the boys shouted back. "We're going to the Holy Land."

"Join us!" called another.

The boy stood watching the group for a moment. Then suddenly he dropped the plow and began running toward them. A celebratory cheer went up from the group as he joined in step with them. As they continued on, they heard a commotion behind them.

"Basile! Wait!"

They turned to see a small boy racing across the field, with a woman running after him, shouting.

"Léonard! Come back here!"

She caught up to the child and grabbed him by the arm. He tried to get free of her grip, frantically twisting and squirming.

"Basile! I want to go with you."

Basile called out to the boy.

"You can't come with me, Léolo. You must stay with *Maman*."

Still holding on to the small boy, the woman raised her other hand and shook her fist angrily.

"You come back here, Basile!"

He shook his head.

"No, *Maman*."

"I forbid you to go!"

"I have to, *Maman*. Forgive me."

Fighting back tears, he turned away and resumed walking, as the anguished wails of his mother and brother pierced the air around him.

"Don't you dare leave us, Basile!"

"Take me with you, Basile!"

Watching the scene, Abel felt deeply uneasy. Was this what going on a crusade meant? Tearing families apart? And yet there was no denying Basile's utter determination to join them.

As the day wore on, it became clear that many of the boys had no knowledge of the world beyond their villages. When the sun dropped low on the horizon, they spied a castle in the distance. "Is that Jerusalem?" a small boy called out. Later, when the group settled down to sleep in a field, Étienne and Abel tried in vain to comfort all the little ones crying inconsolably for their mothers.

Abel felt that things were off to a terrible start. He said nothing to Étienne. Anyway, it was too late to turn back. They were on their way to the port of Marseille, where, Étienne reassured the group, the waters would part for them.

The next morning a few boys changed their minds and started back home. But even that did not break Étienne's cheerful mood.

"This is another test of our faith," he told Abel. "We will put our trust in God and continue on with our journey."

Over the next few days, things began to settle into a rhythm. Their days became structured around prayer — Prime when they arose, Tierce at midmorning, Sext in the afternoon, Vespers in the evening and Compline when they lay down in the fields to sleep. Abel pretended to pray along with them, but kept his own devotions and observed Shabbat by himself as best he could.

As they passed through some of the villages they were heartened to discover that news of the crusade had preceded them. People came out to greet them with offerings of bread, ale, sometimes sweet cakes and apples. No matter how small the crowd, Étienne was undeterred, and in time the two of them got into a routine. At every stop Abel would seek out a spot near the well or church square and set up a bale or wagon from which Étienne could preach and be seen above the crowd.

Each time, Étienne recounted the story of the mysterious stranger who had visited him on the hillside, and who had miraculously transformed into Saint Nicholas himself. By now Abel had heard the tale so many times that he himself had trouble recalling what the original version was, and he suspected that Étienne didn't know either. The story always went over well with the crowds, who clearly loved to hear about miraculous visitations from saints.

At each village, Étienne urged people to join the Crusade of the New Innocents and stressed that it was open to anyone, especially the young and the poor. This never failed to stir up the crowd. People shouted out the same kinds of things they had at Saint Denis, denouncing the lords and bishops who lived in comfort while the peasantry struggled to survive.

Abel was shocked to see just how strong and widespread was the anger of the Christians toward their own clergy. He couldn't imagine his fellow Jews harboring the same kind of resentment toward the rabbis, who certainly did not live lives of wealth and luxury, as so many bishops and priests did. Rabbis did not accept payment for their religious duties, and many made their living doing the same kinds of work as the members of their congregations.

Despite all their passion and anger, many of his listeners drifted away once Étienne's sermons were over, as they had at Saint Denis. Usually no more than a handful joined the pilgrims as they passed through countless villages, whose names became a blur in Abel's mind. At least those who did join up were more enthusiastic and presentable than the ragtag bunch who had left Saint Denis. Abel noticed more and more boys arriving with *oriflammes* and other banners, and wearing crosses sewn onto their tunics. Here and there a few girls joined their ranks, mostly servants escaping the drudgery of their lives.

In a field some boys found an old donkey cart for Étienne to stand on. They ended up bringing it with them from town to town so he would always have something to raise him up above the crowds when he spoke.

When the group stopped in a village not far from Montargis, a boy came tearing into the square where Étienne was preaching. A man running close behind him caught up to him right in the middle of the square, piling on top of the screaming boy and holding his head down to the ground. Then the man pulled him up by his hair, and began dragging him back out of the square.

Étienne went over to see what was happening. The boy looked up him as he approached.

"You're Étienne, the boy preacher, aren't you? I want to join your crusade!"

"You're not going anywhere!" the man shouted. "Your father signed a contract with me!"

"You're not my master — God is!" the boy shouted defiantly, wincing as the man tugged even harder on his hair.

Before Étienne could say anything, several young men from among the pilgrims stepped forward and shouted angrily at the man.

"Do what he says!"

"Let him go!"

"Or we'll make you!"

Unnerved by the boys' threats, the man let go of the boy, who ran straight over to Étienne and knelt in front of him.

"My name is Rémi. Please tell this man God wants him to release me from my apprenticeship so I can take up the cross!"

Without a word, Étienne placed a hand on the boy's shoulder and glared at the man.

"Never mind!" the man finally said, stomping out of the square in disgust. "Take him off my hands. He's a good-for-nothing anyway!"

As they passed through farms and villages over the next few days, similar scenarios were played out again and again. Boys dropped whatever they were doing and scrambled to join the burgeoning parade of pilgrims, in open defiance of their parents and masters. Abel noticed that once they were well on their way, out of earshot of the angry threats and recriminations, the boys were almost giddy with joy at their newfound freedom. He couldn't help worrying, though, how they were going to find food for all these people.

One afternoon he heard shouts up ahead.

"Manna!"

"Manna from heaven!"

The boys were excitedly pointing to what looked like stones lying near the side of the road. As he got closer, Abel saw that they were loaves of bread. He knew immediately that the loaves must have tumbled out of a baker's cart. The pilgrims preferred to view them as a sign of God's favor, like the manna He rained down on the Israelites during their long wanderings in the desert.

Later the same day, as they approached the town of Gien, they saw a large group of people clustered around the town gate. By now they had grown accustomed to being welcomed by gatherings of local people, and they were excited that this one seemed even larger than usual. It was only as they got closer that they saw that it was in fact a group of men wielding scythes and pitchforks. One of the men stepped forward and thrust his scythe out toward them like a weapon.

"Go away!" he shouted at them. "You're not wanted here."

Étienne rushed up to the front of the line of pilgrims.

"No, wait! You don't understand who we are."

"We know exactly who you are," the man replied. "And we're not letting you in our town."

"Please! Just give me a chance to preach my message."

"Sure! And lure our children away, as you have everywhere else!"

Some of the men behind him began shouting.

"Get out!"

"We don't want you here!"

"But we're doing God's work!" Étienne shot back.

A man in clerical garb stepped forward and lifted his hand to quiet the crowd.

"No! You are doing the bidding of Satan himself, exhorting children to defy their parents and abandon their work in the fields. When children rule, the devil smiles. You are forbidden to enter these gates. Begone!"

There was silence as the two groups faced each other. The pilgrims stood nervously, waiting to see what Étienne would do.

"We will not fight," he said finally. "We will not enter your gates by force."

The assembled men broke into derisive laughter at Étienne's surrender. He kept on speaking, shouting determinedly over them.

"The Crusade of New Innocents is a crusade of peace. It is ordained by God Himself, and no earthly force can stop it. So I will preach here from outside the gates, and God will ensure that my voice will be heard. Young people of Gien! Hear me out. I am Étienne, the boy preacher, and I call on you to take up the cross. God wills it! *Dieu le veut!* Come join our march to the Holy Land!"

The pilgrims began to chant.

"Join us! Join us! Join us!"

As the chanting built to a deafening roar, a boy suddenly burst through the line of guards at the gate. A couple of the men tried to grab him as he passed, but he evaded their grasp and kept running till he reached the crowd of pilgrims, who erupted in cheers.

A few men started to run after the boy, but the others shouted at them to come back.

"No! Let him go!"

The men began to argue about whether to try to force the boy to come back. They were so distracted that they didn't notice when a couple of boys leaped from the top of the wall and raced over toward the pilgrims.

"Hey!"

"Get them!"

As a number of men chased after the newly escaped ones, pandemonium broke out. At least a dozen more boys burst through the gate. They ran to the assembled pilgrims, who quickly formed a wall of bodies around them. By now thoroughly rattled, the men of Gien held back, reluctant to charge into the crowd with their pitchforks and scythes for fear they might harm one of their own children. They could only watch helplessly as the mass of pilgrims gathered momentum and marched off, chanting triumphantly.

"Dieu le veut!"

୭

CHAPTER 6
The Vielle-à-roux
May 1212

"I HEAR THERE ARE HUNDREDS OF THEM camped just outside Sancerre."

Blanche's ears perked up to the conversation taking place across the room between Sister Saint Delphin and the novices.

Who are they talking about? she wondered.

"There's a whole slew of boys traipsing through the countryside," one of the novices said authoritatively. "They welcome anyone in their ranks — idiots, lepers. Even some women and girls are traveling with them."

"What kind of girl would leave home to journey in the company of men she barely knew and sleep beside them cheek by jowl in the open air?" Sister Saint Delphin broke in.

"They're following a boy by the name of Étienne, a shepherd from the Orléanais," the novice went on. "He says God has called him to lead a crusade of children to the Holy Land. He says God will part the seas for them, the way He did for Moses, and that the Infidels will fall to their knees and beg to be baptized in the one true faith."

"They can call it a crusade all they want. That doesn't make it one," sniffed Sister Saint Delphin. "Only the pope himself can call a crusade and he has not given this one his blessing."

"Why wouldn't he?" the novice asked. "They say Étienne has performed miracles, that a leper was healed simply by touching the hem of his cloak."

"Stories! People talk all kinds of nonsense." Sister Saint Delphin replied briskly. "The priests say the whole thing is the work of the devil, that heretics are behind it, whipping the pilgrims into a frenzy."

The nun shot a knowing glance in Blanche's direction as she said this. But Blanche was used to Sister Saint Delphin's little taunts. Hearing the word "crusade" upset her far more. A crusade was a terrible thing. Crusaders were ruthless men in armor, not children following a shepherd boy through the countryside. Still, she couldn't help listening, fascinated.

"Do you think they'll come this way?" another of the novices asked. "They're begging alms and food everywhere they go. If there are as many of them as people say, they'll clean our stores right out."

"That won't happen," said Sister Saint Delphin. "We will simply turn them away."

The novices were shocked.

"We must give alms to the poor."

"What about our vows?"

The old nun shook her head emphatically.

"They have disobeyed their priests and their parents. In

God's eyes, they are sinners — they deserve not charity but punishment."

Blanche's head was swirling with questions. Who was this Étienne? What was it about him that made so many follow him? She was so caught up in their conversation that without realizing it, she dropped her bobbin. It rolled along the floor, heading right for Sister Saint Delphin's feet. She quickly scooped it up before the old nun noticed anything amiss and resumed her spinning.

ॐ

The bells were ringing for Sext. As soon as she was sure all the nuns were in the chapel, Blanche hurried through the fields and down the path that led to the spring. She managed to make her way there most afternoons, having tricked the abbess into thinking she usually said midday prayers with the kitchen maids.

As she approached the spring, she felt comforted by the burbling sound of water cascading over the rocks of the small waterfall. She went immediately to a small hazel tree and bent down beside it. After taking a quick look around to make sure she was alone, she pulled back a small mat of earth covering a shallow depression in the ground and lifted out the wooden box with the handle protruding from one end.

It was still there, she saw with relief. Her precious *vielle-à-roux*. Since her return from Chalon-sur-Saône, Blanche had managed to conceal it here in this hiding place by the spring. To her great joy, she found that she remembered much of what she learned from watching the troubadour and in time she could play a number of simple melodies. Whenever she managed to steal precious moments of freedom, she came down here to the little waterfall, confident that the sound of the rushing water would mask the music of the *vielle*. She played carols that lifted her spirit, sang *Chèvrefoil* and other haunting *lais*, songs that took her away, in her mind at least, from her unhappy life at the nunnery.

And always, she found herself daydreaming of her Good Knight.

Sometimes, now, she could barely recall his face. In her mind the Good Knight had become fused with the image of Tristan, and like Tristan he would sweep her up in his arms, cover her face with kisses, take her away from this wretched life, from these cold, unfeeling women. Like the honeysuckle and the hazel tree, they would never be parted.

"What do you think you're doing, missy?"

Jolted out of her reverie, she turned with a start. Looking down on her from the ridge was Sister Saint Delphin.

"What's that you've got there?"

"Nothing!"

She quickly tried to cover up the *vielle* with her dress, but it was too late. Sister Saint Delphin came racing down the path to the stream.

"Give me that thing!"

"No!"

They struggled. She fought like a tiger, but the old woman was fierce too. As Blanche pulled hard on the *vielle*, it snapped upward, and the handle struck the nun in the face, making a gash on her cheek.

Blanche ran, carrying the *vielle*. As she raced along the stream bed, the nun's voice rang in her ears.

"You are a child of the devil. You took in the heresy with your mother's milk. It runs in your veins! Nothing can save you from the fires of hell. Nothing!!"

She ran until she couldn't run any longer and finally stopped to catch her breath. She looked behind her and listened carefully. There was no way Sister Saint Delphin could have followed her all this way. The old nun had probably gone up the ridge and back to the convent, eager to tell the others of the little heathen's latest monstrous transgression.

What was she to do now?

Sister Saint Delphin and the others fully expected her to crawl back and tearfully beg forgiveness. If she went back to the convent, there was no doubt in her mind that they'd destroy the *vielle*. The very thought of it tore at her insides. She loved her *vielle*. It was the only comfort she had in this awful place.

She thought back to the conversation she'd overheard earlier, about the great mass of boys making their way down to Marseille. They were camped at Sancerre, one of the novices had said. If she headed west, she could meet up with them in a couple of days, as they made their way south down the Loire.

She couldn't walk all that way on an empty stomach.

She sat for several hours, waiting for darkness to fall, then made her way back along the stream. There was an

almost full moon, and the land around her seemed illumi-
nated with an eerie glow. As she got closer to the convent,
she heard the bells for Matins, and knew the nuns would be
rousing themselves from sleep and making their way to the
chapel for midnight prayers. But between the end of Matins
until the bells rang again for Lauds in the hours before dawn,
everyone in the convent would be sound asleep.

Once she was satisfied that midnight prayers were over
and the nuns had returned to their beds, she slipped quietly
into the kitchen. Even without a candle, she knew the place
well enough to feel her way around. She took one of the balls
of cheese hanging from the ceiling in a net bag, along with
some sausages also hanging to dry. In the basket in the corner,
she knew, were the loaves for the next morning's breakfast.
She felt down for it and grabbed two.

So now, to add to her many sins, she was also a thief.

❧

CHAPTER 7
The Miracle of Little Guinefort
May 1212

THEY HAD BEEN FOLLOWING THE SNAKY PATH of the river Loire for days, and now they were approaching the city of Nevers, which they could see on the ridge ahead. Below the town the Loire met the river Nièvre, and near that juncture another small stream forked off to the north.

As they approached the forks, Abel saw a number of people standing on the riverbank. The pilgrims around him all streamed over to see what was going on. There were shouts and cries coming from inside the crowd, but he couldn't tell if they were sounds of excitement or fear.

He followed the other pilgrims over to the river and managed to push his way to the front of the crowd. A woman was kneeling on a flat rock in the shallows, her hands gripping something she repeatedly plunged into the river.

"Saint Guinefort, we beseech you to drive out this devil!" one of the women in the crowd cried out.

At first Abel thought the wriggling creature in the woman's grasp was a small animal, but as she lifted it out of the water he was shocked to see it was a child, dripping as he dangled upside down.

"What is she doing?" Abel cried in horror.

The pilgrims around him, amused at his ignorance, explained that the child was a changeling, and that only by praying to Saint Guinefort and dipping him nine times in waters where three rivers meet could the evil spirit be driven out.

"What makes her think the child is a changeling?" Abel insisted. "What's wrong with him?"

His questions were interrupted by shrieks from the crowd. The woman had turned the child around to display the large, ugly growth on his neck, protruding from just under one of his ears to below his throat. Abel had seen goiters before on a few of his father's patients but never one so large. Involuntarily, he shrank back in disgust.

"It didn't work!" someone called out. "The devil's still in him."

Others in the crowd began shouting at the woman to finish off the child, to hold his head under the water and drown him.

"No!" Abel screamed at them. "That thing on his neck is harmless. I know — my father's a doctor."

"What do doctors know about changelings?" one of the village women said dismissively. "Since that thing burst out of him, he's gone deaf as a stone and hasn't said a word. That's what happens when a devil makes off with a soul."

Abel didn't know what to do. He recalled that one of his father's goiter patients was also deaf. His father had consulted the work of the Arab physician Abulcasis of Cordoba, who postulated that the two conditions were related, that the goiter might be causing the deafness. Abel could see it was no use trying to talk sense to the villagers.

There was a commotion behind him.

"Make way for Étienne," someone called.

The crowd parted as Étienne emerged. He looked quizzically at Abel, who began to explain what was going on.

Before Abel could get two words out of his mouth, Étienne reached over and took the dripping child from the woman's grasp. He drew the child's body to his, pressing his own cheek directly against the bulbous growth on the child's neck, and let out a single, anguished sob. For a few moments there was complete silence. Then Étienne lifted his head to the crowd, cradling the child tightly against his breast.

"Did not our Lord say, 'When you do it for the least of my brethren, you do it for me?' Woman, if you will not care for this child, we will take him with us on the Crusade of the New Innocents."

Abel was disconcerted. Was Étienne really serious about bringing the boy along? They already had too many young ones as it was, and this one was barely out of babyhood — he couldn't be more than three or four years old. And the pilgrims were just as convinced as the villagers that the child was possessed. Abel feared what would happen to the child on the march. He'd be shunned, mocked, maybe worse.

Étienne handed the boy to one of the pilgrims and commanded him to carry the child with the group when they departed. Then he hurried off by himself. Abel ran after him, wondering if he should try to get him to change his mind. When he caught up with him, Étienne was trembling.

"Étienne, what's wrong?"

"How could she do that?"

"What?"

"How could a mother abandon her own child?"

Abel started to explain that the unfortunate woman was just misguided but realized Étienne wasn't really listening to him. There was a faraway look in his eyes, and Abel had a strong feeling that he wasn't talking only about the woman at the river. He recalled that he hadn't found out what happened to Étienne's mother, that Étienne had never gotten around to telling him about her.

ؤ

Abel could only wonder what the child thought about the strange turn his life had taken, but he was incessantly cheerful and seemed to love all the doting attention. He was mute and could not tell them his name, so they took to calling him Little Guinefort, after the saint to whom the villagers had prayed to drive out the changeling.

The name caused much merriment among the pilgrims. When Abel asked what was so funny about it, they burst out laughing.

"Don't you know who Saint Guinefort is?" one asked incredulously.

"Saint Guinefort is a greyhound!" another shouted over peals of laughter.

Abel realized he was the only one who was ignorant of the true nature of Saint Guinefort. He marveled anew at the peculiarities of these Christians, making a saint of a dog, no less. Still, it was another reminder that he had to be careful lest his ignorance of Christian matters begin to draw suspicion.

He was relieved to see that his fears proved groundless, that despite the pilgrims' initial wariness, they didn't ostracize Little Guinefort. Instead, they took their cue from Étienne, who showed the boy a special tenderness and frequently carried him on his shoulders as they walked. After a while, some of the girls began to fuss over Guinefort, and pilgrims vied among themselves to see who would carry him, mostly as a way of winning favor with Etienne. Abel overheard some of them speaking in awed tones about Étienne's treatment of the deformed child.

"Étienne took him in his arms and prayed over him."

"Just like Jesus when He healed the leper!"

Abel thought of pointing out to them that Guinefort had not been healed at all — he was still deaf and still had his goiter. He knew that wasn't what the pilgrims wanted to hear. In fact, after the incident outside Nevers, he began to notice a growing intensity in people's response to Étienne. They surrounded him, pressing in close to him. Some asked if they could kiss his clothing, touch the hem of his cloak. Others asked him to lay his hands on their heads and bless them. Though he felt awkward at first, Étienne always did what they asked. He gradually grew more comfortable with the requests, convinced, as he explained to Abel, that it was comforting for people. Still, Able was alarmed at some of their behavior. In one village he saw a woman reach up and tug at Étienne's hair. He pulled her hand away sharply.

"What are you doing?"

"Just a few hairs I want, a relic of the holy Étienne."

"Relic?" Abel said, exasperated. "He's not dead and he's not a saint."

"He will surely be both," the woman replied briskly.

Abel shook his head as she walked away reluctantly. This predilection for relics — bits of clothing, even body parts of saints — was another Christian practice he found very strange.

Although Abel tried his best to lay down rules to protect Étienne, the more people asked, the more Étienne was willing to accommodate them, even allowing people to tear threads of his cloak. Still he was relieved to no longer hear the kind of angry denunciations of Muslims that punctuated Étienne's sermons back in Saint Denis. People's hatred of the Infidels seemed to have been replaced — for the moment at least — with the deep spiritual yearnings they experienced in Étienne's presence.

As more and more people flocked to join them, Abel was coming to see that, in ways he didn't fully understand, Étienne was giving voice to the deepest longings of the poor and dispossessed. Time and again, Abel was shocked by the wretched sight of men, women, whole families who had lost their land, reduced to begging to survive. He had no idea so many were destitute and appreciated how fortunate he was, what a comfortable and even sheltered life he had lived with his family in the Broce-aux-Juifs back in Troyes.

Some who joined the crusade were not only poor, but also outcasts — idiots, crookbacks and others who managed to barely survive on the margins of village society. People took to calling them simply the *pueri* — the boys — despite the smattering of girls among them. Étienne assured them all they would find acceptance in the Crusade of New Innocents, because God loved them more than the rich and powerful, and had promised that He would raise up the lowly on the Last Day.

"Blessed are the poor in spirit, for they shall see God."

They were on a hillside near Lyon one day when they heard shouts coming from below.

"Étienne!"

"Where is Étienne?"

"Here I am!" he called down to them. "What is it?"

"Someone has come! Someone with news!"

Abel and Étienne looked down to see a pale boy in tattered clothes making his way up the hill. He looked so thin that Abel wondered if he had the strength to make the climb. Finally, out of breath, he staggered over to Étienne and began speaking rapidly in German. Étienne shook his head to indicate he couldn't understand. The boy then launched into halting, heavily accented French, but other than picking up that the boy was from Cologne, a city in the Rhineland, Étienne was still at a loss to know what he was trying to say.

"Let me try and talk to him," Abel interjected. Growing up in Troyes, he'd picked up a smattering of German, since the city was on a major trade route and merchants from the Rhineland frequently visited there. Speaking a combination of French and German with the boy, he was able to figure out the gist of his message and convey it to Étienne.

"He says news of the crusade reached the Rhineland … The young people there were excited and formed their own contingent … They set out from Cologne and are making their way across the Alps … They are encountering terrible hardships … near starvation … walking through ice and snow in bare feet … But he says the Rhineland children are determined to keep going … until they meet up with us in Marseille!"

Étienne was jubilant at the news.

"How many are coming?"

Abel relayed Étienne's question to the boy, but he seemed to have no real idea and could only answer "many."

"This is wonderful. Everything we have worked for is coming to fruition," he told Abel excitedly. "Nothing can stop us now! *Dieu le veut!*"

As Étienne spoke, Abel looked down at the great masses of people streaming across the countryside and up the hill. He was astounded at the scene below him. He knew their numbers were growing, but until that moment he had had no real conception of what a phenomenon the crusade had become.

How many more would there be when they were joined by the group from the Rhineland? How would they manage then? How would they feed so many? Where would they sleep?

Kathleen McDonnell

His moment of panic passed. Étienne was right. They had to trust in God. For how could it be anything but God's will, this great swell of humanity marching triumphantly through the villages and towns?

Perhaps the Crusade of the New Innocents really was a harbinger of *Olam Ha-Ba*, the time foretold by the prophet Isaiah, when harmony among all the peoples of the earth would prevail, when wars would cease and the cruelty of human beings to one another would come to an end.

Something great and new was coming into the world. He could feel it. He was part of it. There was no way he could abandon the journey now.

The time had come to let his family know his whereabouts. He would have to send a message to his parents explaining his absence and asking their forgiveness. He thought of the Three Hundred — the group of rabbis and their families who had set out a year earlier for the Jewish homeland in Jerusalem. He had to somehow make his father understand that in embarking on this journey with Étienne, he was following in the footsteps of the Three Hundred rabbis. He was doing his part to bring the world to come into being.

What Étienne said was true: This was a crusade like no other, a crusade grounded in peace and love, not blood and force. A crusade in which Jew and Christian walked side by side.

And very soon, when the time was right, he would tell Étienne who he really was.

CHAPTER 8
Midsummer Eve
June 1212

THEY HAD JUST FINISHED MIDDAY PRAYERS and were preparing to set out when Abel noticed a small boy running along the edge of the crowd of pilgrims. He seemed to be looking for someone and, at his wit's end, began frantically screaming at the top of his lungs.

"Basile! Basile! Basile!"

Abel recognized him as the little brother that Basile the plow boy had left behind many days earlier. The child must have run away and somehow managed to survive on his own until he caught up with the pilgrims. Abel thought back to the heart-wrenching scene when Basile had joined them, and now he could only imagine the mother's agony at finding her other son gone as well.

His home was several days' walk away, so there was no way the child could be sent back to his mother. The only thing to do was to find Basile.

Abel went over to the boy.

"Would you like me to help you find your brother?" he asked.

Wiping away tears, the boy nodded.

Abel took him by the hand. His grip was weak and his arm so thin that Abel figured he had barely eaten on his journey, and resolved to find him some food. For the moment, finding his brother was even more important to him. Together they walked through the crowd, calling out Basile's name. Now that there were so many pilgrims, finding any single person was no easy task, and there were a number of boys who answered to the name Basile. Abel realized they would have to be more specific.

"We are looking for Basile whose little brother is named Léonard," he called out.

After nearly an hour of looking, they finally heard a voice call back.

"Léolo? Is that you?"

"Basile! Basile!"

As he saw his brother bounding out of the crowd, Léolo burst into tears and raced toward him. Basile scooped the child up with a look of dumbfounded amazement.

"Léolo? How did you get here?"

Carried in his brother's arms, Léolo talked rapidly through his tears as the two of them blended back into the great mass of pilgrims.

Watching the joyous reunion, Abel pondered with amazement how much his life had changed in such a short time. Only weeks before, he'd passed his time studying and attending lectures in the Street of the Straw. Now his days were taken up with very different tasks. He was Étienne's trusted adviser, the one person to whom he confided his hopes and fears. Each night they talked, just the two of them, about the events of the day, the new pilgrims who'd joined, what they might expect at the next village or town. And from the moment he awoke the next morning, he was on the move, following Étienne through the crowd of pilgrims.

Everyone, it seemed, wanted to see Étienne up close, to talk to him and ask for his blessing. He listened, with what seemed like endless patience, to their stories and requests, offering comfort where he could. Usually he referred problems to Abel, who would then seek solutions from among the pilgrims.

One day Abel came upon a boy who had a festering sore on his heel and could barely walk. Like most of the pilgrims, he had no shoes and was making the journey barefoot. The boy was having trouble keeping up with the group, and Abel feared his foot might become gangrenous. Footwear would have to be found for the boy.

He spread the word among the pilgrims, and before long a young man sought him out, an apprentice shoemaker who had brought his tools with him when he left his master's workshop and quickly fashioned a simple pair of boots for the boy out of goatskin.

Again and again, Abel found himself moved by the pilgrims' generosity and heartened by their ingenuity. As time went on, he noticed they were dealing with problems on their own rather than coming to him. Some difficulties defied all his best efforts to find solutions. In such a large group of people, there were the inevitable arguments and petty disputes, which Abel was frequently called upon to settle. Many of the arguments, he noted, involved Rémi, the hotheaded cutler's apprentice whose master had dragged him by the hair.

And there was the great overriding problem that occupied their every waking moment. In the earliest days of the march, there had been more than enough food to go around. Every day local people had brought them bread, salt pork, sometimes even cakes and honey. Those blessed days had came to an end, giving way to a never-ending search to find things they could eat.

They picked wild leeks and other herbs. They scavenged the small, underripe pears and apples that had fallen to the ground. At every stream they fished for trout and salmon, and the boys put their hunting skills to use, snaring grouse, rabbits and whatever else they could find. When they stopped to make camp in the evening, the servant girls put their kitchen skills to good use, skinning and preparing the animals for cooking while the younger boys scavenged for firewood.

But for all their efforts, there was never enough. Abel tried as best he could to make sure the food was divided fairly, that everyone had a share. But hunger was the pilgrims' constant companion.

He had to trust that Étienne was right: God would provide. Still, his mind was often heavy with worry. He sometimes asked himself whether, if he'd known what an enormous undertaking it would turn out to be, would he have set off for Saint Denis that morning with Étienne. And he brooded over what his father would say when he learned that Abel had left the university.

He couldn't put it off any longer. The letter to his family had to be written. In the city of Roanne he was finally able to secure some vellum and ink. He decided to steal a few moments by himself to compose the letter, when he saw a commotion in the cathedral square.

Étienne, preaching on the steps of the cathedral, was interrupted by a local priest, who exhorted the crowd not to listen to the boy preacher. By now the crusaders were used to opposition from the local clergy, and Étienne resumed speaking. The priest broke in again, and what he said this time took Étienne aback.

"The Holy Father himself denounces your crusade."

A collective gasp went up through the crowd.

"That can't be true," Étienne said.

"Oh, but it is," the priest insisted.

"How do you know that?" someone in the crowd called out.

"The bishop of Lyon himself has just returned from Rome. He said the Holy Father expressed great displeasure at the idea of so many children defying their parents and wandering the countryside, daring to call their disobedience a crusade."

"But Étienne was visited by Saint Nicholas!"

"In following him we're doing God's will!"

"That is for the Holy Father to decide. He alone has the divine authority to call a crusade, not some shepherd from the Orléanais whose head is swelled by the sin of pride."

The crowd, in no mood to cave in to the priest's demands,

bade Étienne to continue, and he did. As he and Abel talked later that night, he was still agonizing over what to do.

"What if the priest was right?" he asked Abel. "What if the Holy Father opposes the crusade?"

Abel was surprised at how tortured Étienne seemed to be. He had openly defied the priests, but opposition from the pope was clearly a different matter. This elevation of a single religious figure over all others mystified Abel. In Judaism, there were no all-powerful earthly leaders; only the word of God was supreme. All ideas were open to discussion and the rabbis carried on lengthy, spirited debates. If the opinion of any one of them was regarded as superior to the others, it was because he had argued his position more persuasively.

"That's just it," he tried to reassure Étienne. "You don't know if what he said is true or not. Wait and see what happens."

"You're right," said Étienne. "It's always so helpful to talk over things with you. I value your counsel so much, my friend. Sometimes I wonder what would have happened if you hadn't decided to come to Saint Denis with me that day."

Listening to Étienne's words, Abel felt a deep happiness. In some ways he'd come to feel closer to Étienne than he'd ever felt to another person. This country boy from the Orléanais, he realized, was the brother he never had.

As they sat in silence, Abel decided the moment had come. The moment to end secrecy and say the things he'd been holding back.

"I feel the same way about our talks together," he began. "And there is something else we should talk about …"

His voice trailed off. Étienne was not listening. His eyes were shut, his hands cupped together in front of his face, lost in prayer. After a few moments, he opened them and looked at Abel.

"I feel at peace, now that I have prayed for guidance. I'm ready to go to sleep."

With that, he lay down on the ground and closed his eyes again.

Another time, Abel thought. But soon. Soon.

୨

The pilgrims were massed around a bonfire in a field outside Saint-Foy when Étienne first heard the mysterious droning sound.

Earlier, he'd watched from a distance as they gathered wood and assembled the enormous bonfire. The thought of Midsummer Eve revelry made him uneasy, and he wondered if he should step in to call a halt to the preparations. He looked around for Abel to ask his opinion, but for the moment Abel was nowhere to be found.

On this night, all across the countryside, people were setting bonfires in celebration of Midsummer Eve, the longest day of the year. There would be much dancing and drinking, and when the fires burned down, couples would join hands and jump over the embers, then run off together into the bushes or somewhere else they could be alone. The church authorities made halfhearted attempts to discourage the wild festivities, which dated back to pagan times, before the great Charlemagne had embraced Christianity. They knew that if they banned outright the celebration of Midsummer Eve, the people would just ignore them and carry on anyway. So the bishops decreed that the building of bonfires was permitted in honor of the feast day of Saint John the Baptist, which fell around the same time.

Once again Étienne recalled the words of the mendicant back in Vendôme: "We are never closer to God than when we are joyous and high-spirited as children." Most of the pilgrims were little more than children themselves. They needed to play. He would not be like the bishops, Étienne decided, trying to squelch the people's natural exuberance. Midsummer Eve was exactly what the pilgrims needed right now to take their minds off the gnawing hunger in their bellies.

When the strange drone rose up from somewhere near the edge of the field, he was moved to join the throng around the bonfire. After a few moments, the drone was layered over by the notes of a lively dance tune. One by one pilgrims got up and began to dance with joyous abandon around the fire. Soon a huge circle dance formed.

A female voice began to sing an old ballad.

It's rosebuds in June and violets in full bloom
And the small birds are singing love songs on each spray.
We'll pipe and we'll sing, love, we'll dance in a ring, love,
When each lad takes his lass all on the green grass.

Many of the pilgrims were familiar with the words and joined in. After a few moments, Étienne himself stood up and joined the ring dance. A raucous cheer went up.

"Our Étienne dances!"

When the dance was over, he was nearly out of breath. He felt exhilarated. He turned and saw a large group of boys clustered in a circle. In the center was a girl he hadn't seen before. She was holding a wooden box with a crank on its side. She was turning the crank with one hand, and Étienne realized that this girl and her box were the source of the lively music.

He walked over toward the group. As he approached, the girl began to play another tune, slow and haunting, one that seemed to weave an even more intoxicating spell, leaving him disoriented, light-headed.

When the tune ended, he stepped into the circle.

"Who are you?" he asked the girl.

"My name is Blanche," she replied. "Who are you?"

He realized she must have been a very new arrival. A boy standing nearby spoke up.

"He's Étienne, of course!" he shouted indignantly.

The girl looked startled.

"You're Étienne? The one they call the boy preacher?"

"You've heard of me?" Étienne said, knowing full well he was being falsely modest.

"Of course. The name of Étienne the boy preacher rings up and down the fields of the Lyonnais."

She had come from a convent near Lyon, she told him. When she heard about the crusade, she knew immediately that she wanted to join the pilgrims on their march to the Holy Land. He was eager to know more about this mysterious newcomer, but for the moment she didn't seem to want to say much about herself. He believed that for her to leave the safety and comfort of the convent behind, her faith had to be very strong indeed.

The bonfire was dying down. Suddenly there was a mad scramble. Some of the older boys were racing toward the cluster of girls at one end of the crowd. A few of the girls ran away, but most stood laughing, not resisting as they were captured by the boys and pulled toward the fire. In pairs they jumped over the pile of embers, and several couples, still laughing, raced off into the darkness at the edge of the field.

Now Étienne was standing so close to the new girl that he could feel her breathing. Almost without thinking, he held out his hand to her. She looked at it a moment, then pulled the strap over her head and laid the *vielle* on the ground beside her.

She took his hand, and together they jumped over the red-hot embers.

ဢ

Earlier, as she had watched them from a distance gathered around the roaring fire, Blanche had sorely regretted what she'd done. What madness had driven her to leave the security of the nunnery, where she had food and a bed and safety? What was she doing here with all these rough peasants who were nothing like her, who called themselves crusaders and carried the banners of the church that had murdered her family and laid waste to her city?

She could still go back. It wasn't too late. Of course, she'd be severely punished for her behavior to Sister Saint Delphin, but it might be preferable to the hardscrabble life of these pilgrims. Yet when she imagined herself going back, crossing the threshold into the nunnery, making her way down the dark corridor to her little room, an overwhelming sense of despair came over her. It was the same feeling she'd had when the Good Knight left her at the convent. She felt a sharp ache, a longing for her mother, for her old, dimly remembered life, now gone forever. She realized anew that she had nowhere to go. She was all alone in the world.

No. She would not go back there.

She summoned up the courage to go out and walk among them. At first she was relieved to be unnoticed. No one spoke to her or asked who she was. She saw a few girls here and there, but they seemed to sense she was different from them and kept their distance. She noticed a few of the peasant boys staring hard at her, which made her anxious and uncomfortable. She'd lived with only women for so long. She wasn't used to being around males, especially not these coarse peasant boys.

She was startled by a voice behind her.

"What's that?"

She turned to see a boy, pointing to the *vielle*, carried by a strap across her back.

"It's a music box."

His question attracted the attention of others nearby, who came over to see for themselves.

"A music box?"

"What's that?"

She swung the strap around to her chest, and began to turn the crank on the *vielle*.

A large group clustered around her, their eyes wide with curiosity. Clearly they'd never seen or heard anything like it before. They listened attentively, which only unnerved her. No one else had ever heard her play.

Then she noticed him looking at her.

She knew right away who he was — it was obvious from the way the others treated him — but she pretended not to. Even in his rough peasant tunic he was handsome, almost regal in his bearing. They spoke only a few words, but when he looked at her, his eyes burned with an intensity that sent a shiver down her spine.

She was surprised when he motioned to her to jump over the fire with him. She expected him to be too reserved, too aware of his position to indulge in such antics. But she laid down her *vielle* and took his hand. They broke into a run and took a flying leap over the embers, and when they landed the crowd erupted in cheers.

From that moment, the pilgrims treated her differently. Even the boys who had been teasing and leering at her earlier now approached her with a certain deference. They understood that Étienne had a special regard for her.

For so long she had prayed for the Good Knight to take her away from the miserable, loveless existence of the convent, and he had not come. But God had answered her prayers. She had found her savior.

❧

Abel wasn't at all happy to have this new girl around — the one who had emerged out of the darkness on Midsummer Eve playing a strange music box. Its eerie drone made him think of the Sirens, those dangerous female spirits in Homer's epic poem whose call lured the hero Odysseus away from his true purpose.

When he saw Étienne hand in hand with the girl, jumping over the bonfire, he was shocked. The pilgrims looked up to Étienne. How could he have let them all see him carrying on like that, no better than those wild boys?

He didn't fully understand why he felt so unsettled, even resentful of her presence. He knew what Étienne would say if he found out he felt that way. He'd say that Abel was being un-Christian, that as a leader of the crusade it was his duty to make everyone feel welcome. Abel was careful to hide his feelings toward the girl, especially when Étienne was around, but he couldn't help the fact that he just didn't like her.

After a few days, Étienne took to including her in the nightly talks with Abel. He said he needed them both at his side, constantly reminding him that he was only the vessel of God's grace so he wouldn't succumb to the sin of pride. He valued their counsel, he said, because they weren't simple, impressionable peasants like the other pilgrims, who treated him like a saint. Abel knew there was more to it than that.

Blanche mystified him. She wasn't like the other girls who had joined the crusade. She could read, and he could tell from the way she spoke that she was no peasant. It made no sense for a girl like that to leave the secure life of the convent to take to the road, to scramble for food and sleep in fields under the stars.

What was she doing here?

CHAPTER 9
A Beautiful Fire
July 1212

It was scorchingly hot, and dry as bones baking in the sun.

The first weeks after they left Saint Denis and trekked through the Loire Valley, they'd been blessed with glorious summer weather. Once they had crossed the Rhône in early July and headed south toward Provence, the days grew hotter and hotter. They began to see dry creek beds, parched fields dotted with crops shriveling in the unrelenting sun. The old people said it was the hottest summer in living memory.

They were finding it harder than ever to find food. The bountiful charity they'd received in the early days of the crusade was a distant memory. The peasants were keeping what little they had for themselves. Worn down by hunger, exhausted from the heat, the pilgrims no longer sang as they marched. Instead, tempers flared. There was much grumbling and complaining.

Étienne tried his best to keep their spirits up and pull them together.

"This is another of God's tests," he told them. "Think

of your fellow pilgrims from the Rhineland, who are at this moment trudging across the frozen Alps. They are famished, they shiver in the cold, but do they complain? Do they waver in their faith? No. They keep going, and trust in God Almighty to lead them to meet us in Marseille."

Whenever he spoke, things would settle down for a while, but it was never long before the complaints started up again, and boys were at one another's throats. One afternoon Abel happened upon an argument over who would carry Little Guinefort. Because of the weight and pressure of his goiter, the child's breathing was labored at the best of times. In the oppressive heat, he barely had the strength to move and needed to be carried constantly. No one, it appeared, was willing to carrying the child any longer, and the argument quickly degenerated into a shouting match between those who wanted to leave Little Guinefort behind and a handful of pilgrims who objected.

"We can't abandon him. He'll die," said one of the girls.

"Then you carry him!" someone yelled.

"I can't!" she shot back. "I'm too weak!"

"We all are!"

"He's not going to last much longer anyway! Look at him. He can hardly draw a breath."

"We'll all die soon if we don't find something to eat!"

The child, who seemed to know the argument was about him, quivered as the angry voices shook the air around him. Abel listened to the heated talk with great discomfort. His instincts told him that the boys were right. Little Guinefort couldn't survive much longer in this heat, but he couldn't countenance abandoning the child to die alone.

He looked around but couldn't see Étienne anywhere. He'd have to find a way to resolve the dispute himself. He was just about to speak when the girl Blanche stepped out of the crowd.

"I'll carry the boy."

She marched through the circle of boys assembled around Little Guinefort and scooped the child up off the ground. He threw his arms around Blanche's neck and burrowed into her bosom. For a few moments there was a shocked silence. Then one of the boys who had been at the center of the argument called out to her.

"Fine. See how long you last in this heat."

"Down here in the Languedoc we're used to a little hot weather. And I've got more strength than the rest of you. You've barely eaten for weeks. My belly is still full of convent food. Let's get moving."

She lifted Little Guinefort up onto her shoulders and resumed walking. Noticing that she still had her music box slung onto her back, Abel was even more surprised at her willingness to take on the extra weight of the child.

He felt a swirl of mixed emotions. Blanche's action had gotten him out of a difficult situation and nipped another argument in the bud. What's more, she'd set an example of self-sacrifice that would win her even more favor with Etienne when he heard about the incident, as he surely would. Until now she had been the mysterious, beguiling stranger. Now, in Étienne's eyes, she would become an angel of mercy too.

The thought of it made Abel hate her more than ever.

❧

Little Guinefort was quite taken with the unusual instrument slung on her back. At first he tried to reach down and play with the buttons, but his squirming and stretching threw her off balance. She looked up at him with a piercing gaze, to let him know that he was to sit still and leave the *vielle* alone. Then she took his hand and squeezed it so he would understand that she wasn't really angry at him. The child seemed to understand, and settled down to ride quietly on her shoulders.

She wondered what was going in his mind. It had to be very lonely to live in a silent world — to have no ability to speak or understand those around him. It was an isolation she understood. Only days earlier she too had felt profoundly lonely, cut off from life. Now the weight of Little Guinefort perched on her shoulders felt uncommonly light, even with the *vielle* slung across her back. It was as if nothing could weigh her down, because there was such a lightness in her heart.

To think she had almost turned around and gone back to the convent. And not met Étienne.

Thinking of him, she felt strange and unfamiliar stirrings in her body. She didn't try to push them away. It was true that Good Christians considered carnal desires evil, part of the matter that keeps the spirit mired in the physical world. They also believed in enjoying the sweet delights of the material world while they dwelled in it, which was why most Good Christians delayed taking the *consolamentum*, which entailed the renunciation of carnal love and the eating of animal flesh, until they were on their deathbeds.

For the first time since that terrible day in Béziers, she again belonged somewhere — here, by Étienne's side, walking with the pilgrims to Marseille. They accepted her as one of them.

Not all of them, of course. She saw how the one called Abel glowered at her, as if he had daggers in his eyes. He seemed to resent the attention Étienne paid to her.

There was also something that she couldn't put her finger on at first. She knew he was educated, of course. The pilgrims talked about how he had left his studies at the university in Paris to help Étienne start the crusade. But there was something else that set him apart. Gradually, it dawned on her how much his manner and way of speaking reminded her of the Jewish students she used to see every day leaving the synagogue in Béziers, carrying their slates, on which they had written words in the Hebrew script.

Surely he couldn't be a Jew, marching with all these Christian pilgrims. Not that any of them would know it if he was. Few Christians had the day-to-day contact with Jews that was normal in Béziers and the other cities of the Languedoc. Most of the pilgrim boys came from the north, where Jewish people lived apart, in their own districts.

Whatever it was, Abel clearly wasn't happy having her around. It didn't matter what he thought about her, though. Only Étienne's feelings mattered. And he cared for her, like Tristan for his beloved Isolde.

She could see it in his eyes when he looked at her.

ॐ

Back in Roanne, Abel had begun to compose the letter to his family. It proved to be a far more difficult task than he anticipated. Whenever he sat down to write, he would imagine his parents reading the letter, and the look of pained bewilderment on their faces would stop him cold. How could he possibly find the right words to make them understand what he was doing, and why?

It didn't help that there were so many other demands on his attention. Invariably a group of pilgrims would cluster around him, curious about the strange symbols that seemed to magically flow from the quill in his hand onto the vellum. Most had never even seen words written down before.

Now, as they took refuge from the afternoon heat under a canopy of walnut trees, Abel managed to steal a few moments by himself to finish the letter. This time, he stopped trying to explain himself and simply wrote from his heart.

> I would never intentionally cause you pain, and I hope that in time you will forgive me for not seeking your permission before leaving Paris. I know that my actions must seem strange and difficult to understand, but I feel strongly, in a way that I cannot put into words, that it is somehow right for me to be here. Father, you have said many times that we Jews cannot simply wait for *Olam Ha-Ba*, that we must do our part to bring it

about. The followers of Étienne have been drawn together by the same glorious dream of peace and understanding among all the peoples of the earth. We are walking side by side, on a journey toward the world to come.

I will not be absent from the university much longer, and I promise that on my return I will study very hard and make up all the work I missed.

With the deepest affection and respect,

Your loving son,
Abel

He was waiting for the ink to dry when he spied some boys around the donkey cart that Étienne had been using to deliver his sermons. The boys had tied several poles to its sides and were stretching some cloth over top of the poles. He went over to them.

"What are you doing?"

"Fixing up the cart for Étienne to ride in," they said.

"It's for his preaching. Why would he need to ride in it?"

"So this canopy can shield him from the burning sun."

"You don't mean to pull him in that thing?" Abel asked them.

They all nodded eagerly.

"We already showed it to him," said one proudly.

"And he didn't tell you to stop?"

"Oh, no. We told him we would pull him in the cart so that he could save his strength for preaching, and he agreed."

Abel went immediately to find Étienne.

"What are you thinking? You can't let them pull you in that cart."

"Why not?"

"You can't let them treat you like some kind of saint. They already give you their food and go without themselves."

"They want to do it. It takes their mind off their empty stomachs."

"It sets a bad example, putting yourself above the rest of the pilgrims. You yourself say that we're all equal in the eyes of the Lord. Shouldn't we all undergo the same hardships?"

"You don't understand, Abel. I'm doing this for them, not for my own comfort. This way I can be seen above the multitude. I can bless them and give them the strength to keep going."

Abel sighed. There was no use arguing. It was clear that with every passing day he was losing influence with Étienne. The evening talks had stopped, and the rift between them was coming more and more out into the open. Étienne now spent all his time with Blanche. It was she who was at his side constantly, who had become his confidante.

❧

The heavy wooden door of the monastery loomed over Léolo as he stood surrounded by a clutch of other children.

Hunger had reached the point of desperation. Many of the pilgrims had had nothing to eat for several days. Their hopes rose when they spied the monastery of Saint Sauveur in the distance.

"The monks will not turn us away."

"They must practice Christian charity and share what they have."

Abel feared the boys' confidence was misplaced. He wasn't at all sure they'd be welcome at the monastery. There were just too many of them, and with the severe drought here in the south, few people had enough to even feed themselves. He decided that rather than descend on the monastery in a great mass, they might have better luck sending a group of the youngest children to appeal to the monks.

Now, as Abel watched anxiously from a short distance away, Léolo lifted both his frail arms and pounded with all his might on the monastery door. They waited a few moments in silence. Léolo was about to knock again when they heard a voice call out from behind the gate.

"Who's there?"

"Alms for the poor!" the children called out in unison, as they had been instructed to. "Alms for the poor!"

The voice came booming back.

"We have nothing to give. Go away."

The children looked at one another in shock. After a moment one of them spoke up.

"Please, Father. We are hungry."

"So is everyone here," the monk shot back.

Léolo and some of the other children chimed in.

"Please!"

"Alms for the poor."

"Any small thing you can give."

"Go see what you can find in the garden," the monk finally answered. "Then you must go."

The children were jubilant.

"Thank you, Father."

"God bless you, Father!"

Abel caught up with them as they raced around to the other side of the stone wall and descended on the neatly tilled rows lined with parched, pale green turnip leaves. As they dug into the dry, dusty soil with their hands, they pulled up nothing but clumps of shriveled roots.

☙

After the crushing disappointment at the monastery, it was harder than ever to keep going.

Later that day, Abel heard a piercing scream behind him. People streamed in the direction it had come from to see what was the matter. Abel followed them.

He pushed through a group of pilgrims and saw Basile, bent over and sobbing. At his feet lay his brother, his face ashen, his body limp and lifeless.

Léolo was dead.

Abel knew how weak the boy had grown in his solitary wanderings. Still, the onlookers were shocked. This was not the sickly Guinefort, whom everyone expected to die, but an able-bodied child like themselves.

A few boys dug a small grave by the side of the road, and Étienne led them in singing *Veni, Creator Spiritus* as Léolo's body was placed in the earth. As they walked away from the grave, Abel overheard some of pilgrims talking among themselves about going back home.

The next morning another boy was found dead where he had lain down to sleep. Word spread rapidly, and waves of panic spread through the crowd. More and more people began to talk openly of abandoning the crusade and going home.

Étienne angrily warned them that by breaking their sacred pledge to take up the cross, they were risking the fires of hell.

"What's the difference?" someone retorted. "This is like being in hell already."

"Everything that happens is part of God's divine plan," he reminded them. "For all we know, God has sent the terrible heat to dry up the sea. It is not a scourge but a miracle that will allow us to walk to the Holy Land!"

Étienne's arguments worked for a while. Many pilgrims changed their minds, and the mass exodus failed to develop.

ॐ

They trudged on in the blistering heat. They were about a day's walk south of Valence, preparing to settle in for the night, when they spied the two figures on horseback at the top of a ridge.

At first they were little more than specks on the horizon. The pilgrims stood watching as the figures became larger and more distinct, and the pounding of the horses' hooves grew louder and louder. Who, they speculated, might these riders be? Knights, perhaps? Emissaries out on business for the local viscount? It quickly became clear that this was no random encounter, for the two figures were riding right toward them.

When they came to the edge of the crowd, they spoke to a number of pilgrims, who nodded and pointed them in the direction of the canopied cart. The two men dismounted and started walking toward the cart. It was then that Abel saw that they were wearing clerical robes.

At first he was reluctant to go over and investigate. He hadn't even spoken to Étienne in several days. The very sight of him riding under the shelter of the cart, while all around him were exhausted, starving pilgrims at the limit of their endurance, made Abel grit his teeth in fury. Now he saw Étienne and Blanche heading toward the visitors, surrounded by pilgrims. He watched as the two groups met, and when the conversation quickly became heated, he could no longer keep his distance and hurried over.

Étienne was in a state of extreme agitation. The friars had been sent by the bishop of Avignon to investigate charges that the Crusade of New Innocents was tainted with the Albigensian heresy. Its adherents, popularly known as Cathars, were still numerous in the Languedoc, despite the efforts of the Church to put them down. According to reports that had reached Pope Innocent III in Rome, the

Cathars had infiltrated the crusade and were manipulating the impressionable young pilgrims, filling their heads with notions of rebellion against the authority of the Church in order to spread their heretical beliefs.

"How could the Holy Father think the crusade is under the control of heretics?" Étienne objected. "I don't even know any heretics. I've never met one in my life."

"That's just it," said one of the friars. "You wouldn't know one if you had. They hide their true beliefs, going stealthily among the faithful until they decide the time is ripe to pounce."

"The Holy Father calls them 'foxes in the vineyards of the Lord,'" said the other.

Abel didn't know what to think. He knew little of these heretics, other than the fact that their disagreements with Church authorities had been the cause of much bloodshed here in the south. He looked over at Blanche, who seemed deeply unnerved by the whole exchange. All the color seemed to have drained out of her face.

"Our faith is strong," Étienne insisted to the friars. "Look at our numbers. What power could a few heretics have over so many? And when we are met in Marseille by the faithful who have made their way over the Alps —"

One of the friars cut him off sharply.

"That will not happen. The Rhineland children will not be meeting you in Marseille."

"What?"

Étienne was so flabbergasted that his mouth could barely form the words.

"What do you mean, they won't be meeting us?"

The Rhineland contingent, the friars explained, had turned back and gone home, by order of Pope Innocent himself.

"A few of their number came to Rome to meet with the Holy Father. He told them they were too young to be on a crusade, that they should return to their homeland and submit to the will of their parents. The bishop of Avignon believes you should do the same."

"Go home?" he said. "Turn back now? We can't do that."

"There were a few among the Rhineland children who ignored the Holy Father's decree and have pushed on to Genoa," one of the friars replied. "Where, like you, they hope that God will part the seas for them. As the rebellious ones will soon discover, God bestows not grace but divine retribution on those who defy the scepter of Saint Peter."

For a few moments there was uneasy silence. Everyone waited to hear Étienne's response to the friar's thinly veiled warning.

Étienne turned to Abel with a look of desperation.

"What should we do?" he whispered.

Abel felt a surge of joy in his breast. Étienne was asking for his counsel. He still needed him!

He also knew well that the pope's disapproval was the thing Étienne feared most. But after all the trials they'd been through, after they'd already defied numerous priests who opposed the crusade, how could he contemplate disbanding the crusade now?

Abel knew he had to choose his words carefully. He turned to the friars.

"With all respect to his excellency, the bishop of Avignon has been misinformed," he told them. "These allegations of heresy are false rumors spread by those who are jealous of Étienne and wish to undermine his work. They are the same enemies we have encountered again and again, and the more they have opposed us the greater have our numbers become. These thousands of followers have faith that Étienne is carrying out the Divine Will, conveyed directly to him through the intercession of Saint Nicholas. He has no choice but to continue the crusade."

Abel could see that his words had just the effect he hoped for, for Étienne's expression quickly changed to one of clarity and resolve. Emboldened, he turned to the friars.

"My friend is right," he said. "I owe it to the pilgrims to carry on. But I understand that the bishop is very concerned for the welfare of the faithful and Holy Mother Church, and I will travel with you to Avignon so I can speak with him face-to-face, and put his fears to rest."

When they heard this, ripples of anxiety swept through the crowd of pilgrims surrounding them.

"No, Étienne," some called out. "Don't go."

"Don't leave us."

"What if the bishop won't let you come back?"

"Don't worry," Étienne reassured them. "Once I've seen the bishop, all this talk of ending the crusade will be swept aside."

"I'll go with you," said Abel.

"No," Étienne said firmly. "I need you and Blanche to stay here with the pilgrims and take care of things while I'm gone."

He got on the horse behind one of the friars. As they galloped away, Abel watched them with a feeling of deep apprehension. He wished he'd been more insistent about going along. Étienne had stood up to many adversaries in the course of the crusade — priests, the angry men with pitchforks at the gate of Gien.

Would he be able to hold his own with someone as powerful as the bishop of Avignon?

ç

In Étienne's absence, Abel tried his best to keep things under control, but the seeds of fear had been planted. Pilgrims again began leaving, and among those who stayed there was constant anxiety, wondering who in their ranks might be secretly polluting the crusade with heretical beliefs. They indulged in wild speculation about the Cathars and their rituals.

"I hear they stand in a circle and lower the cat on a rope so each one can get a good lick. Then they burn the animal and consume the ashes."

"Yes! That's why they're called cat-ars."

Abel was appalled by some of these bizarre notions, which were similar to the kind of ridiculous claims sometimes made about Jews.

He also noticed that a lot of the talk was spearheaded by Rémi. From the beginning the cutler's apprentice had seemed resentful of the way the pilgrims exalted a mere shepherd boy, and he engaged in a simmering, unspoken rivalry with Étienne. Now, in Étienne's absence, he grew bolder, seizing on the pervasive sense of unease to gain more influence among the young men.

"We know there are heretics among us. Why aren't we doing anything to root them out? Étienne would like to be held in the same high regard as Peter the Hermit. But Peter the Hermit was ruthless in battling the enemies of Christ. He told his followers to slaughter as many Jews as they could."

Abel was taken aback when he heard this.

"That's not true," he retorted. "Peter the Hermit was a great holy man. He wouldn't have said such a thing."

Rémi let out a loud snort of laughter, and the boys around him looked at Abel as if he was an idiot.

"Of course he did!"

"Everybody knows that."

Abel quickly realized he should hold his tongue and said no more. Once again, he had blurted out something that revealed his ignorance of Christian ways.

Rémi resumed his tirade.

"If you ask me, God is angry we let so many Jews live in our midst. That's why he put the curse of drought on the land. In the eyes of God, Jews are an abomination, worse even than the Infidels. You've heard of the child named William, who lived up in Norwich? He was kidnapped and murdered by Jews, to get the blood of a Christian child. That's what they use to make that strange flat bread of theirs."

Abel could hardly believe what he was hearing. The story about the child murder in Norwich had swept the country-side a few years earlier. His father and the Elders had laughed it off, regarding the accusations as preposterous, evidence that England was a land full of rude, ignorant people.

He had to fight to keep from speaking. He didn't dare voice his objections, not in the midst of the frenzy Rémi was stirring up.

He heard a voice from behind him.

"How could one who considers himself a Christian possibly believe such lies?"

Abel whirled around. To his astonishment, the person who spoke was Blanche. She marched into the group.

"Don't listen to him," she said, pointing straight at Rémi. "Those stories don't have a scrap of truth. People say all kinds of things about Jews just because they have different beliefs from Christians. What's so terrible about that?"

"It was the Jews killed Christ our Lord!" Rémi retorted.

"The scriptures say God that sent His son to be crucified to atone for the sins of mankind," Blanche shot back at him. "How can the Jews be blamed for doing God's will?"

Rémi glowered at her.

"You think just because Étienne favors you, that means you can say anything you want. I wonder what he'd say if he was here right now, listening to you defending the Jews and blaspheming Almighty God?"

"I know exactly what Étienne would say," she replied. "He would put an end to these accusations and suspicions once and for all. He would tell us to love one another, as Jesus Himself commanded."

For a few moments the boys just looked at her, chastened into silence. Then, one by one, they began to drift away.

❧

She went off by herself, where no one could see that she was quaking with fear. What was she thinking? Openly challenging the blowhard Rémi like that?

Of course, she knew perfectly well the rumors were false. There were no Good Christians secretly manipulating the crusade. But when she heard Rémi repeating those slanders about her people kissing the asses of cats, about Jews drinking babies' blood, she couldn't help herself. Her rage got the better of her. She couldn't afford to let it happen again. She had to be careful not to arouse suspicion, knowing all too well the brutality these so-called Christians were capable of.

In the beginning she'd been afraid of the hardships of joining the crusade; now it was her own safety she feared for. She'd cast her lot wholeheartedly with these people. She had no one to turn to, nowhere else to go.

Rémi's words came back to her now like a fist in the stomach. What would Étienne have done if he'd been there?

What if he found out who she really was?

❧

After so many weeks of living in the open air and scrambling for food, Étienne found it strange to be ushered into the richly decorated private chambers of the bishop of Avignon.

He had told the story of the relic peddler revealing himself as Saint Nicholas so many times, and it had never failed to move anyone who heard it. As he told it now, the bishop listened with stone-cold eyes.

"What they say about you is true," he said, when Étienne had finished. "Indeed, you have the storyteller's gift. But Satan has taken hold of your tongue and made it a weapon to cast his spell over the ignorant."

It was then that he directed his attendant to unfurl the scroll and pointed to the papal seal at the top. Étienne had no way of knowing whether it was truly the seal of Pope Innocent III, of course, for it was as meaningless to him as the lines of letters on the scoll. But the bishop had the attendant read the words aloud, and there was no mistaking the gist of the message. For a moment he felt as though he would fall into a faint on the floor in front of the clergyman.

As he watched the bishop turn his back to him and walk away, Étienne was speechless. He'd been so sure he could win the bishop over. How could it all have turned out so badly?

How could he go back and face the pilgrims?

੭

As he lay on the ground surrounded by sleeping pilgrims, Abel heard angry shouts in the distance. There was a fight brewing among some of the boys. Normally he would have immediately roused himself, figured out where the noise was coming from and gone to settle the altercation. Tonight he was too consumed by his own inner turmoil to care about the pilgrims and their petty disputes.

It never bodes well for Jews when Christians go after unbelievers.

He'd convinced himself that in embarking on the crusade with Étienne, he was following in the footsteps of the Three Hundred rabbis. The horrifying realization was dawning on him that he was actually dishonoring his own heritage. How could he have been so blind to the true nature of these Christians?

And worse, he had stood silent as Rémi and the other boys spewed forth their hateful lies about Jews, while Blanche, the girl he disliked so intensely, appeared to be the one person in the whole crusade willing to stand up for his people. He had no idea why she did what she did, but it was clear that she was braver than he was.

He felt a deep shame and anger at himself. How could he have left his home, his beloved family for this?

Finally he dropped off into a fitful sleep. He felt someone shaking him by the shoulder. He opened his eyes and saw a figure looming over him in the darkness.

"Étienne!"

Étienne opened his mouth to speak but all that came out was great heaving sobs.

"Étienne, please, tell me what's wrong."

"It's over, Abel. The crusade is finished."

"What do you mean, the crusade is finished?"

"We've been ordered to disband the crusade and return home."

"I know the bishop said that, but —"

"No, Abel. It's not the bishop. It's a direct command from the Holy Father himself. The bishop read the proclamation to me and showed me the papal seal. He says we must wait until we are older to fulfill our crusading vows. I can't go against the Holy Father. I'm afraid I've made a terrible mistake, Abel. Maybe the king was right. Maybe we've been doing Satan's bidding, not God's."

Abel had never seen Étienne look so forlorn, so utterly defeated. He thought back to Saint Denis, remembering all the times when Étienne had begun to lose heart, and how he'd always managed to find the words to console him and bolster his spirits. Now he couldn't think of a thing to say.

Étienne fell to his knees and raised his hands to the sky.

"Please, Lord," he said, tears streaming down his face. "Help me. Show me what you want me to do. If you want me to go on, I beg you. Give me a sign."

So this is it, Abel thought. After all they'd gone through, the crusade was coming to a halt here, in the parched fields of Provence. The world to come was not at hand, after all. The letter to his parents still lay in his pouch, and now there was no longer any need to send it. Tomorrow he would set out for Paris and return to his studies.

He was relieved when Étienne finally fell asleep beside him, exhausted.

❧

Abel woke up with a start. He'd been having restless dreams. In one, he was locked in a fierce fight with another boy, whose face was indistinct. Abel had the sense that his opponent was some kind of beautiful, divine being, like the angel Jacob wrestled with.

He looked over at Étienne, now sleeping peacefully, his chest rising and falling in an easy rhythm. He got up and walked a short distance away so as not to disturb him. It was a warm, still night. There was a heavy moisture in the air that felt like a prelude to rain. There had been many other nights that felt like this, and still no rain had come.

He heard steps behind him. He turned to see Blanche walking toward him.

"Étienne's back from Avignon," he said.

"Where is he?"

"Over there," said Abel, pointing to the sleeping Étienne. "Let him sleep awhile longer. He's exhausted."

"What happened in Avignon?"

Abel recounted what Étienne had told him about the pope's proclamation.

"What do we do now?"

Abel shrugged.

"We go home."

"Just like that?"

"Étienne says he can't go against the pope."

"The pope be damned! It's because of him that —"

She was about to say more but stopped herself. She could see how shocked he was to hear her talk about the pope in such terms. To her relief, Abel didn't chastise her for it.

"I know you're upset for Étienne," he said. "But maybe it's for the best. The pilgrims can't go on like this much longer. And I should return to my classes at the university. I suppose you'll go back to the convent?"

She shook her head.

"To your home, then?"

"I have no home."

"What do you mean, you have no home?"

To Abel's amazement, Blanche suddenly burst into tears.

"I had a home! I had a mother and father and sisters in Béziers, and they are all gone."

"Béziers? Isn't that where —"

She cut him off sharply.

"Where all the heretics were slaughtered? Yes! By order of your pope!"

He stared at her blankly for a few moments, unable to make sense of what she telling him. Then, in a flash, he understood.

"Then you —"

"Yes. I am one of them. Go on. Tell Rémi and the others."

"I wouldn't do that. It's just —"

"You expected some devil who burns cats alive?"

"No, no. I know those things Rémi said aren't true. I thought you were brave to stand up to him like that."

She stared at him for a moment, trying hard to decide if she should trust him, if he really meant what he was saying.

"I don't understand. If you're one of the Cathars, how did you come to be here, on a crusade?"

"When the pope's army attacked Béziers, the men stayed on the battlements while the women and children all fled to the cathedral. On the way I got separated from my mother and sister. I was looking for them when the soldiers stormed the gate and spread out through the city. A merchant found me and hid me in his cart under some wool bales. I stayed there a long time and saw some terrible things. After many hours, a knight discovered me hidden in the wool. He pulled me up onto his horse and took me to the convent in Lyon. Why he let me live I'll never know. He thought he was saving my soul, taking me to the nuns, but I hated it there. One of them used to taunt me, telling me my parents were burning in hell. It's she who will one day burn in hell, while my parents look down with pity from their place in paradise. That's why I ran away from the convent. And why I hate the pope," Blanche said, practically spitting out the words. "What these people call religion is just their excuse to kill and rob those who don't agree with them."

Blanche paused a moment before she resumed speaking, more quietly.

"Now you know my secret. I suppose you feel you must tell Étienne."

Abel shook his head.

"No. I will keep your secret. If you will keep mine."

He felt a rush of terror as he heard himself saying the words.

"What do you mean?"

"You are not the only one hiding your true self."

She eyed Abel curiously and for a few moments neither of them spoke. Finally Abel broke the silence.

"Blanche, I am a Jew."

"I know."

"You do?"

"Yes."

Abel felt great sobs of relief welling up in him. Finally the terrible burden of secrecy was lifted. For a few moments he could barely speak.

"How … how did you know?"

"I just knew. In Béziers, Jews and Christians live and work side by side. Nobody thinks anything of it. We are of different faiths, that's all. The man who hid me from the soldiers was a Jew. These people are ignorant; they don't know any better. Especially the young ones. Most of them have never even met a Jew. But I have to ask you the same question you asked me: What is a Jew doing on a crusade?"

"I barely know the answer to that myself," said Abel. "I met Étienne one day in Paris, and somehow his words just swept me along, as they do with everyone he meets. I believed in the things he said, but I don't know what to think anymore. He preaches love, but he seems blind to the hatred all around him."

"Maybe we're the ones who are blind to the truth," said Blanche. "I wonder, if Étienne knew who we really were, would he still want us by his side? Or would he despise us the same as Rémi and the others do?"

Abel wanted to argue with her, even as the tightening sensation in his chest told him that she was saying the very thing he didn't want to think about.

They were distracted by the sound of a distant rumble.

"What was that?"

They stopped talking and listened.

"Thunder?"

She pointed to the horizon. A bolt of lighting touched down in the distance.

Some children sleeping nearby were roused by the noise.

"Is there a storm?" one asked.

Abel tried to get them to go back to sleep. There had been brief, all-too-tantalizing hints of rain before. This would probably add up to no more than a few scattered drops.

The thunder grew louder, the bolts of lightning stronger, closer. Throughout the fields, pilgrims woke up and rose to their feet.

Rain was coming down, first sporadic drops, then a gentle drizzle.

Suddenly there was a shout from within the crowd.

"Look out!"

Lightning zigzagged across the sky and slashed down the side of a nearby tree, which burst into flames.

The pilgrims stood watching in amazement. The rain was coming down more heavily, but not enough to douse the burning tree, which was now completely ablaze. Two large branches, jutting out on either side of the tree to form a cross shape, groaned as they crackled with flames.

"This is it!"

The voice of Étienne came out of the darkness. He raced to the head of the throng and raised his arms to the sky.

"This is the sign!" he cried. "The beautiful fire of the crucifix on which He sacrificed His only begotten son. There can be no mistaking it! God means for us to continue the crusade!"

As his voice rang through the night, the tree sent up a final roar of flame. Then the heavens opened up and released a massive downpour. All around Étienne pilgrims fell to their knees, kissing the wet ground, catching the raindrops on their tongues.

"Our time of wandering in the wilderness is over. We will march in glory to Jerusalem!"

୬

The rain pounded down, and the pilgrims reveled in it, laughing, singing, soaked to the skin in their drenched clothes. The boys hoisted up Little Guinefort and bounced him along from shoulder to shoulder.

The long drought had ended. The spirit of the crusade was reborn. Now all their doubts were swept aside. God had sent them a miracle: the flaming cross and the great quenching rain. There was no question now that He would part the seas for them, as Saint Nicholas had promised. They would follow Étienne to Marseille. They were ready to follow him to the ends of the earth if necessary.

Rémi made one last effort to undermine Étienne.

"What's the matter with you people? Rain is not a miracle. Haven't you seen trees struck by lightning before?"

His words made Abel uneasy. The ideas he'd been immersed in back at the university strongly favored trying to understand God's creation through reason and the workings of natural law. He couldn't say it out loud, but he knew that Rémi was right: the lightning that struck the tree could have been a perfectly natural phenomenon, and even the most severe drought comes to an end eventually. Still, who was he to say with any certainty what was a miracle and what was not?

Rémi's arguments fell on deaf ears. In the eyes of the pilgrims, Étienne was once again a divine instrument of God, with the ability to work miracles. In the end Rémi left, able to persuade only a disgruntled few to depart with him.

Abel decided to keep his doubts to himself. He didn't want anything to take away from the deep happiness he was feeling now. Things had changed completely between him and Étienne. It was to him that Étienne had turned to confide his anguish and doubts. It felt as if their bond was stronger than ever, and Abel wanted to be at his side as they marched in triumph into Marseille.

৭

Blanche was relieved to see Étienne back to his old self again, talking animatedly with the pilgrims. It was as though the rain had restored his body's vitality, and he strode through the crowds with the proud grace that had beguiled her by the fire on Midsummer Night.

But she'd also begun to see things that she'd been blind to before. Much as she loved Étienne, much as she wanted him to be her Tristan, her Good Knight, she found the pilgrims' unswerving belief in his ability to perform miracles more and more unsettling. And having felt the depths of their hatred for Good Christians, she could no longer walk among them with the same feeling of safety. The events of the past few days had opened her eyes irrevocably, and now she had to put aside the things of a child. She had to cast a cold eye on her situation and see it for what it was.

No one would save her. She had to take care of herself, and of the child whose fate she felt somehow entwined with her own.

For, much to everyone's amazement, Little Guinefort had survived. He seemed almost miraculously rejuvenated, Blanche thought, feeling the tight grip of his small hand as they walked together. He still needed to be carried much of the time, but slowly his strength was coming back, his breathing becoming easier.

In the face of great terror and trials he had survived, as she had. When they stopped to rest, or at night before sleep, she would wrap his body in her arms, as the wool bale had once enveloped and protected her. Without ever having consciously decided it, she had taken on, as an almost sacred trust, the task of protecting Little Guinefort.

Drifting along in her thoughts, she noticed Abel was walking near her. They had been avoiding each other, both fearing they'd revealed too much in their talk that night. It was as if they wanted to pretend that the conversation had never happened. Still, she trusted him to keep her secret, as she had pledged to keep his. There were things weighing on her mind, though, and he was the only one she could talk to about them. She broke the awkward silence between them.

"What's going to happen when we get to Marseille?"

"What do you mean?"

"What if the sea doesn't part?" said Blanche. "What do we do then?"

He realized she'd given voice to the burning question in his own head. From the beginning he'd tried to push it aside, reluctant to think that far ahead. Perhaps he never even believed, in his heart of hearts, that the crusade would get this far. Now that they were approaching Marseille, he knew the moment of truth was not far off. Why did she have to bring it up now, when he was finally feeling free of care for the first time in weeks?

ও

After a couple of days, the rain finally let up. In the cooler air they felt energized and found they could cover more ground than ever. They felt no fatigue, and even though food was still scarce, they forgot their hunger. On the third day, they began to notice a new freshness, a kind of bite in the air. It took a while for them to realize what it was.

Salt. The smell of the sea.

A couple of boys went on ahead and soon returned to report that they'd climbed a ridge, where they spied a sliver of blue water on the horizon and sails in the distance. It was clear that they were within a few hours' trek of Marseille. If they hurried, they could get there by nightfall.

There was great excitement as they crossed the valley and headed toward the ridge. Étienne went through the crowd, encouraging them to walk quickly and leading the hymns.

Suddenly they heard shouts. Up ahead of them, a cluster of pilgrims were standing on the crest of a hill, looking down.

"There it is!"

"The sea!"

"Marseille!"

Now the multitude broke into a race up the hill.

"Make way for Étienne!"

He walked through the crowd to the top of the hill and lifted his arms to heaven.

"As did the Red Sea for Moses, I command these waters to part!"

ૐ

CHAPTER 10
Marseille
August 1212

SEVEN DAYS HE HAD WALKED OUT AT DAWN to the edge of the harbor. Seven mornings he had raised his arms, crying out in supplication to Almighty God. But no matter whether the waters were calm or waves splashed against the wharf, seven times the seas did not part, seven times no pathway appeared.

Poised on the ridge overlooking , he had, at first, been crushingly disappointed. But it was too soon, he told himself. It was late in the day, they hadn't even come to the gates of the city yet. How could he have been so foolish, so full of pride, as to expect the waters to part on his command? The way had to be prepared. Why, if the sea had suddenly cut a path without warning, the ships moored in the harbor would have been swamped in the waves, causing destruction and even death. No, he had to be patient. The miracle would happen by the power of God, in His own time.

So it was with joy and anticipation that Étienne led the multitude of pilgrims through the gates of Marseille as the sun was setting. They found, as so many times before, that

Kathleen McDonnell

word of the crusade had gone before them, and the inhabitants of the great port came out to welcome them with cheers and banners.

As usual, too, there were naysayers. Étienne could tell from the faces of some in the crowd, and from snatches of conversation he heard, that some of the Massilians thought the crusade was an enormous folly. He'd learned to ignore these types, because at every turn his faith had been vindicated. God had provided.

And clearly there were just as many in the city who welcomed them with open arms and believed in their cause. Marseille hadn't suffered nearly as much as the rest of Provence from the recent drought, and with all the cargo going in and out of the harbor, there was plenty of food to share with the pilgrims. Étienne, Abel, Blanche, Little Guinefort and a few others were put up for the night in the villa of the count of Marseille. Other Massilians took some of the youngest pilgrims into their homes. After sleeping for so long on the unforgiving ground, even the older ones who passed that first night on beds of straw in the streets of Marseille, felt as if they were living in comfort.

Even the next morning, when the waters again failed to part, Étienne took it in stride. God was telling him that the pilgrims needed a day of rest, he decided. So they spent the time wandering the streets of the bustling city, marveling especially at the shipyards, where teams of craftsmen constructed magnificent wooden ships that, they were told, would be added to the count's own merchant fleet.

The same thing happened the next morning, and the

morning after that. Étienne watched in dismay as the now-familiar cycle of disbelief and discouragement repeated itself. He reminded them what they'd already endured, and how, when things looked bleakest, God had led them out of the desert of drought. This calmed things down for a while, but by the fifth day pilgrims were starting to drift away, and many were on the verge of leaving to go home.

"We should have listened to Rémi," some said.

Étienne found he had no more words. Until now he had always known what to say to bring them back, but this time nothing came to him. He felt he was at the end of his endurance, a Job facing catastrophe upon catastrophe.

Was this his punishment for going against the express wishes of the Holy Father?

Blanche came over to try to comfort him. On other occasions, she would touch him on the shoulder or gently take his hand, but this time she took him in her arms, laying his head on her shoulder and stroking his tear-stained face. Even in the extremity of his anguish Étienne felt a powerful surge of desire for her.

He'd fought so hard against these feelings, and until this moment he had thought his struggle was successful. Now he was flooded again with thoughts of kissing her mouth, pressing her body against his, losing himself in her. It was as if nothing else mattered — not the crusade, or the pilgrims, or even God Himself. Which made him, in his heart of hearts, the most monstrous of sinners.

He resolved once again to push down these desires, to keep his distance from Blanche, as more and more he felt as though something had broken in him. He didn't want to admit it to himself, but he was almost relieved the seas had not opened a path to the Holy Land. He was at the end of his endurance. He longed to be delivered of this great burden. He wanted to be an ordinary young man again, to go home to Cloyes and tend his flock. And marry Blanche.

For Saint Paul himself had said it is better to marry than to burn.

ഉ

Abel fought back hot tears as he watched the two of them, their arms intertwined, their cheeks pressed together. For a moment he felt such hatred for Blanche that he wished a thunderbolt would come out of the sky and strike her dead. How could he have been foolish enough to believe that things were ever going to be the same between him and Étienne? A short time ago he had been on the verge of abandoning the crusade. It was only the belief that Étienne really needed him that drew him back in, he thought bitterly. What was the point of staying on and watching Étienne go out to the wharf morning after morning, open his arms to the sea, only to collapse in tears in her arms?

He decided then and there to leave the next morning for Paris. He would return to his studies and then to the Broce-aux-Juifs and the bosom of his beloved family. Still, he dreaded telling Étienne of his decision. He knew Étienne would be angry and hurt. He would view Abel's choice as a huge betrayal and compare himself to Jesus when He was denied by His apostle Peter.

He was trying to muster up the courage to face Étienne, when Blanche came and sat down beside him.

"I don't know what more to do for him," she said with a weary sigh. "What are we going to do?"

"What do you mean 'we'?" he shot back.

She looked at him quizzically.

"What's the matter with you?"

"Nothing. I'm just tired of all this. Maybe it's time we all gave up and brought this folly to an end. I'm going back to the university."

"When?"

"Tomorrow."

"You're leaving? Just like that?"

"Why shouldn't I?"

"Étienne needs you."

"No he doesn't. Not since you came along. He hardly talks to me anymore. Me — the one who was with him from the beginning!"

As he heard himself saying the words, Abel wanted to take them back, but it was too late. He saw from the shocked look on Blanche's face that she was completely surprised by the intensity of his feelings. He barely understood them himself.

"I didn't know you felt that way," she said finally. "I'm sorry. I thought we were friends."

He was on the verge of offering his own apology, when they were distracted by a commotion nearby. A group of pilgrims were pointing at them and carrying on an animated conversation with a Massilian boy. Moments later they all rushed over to Blanche and Abel.

"This is it!"

"What?" said Abel.

"The answer to our prayers!"

The Massilian boy spoke, barely able to catch his breath.

"Come with me," he said.

"Who? Me?" said Abel.

"Both of you!" cried the boy impatiently.

"Where?" Blanche asked.

"To the wharf to see Ferrous and Porcus."

"Who?"

"Iron Hugh and Will the Pig!" said one of the pilgrims. "They have ships!"

"Why us?" Blanche persisted.

"They need to talk to someone who can read!" shouted the Massilian boy, pulling Blanche by the hand while the pilgrims pushed Abel to follow her.

༶

It seemed to be yet another remarkable reversal of fortune. Abel was beginning to think differently about this Christian preoccupation with miracles. Maybe Étienne was right, after all. Maybe the crusade's success was foreordained by God.

It took him a while to grasp the magnitude of what was happening, as he and Blanche stood in the hut on the wharf with Hugh Ferrous and Will Porcus, the shipowners known in Marseille as Iron Hugh and Will the Pig. Their seafaring nicknames suited them perfectly. Hugh, angular and unsmiling, wrote on a long sheet of parchment, saying little. Loud, gregarious Will, his belly jutting out of his tunic, did most of the talking. And what he was proposing left them thunderstruck.

"You're serious?" Blanche said. "You'll take the pilgrims to the Holy Land?"

Will nodded eagerly.

"All of us?" said Abel.

"As many as want to come. We have a vast fleet of ships."

"But what about the fee?" Blanche said. "We can't possibly —"

Will cut her off.

"No, no, don't worry about payment."

Hugh broke in.

"All we need is for you to sign this contract," he said, thrusting out the sheet of parchment.

"That's why we needed someone who could read!" Will added. "To think there are two such educated young people on this crusade, and one a lovely young girl. What you must have sacrificed to take up the cross. God loves you both."

In spite of his invoking the name of God, something in Will's manner made Blanche uncomfortable. To avoid his gaze, she looked down at the document.

Abel read aloud.

"Each passenger will receive a day's rations of two hard

biscuits and a pint of beer, with a slice of salt mutton every third day."

"That's more generous than most," Hugh said a bit testily.

"It says here you'll take us to the port of Gaza, or as far as the weather allows," Blanche pointed out.

"Oh, that's a standard clause," said Will garrulously. "You can never predict the weather, even in the service of Almighty God. Don't worry. I'm going to captain one of the vessels myself, just to make sure you reach your destination."

"And you're going to do all this for no payment of any kind?" Abel said.

"Absolutely none."

"*Causa dei absque pretio,*" said Hugh. "No price is too high for God's cause."

"So, young man and lovely lady," said Will, holding out the quill. "Will you sign?"

Abel signed the parchment and passed the quill to Blanche. She hesitated a moment, her hand poised over the document.

"What about the return voyage? Étienne and some of the pilgrims may wish to stay for a time in Palestine, but these are poor peasants. Most of them will need to return home very soon, to their families and their work in the fields."

For a moment, the shipowners seemed rattled by the question.

"Our ships will be spending a few days in port," Hugh said quickly. "Then of course we will transport as many as wish to come on the return voyage."

"What, did you think we would leave them all stranded on the dock?" Will said with a loud guffaw.

"If you don't wish to avail yourself of our generosity —" Hugh began.

"Of course we do!" Abel interrupted, turning to Blanche and nodding firmly.

She lowered the quill to the parchment and signed her name.

Hugh stood up, making clear that the meeting was over.

"We set sail at dawn tomorrow," he said brusquely. "Tell your pilgrims not to be late or they'll be out of luck."

They left, still stunned at this turn of events.

"I can't quite believe it," said Blanche.

"Don't you see?" Abel said excitedly. "Étienne was right to have faith! This is the fulfillment of Saint Nicholas's promise. The waters won't part by themselves — they'll be parted by the prow of a ship!"

"How do we know we can trust them? I don't like that Will."

"Oh, you're just not used to being around rough characters like that," said Abel.

"It's not that," Blanche insisted. "I just don't understand why they're they doing this. They're merchants. They didn't get rich by giving free passage on their ships."

"Perhaps the count has made some sort of arrangement for our passage," Abel suggested. "He has been so helpful, and the Massillians have been so generous to us. Why do you have such trouble believing that there are some Christians who genuinely believe in charity, who do not think only of their own personal gain?"

They raced off to find Étienne. He was out on the wharf, still staring forlornly out at the sea.

Étienne's reaction to the news seemed to Abel a bit odd. Perhaps he had fallen so deeply into his own melancholy that at first he didn't really comprehend what they were telling him.

"You see, Étienne?" Abel said excitedly. "You misinterpreted what Saint Nicholas was trying to tell you! You thought he meant that the sea would part of its own accord. But it's the ships of Iron Hugh and Will the Pig that will part the waters! Isn't it wonderful? Once again, just when everything seemed hopeless, the Lord has come to our aid!"

As Abel kept talking, Étienne gradually seemed to emerge from the fog of his confusion.

"Truly, the ways of God are a mystery!" he exclaimed, drawing them both to him. "The three of us will march, hand in hand, into the holy city of Jerusalem! God wills it!"

Yes, Abel thought. The three of them, together. He felt a weight lifting from his heart. Everything had changed. He would not leave the crusade. He would not let his feelings about Blanche come between him and Étienne. They would be of one mind, as they had been at Saint Denis.

As they raced off to spread the word among the pilgrims, the words of Hugh Ferrous echoed in his mind: *Causa dei absque pretio.* At long last, he was ready to accept that what had transpired in the hut on the wharf could only be understood as a miracle, that God really had chosen Étienne as His instrument. The Crusade of the New Innocents truly was divinely ordained. This was the path God Himself had set him on when he was led to Étienne's side that day in Paris.

Tomorrow, before they set sail, he would ask Hugh Ferrous to arrange for a messenger to carry his letter to his family in Troyes. He would follow in the footsteps of the Three Hundred, after all. He would walk in the sacred city of Jerusalem and worship in the temple on the holy mount. And when he returned from his travels, what remarkable tales he would have to tell them!

℘

Blanche suddenly sat bolt upright in the dark room. For a few moments she had no idea where she was. Then the sound of Little Guinefort's strained breathing brought it all back. She was at the villa of the count of Marseille. Étienne and Abel were spending the night on the wharf with the younger boys. At dawn she and Guinefort would meet up with them, and they would board the ships with all the other pilgrims.

It had been so long since she had dreamed about her mother. In the beginning, after the Good Knight had left her at the convent, she had dreams almost every night, comforting dreams of life as it had been before, with her mother and Perrine doing ordinary things — spinning wool, peeling apples for cider. As time wore on the dreams grew less frequent. Occasionally she had trouble summoning up her mother's face in her mind, which made her almost crazy with grief.

Tonight she awoke with an almost palpable sense of her mother's presence in the room. In her dream they were running up the hill to the cathedral again. Her mother suddenly turned to Blanche and began shaking her by the shoulders. "See with your eyes!" she commanded Blanche. "See where evil lies." Her mother spoke with the same tone of urgency as when she urged her to always honor the memory of her namesake, Blanche de Laurac.

As she looked at her mother's face, Blanche gasped in horror. Suddenly she realized there were empty cavities where her mother's eyes should have been.

Then, in an instant, her mother was gone, and when Blanche looked up she saw a knight in armor riding toward her. His armor looked much thicker and heavier than normal, almost like slabs of iron rather than steel plate. He rode up beside her, stopped and opened his visor. Underneath the helmet was the face of a pig, grinning ominously down at her.

She lay awake, her stomach churning with anxiety, her eyes wide open. The dream wouldn't leave her — the horrifying sight of her mother's empty eyes, the tight grip of her hands on her shoulders, the desperate urgency in her voice.

Open your eyes. See where evil lies.

What did it mean? She wanted to cry out to her mother, *What evil? Where?*

Finally, exhausted, she drifted back to sleep. When she woke up, the sun was already high in the sky. She looked around. Little Guinefort was gone.

She grabbed her *vielle* and raced down to the wharf, already crowded with people. Frantically, she looked around. Finally she spied Abel.

"Little Guinefort is gone!" she cried.

"It's all right — he's with us," he reassured her. "We came at dawn to get you both, but you were sleeping so soundly that we decided to let you rest a little longer. I was just coming to the count's to get you."

"Where's Étienne?"

"He's already on board. He told me to make sure you got on the lead ship with us."

Blanche looked out on the harbor and saw Étienne on the deck of the lead ship, surrounded by pilgrims carrying *oriflammes* and a large wooden cross given to them by the citizens of Marseille. Little Guinefort, grinning widely, rode on his shoulders. They both spied Blanche, and Étienne waved excitedly at her to join them.

She wanted to shout at him to get off the ship, to come back to her on the shore. She knew it would be useless. He wouldn't do it, not even for her.

"Come on," said Abel. "We have to go now."

Blanche held him back, clutching his arm.

"I can't."

"What do you mean?"

"I'm not going."

"I know how you feel, Blanche. No one gets on a ship without being afraid. But these are experienced seamen. Everything will be all right."

"No, that's not it."

Quickly she told him about the dream and her fear that it was some kind of warning from her mother.

"Warning?" Abel said. "About what?"

"The pig in iron armor, Abel. Don't you see? Iron Hugh, Will the Pig — maybe they're the evil my mother's trying to make me see."

"You don't know that."

"No, but I'm afraid. What if it's true?"

"How could they hurt us? They're giving us free passage. Will's even commanding the lead ship himself."

The pilgrims were piling into small skiffs ready to ferry them out to the ships. Étienne looked anxiously toward Abel and Blanche, gesturing to them to board the lead ship before it got too crowded.

"Come," Abel said, taking her hand again.

She shook her head.

"I want to go, but I can't."

She stood motionless, frozen to the spot. She felt herself almost torn in two. Something wouldn't let her move in the direction of the ship, as strong as if a hand was gripping her shoulder and holding her back.

One of the sailors shouted to Abel, telling them to hurry up, that the lead ship was almost full.

"You have to go now," she told Abel.

"You're really not going to come?" he said, shaking his head in disbelief. "Because of some dream?"

"I can't explain it," she said, fighting back tears.

"But what will you do?" he asked urgently. "Where will you go?"

"I don't know."

He could see that for all the torment in her eyes, her mind was made up. A shiver went up his spine. How could she be so certain of her decision? Could there be any truth to these ominous premonitions? He had to put such thoughts out of his mind. He had to board the ship. They could not both abandon Étienne now.

"Here." He suddenly took off his cloak, and held it out to her.

"Why are you giving me this?"

"The nights will be getting cold. Here. Take this, too."

He took her hand and placed his knife in it, the one his mother had tucked under his pillow when he was a baby.

"No, Abel. I can't take this."

"You'll be traveling alone. You'll need it more than I will. Take it," he said firmly.

"Thank you. Goodbye, my friend. Take care of Little Guinefort."

"I will." He squeezed her hand and headed toward the ship. After a couple of steps he suddenly turned and called back to her.

"What should I tell Étienne?"

"Tell him …"

Her voice trailed off. She didn't know how to answer him, and soon Abel was lost in the crush of people on the wharf. From a distance she watched him clamber onto one of the skiffs.

As the last of the pilgrims were rowed out to the ships, the sailors loosened the anchor chains and held back the sheets. On shore, the assembled Massillians began to sing *Veni Creator Spiritus* as the last skiff was emptied. Will Porcus gave the signal, and the sheets were set free. They billowed in the wind as the anchors were hoisted out of the water.

In quiet stateliness, the seven ships began to move out toward the mouth of the harbor. It was then that Abel realized that in his shock and confusion over Blanche's decision to stay behind, he had neglected to give the letter to Hugh Ferrous to send to Troyes.

∽

CHAPTER 11
𝕿𝖍𝖊 𝕳𝖊𝖗𝖒𝖎𝖙 𝖔𝖋 𝕾𝖆𝖓 𝕻𝖎𝖊𝖙𝖗𝖔
September 1212

As the ships passed Notre-Dame-de-Garde, the chapel of the sailors, hundreds of well-wishers lined the wharf, waving and cheering. Gradually the crowds of people shrank to tiny specks, and Abel felt a fleeting sadness as he watched the land recede. Though some pilgrims kept singing hymns to try to bolster their spirits, many others gave in to tears. Abel thought this melancholy had to be a sentiment familiar to sailors as they left port.

It didn't take long for all their fears and superstitions about sea travel to come to the surface — things that they hadn't dared to speak aloud until now.

"People say the seas around the coast of Africa are boiling hot."

"It's because Mohammedans live there."

"Everything is reversed there — their north is our south."

"And their shadows fall on the opposite side to ours."

Abel knew these ideas weren't based on real knowledge but tales woven as a way of explaining the unknown. He tried to calm them down, fearing that too much of this kind of talk would spread panic, especially among the younger ones, who were the majority now, since many of the young men had left and gone home. It didn't help matters that their vessel was terribly overcrowded. So many pilgrims had pushed their way onto the lead ship because they wanted to be with Étienne.

Sensing the growing unease, Étienne called for music.

"Not hymns," he said. "Carols. Let's have some dancing."

A couple of boys struck up a tune on their pipe and tabor. Étienne got a couple of little ones to start a ring dance, and soon others joined in. When the dance finished, Étienne motioned to the players to keep going and they struck up another tune. Abel saw a look of pain flicker across Étienne's face. He realized it was one of the melodies Blanche had played that first night.

"I'll bet one of the other ships is enjoying the music of the *vielle* right now," Etienne said wistfully.

Abel said nothing, but inwardly he winced. He'd told Étienne that Blanche, caught up in the crush of bodies on the wharf, had gotten on one of the other ships. He didn't dare tell him the truth, Abel decided. Not yet. The thought that he'd never see Blanche again might have crushed Étienne's spirit completely.

Abel pondered his own motives. Was he hiding the truth because he was afraid Étienne would blame him for Blanche's decision? Because he hadn't tried hard enough to persuade her to get on the ship? Deep down, was he glad she'd stayed behind?

Now, as he watched the scene of revelry on the deck, Abel felt reassured that keeping the truth from Étienne was the right thing to do. Instead of trying to talk sense into the pilgrims, as Abel usually did, Étienne got them dancing and singing so that they forgot their fears, for the time being at least. Abel saw once again what a natural leader Étienne was. The pilgrims hung on his every word, and even the ones who were older than Étienne treated him like a benevolent, wise father.

The music continued long into the night, until most of the pilgrims dropped off to sleep in exhaustion. Abel lay awake for a time, thinking of his family. He knew they would worry when he did not come home for the feast of Purim, but he consoled himself with the thought that it would not be too long before he would return to Troyes and set their fears to rest.

The next morning brought a brilliant blue sky and favorable winds, which kept their spirits high. The other ships were all within sight, and occasionally one would veer close enough to exchange shouted greetings. After all the terrible hardships they'd endured, this time at sea became for many of them the happiest they'd ever known.

The one sour note was Will Porcus, who seemed preoccupied and much less jovial than he'd been back in Marseille. When Will approached him asking where the girl was — meaning Blanche — Abel replied that she wasn't on the ship, that she'd stayed behind.

"She stayed behind? Why?"

"I don't know."

Abel looked around nervously, worried that their conversation might get back to Étienne. Will said no more but glowered at him for a moment before stomping off angrily. Abel found the captain's behavior mystifying and a bit disturbing. Perhaps, he speculated, Will was simply preoccupied with all the responsibilities of commanding the ship.

Later in the morning, land was sighted on the western horizon. The little ones cried out excitedly.

"Are we there?"

"Is that Jerusalem?"

The crew members smiled indulgently at their ignorance.

"No, Corsica," said one sailor, laughing.

The excitement of the voyage finally began to take hold. They saw that they were on the final leg of their great journey and their trials and sufferings were behind them. Three times a day they were given their provisions, as Will had promised. They were surrounded by crisp sea air instead of scorching heat. They were being ferried over these long miles to the Holy Land, instead of having to trudge on their own feet. In fact, their biggest problem now was finding ways to pass the time on board the ship.

It was as if the happy times of earliest childhood had been restored to them. All day long they played rambunctious games like Hoodsman's Bluff or pretended to be chickens chased by a wolf in Que Loo Loo, until the crewmen would scold them for getting underfoot. Below deck there was music, dancing and fierce matches of Ringers and Fox and Geese.

When night fell they all gathered on deck. It was a clear night, with still waters and only the gentlest of winds to drive the sails. They looked up into the glorious night full of stars and gave praise to the wondrous ways of God.

"The stars are holes in the floor of heaven, made by God's finger to let His light shine through," said one boy.

"No — the stars are the great spray of milk from Our Lady's breast," another insisted.

"Neither of you is right," an older youth broke in. "The stars are the tears of the angels, weeping for the folly and wickedness of mankind."

Listening to them, Abel smiled to himself. Of course, he knew from his reading of Ptolemy and other ancient thinkers that the stars were distant celestial bodies, not angels' tears or drops of Mary's milk. But who was he to dismiss their stories? Maybe they were as true, in their way, as the scientific ideas he'd studied at the university, all different ways of giving praise to the beauty of the starry sky and the glory of the Creator.

As the night wore on, Abel found himself alone on deck, with only a few crewmen. As he looked up into the vast sky, a feeling of elation swept over him, a glimpse of the unity of all creation, the essential being-ness of all things that Plato had written about. In that moment he felt himself enveloped by a palpable sense of the presence of God, the One who had told Abraham long ago, "My name is Yahweh: I Am Who Am."

He realized, with great joy and enormous relief, that it was right for him to be here. Now he understood, beyond all doubt, that the God of the Jews, the God of the Christians, the God whom the Muslims called Allah — all were one and the same, a Divine Being vast beyond all measure or understanding. He also understood, with a new clarity, his father's belief in the coming of *Olam Ha-Ba*, the time of peace and reconciliation of all people on earth. He vowed to himself that no matter what more setbacks the journey might encounter, no matter what difficulty and devastation his life might bring, he would never forget this moment under the glorious sky. He pledged to God, in whom all things are possible, that he would do everything in his power to bring about *Olam Ha-Ba*.

∾

The next day they awoke to stiffer winds and more turbulent waters. As the ship tossed in the waves, Étienne made sure their spirits remained high, reminding them that the strong breeze was a gift from God that would sweep them on to the Holy Land that much more quickly.

Just as they were kneeling down for lauds, there was a volley of shouts.

"Land!"

They had been sailing within sight of the coast of Sardinia for some time, but some of the pilgrims were pointing in the opposite direction. The others all swarmed to the edge of the deck to see. Out of the vast expanse of open sea loomed what looked like a large, rounded mountain, on top of which was an edifice that glistened in the sun.

"That must be it!"

"Jerusalem!"

The crewmen laughed heartily.

"Palestine is still many days away."

"Then what is it?" they asked.

One of the sailors spoke up.

"It's an illusion conjured up by the hermit of San Pietro. See how the mountain appears no closer to us, even though the ship is speeding right toward it? The hermit is playing tricks on us, the way he does with all seamen who sail these waters."

The sailor explained that many years earlier a man, disgusted with the sinful ways of the world, had retired to a remote spot off the Sardinian coast, the Isle of Falcons. He renamed the place San Pietro, in honor of Saint Peter, and lived out his life there, eking out an existence, growing food in the island's rocky, unforgiving soil. Like many in those days, the hermit of San Pietro believed that only in complete solitude could he truly worship God, though few chose lives of such extreme isolation.

For many years, sailors used to catch sight of the hermit standing by his hut on the cliffs of San Pietro. They would wave and shout greetings, and often he would respond in kind. As the years wore on, he took to ignoring the passing ships completely, and seamen speculated that the isolation had driven him mad. Eventually a time came when the hermit was no longer seen by passing seafarers, who concluded that he must have died. Over the years, there were more storms than before in the vicinity of San Pietro, and strange phenomena, such as the mysterious mountain with the glittering palace, were frequently sighted. The hermit of San Pietro, mariners said, played tricks on passing ships, in a perverse effort to make others join him in his madness.

"And sure enough," said one of the crew, pointing ahead, "take a look now."

The mountain with the glittering palace had completely vanished from the horizon.

Seamen always had a full store of these fantastic tales, Abel knew. Yet he'd seen the strange mountain with his own eyes. Surely there must be some kind of natural explanation, he told himself. He found the whole incident unsettling.

So did others. The turbulent weather combined with the sailors' story of the hermit of San Pietro brought on a mood of anxiety among the pilgrims. Étienne called on them to resume their morning prayers.

"Let us pray not only for our safe passage but also for the hermit of San Pietro, that his soul might be delivered from its restless wandering."

A little while later, they were sitting below deck eating their noon rations when the ship began to rock violently. It was clear that a large storm was brewing, and fearful murmurs again went through the crowd. Étienne held up his hand.

"O ye of little faith! Don't you know by now that God is with us every moment? That He is guiding us to the Holy Land with every step, every league?"

As the storm grew more fierce, the pilgrims clung to one another. Some, unable to stave off the queasiness in their stomachs, spat up their food. They heard a commotion on the deck. There were frantic shouts back and forth.

"It's one of the other ships!" cried one of the pilgrims from the top of the stairs.

"It's heading right for the cliffs!"

They all surged toward the stairway.

"Don't come up!" the crewmen shouted at them. "Stay down!"

Abel tried to hold some of the little ones back, but they wriggled away. As the mass of pilgrims streamed onto the deck, even Étienne's pleas to stay down had no effect on them.

Swarms of screeching falcons hovered over the nearby island of San Pietro. Through the driving rain they could make out two of the ships moving perilously in the direction of the island. They watched, terrified, as both ships were tossed in the white breakers, zigzagging toward the shoreline strewn with boulders.

Étienne's voice rose over the roaring winds.

"Saint Nicholas! Patron of those in peril at sea! Save your pilgrims now, as you saved the Three Mariners!"

There was a moment of utter stillness. Then a mighty billow hovered over both ships.

"Help them, Saint Nicholas!" Étienne shouted, hoarse with agony.

The next moment the air was filled with shrieks and cries as the breaker pounded onto the deck of one of the ships, tossing it on its side and sweeping dozens of bodies into the raging sea. They could see some pilgrims clutching the masts, holding on for dear life, only to be pulled down by the next breaker. Wave upon wave followed, pounding the deck of the second ship until everyone on it was swept into the sea. Then both ships were smashed to pieces on the rocks. There were loud cracks as hunks of timber were tossed high into the air, tumbling back down into the churning waters and dashed to splinters against the rocks.

ೲ

The crew on the lead ship finally managed to hustle the pilgrims back below deck, where they huddled, weeping and wailing. Abel looked around for Étienne. He'd lost sight of him during the shipwrecks. Now he felt a churning fear in the pit of his stomach that Étienne might have thrown himself into the waves in a desperate, crazed effort to rescue some of the pilgrims on the doomed ships.

After a while the storm let up. Most of the pilgrims fell into exhausted sleep. Abel went back up on deck and spied Étienne standing alone, staring out to sea. He approached him and softly called his name.

He turned and looked at Abel with an expression both haunted and uncomprehending. It reminded Abel of the wounded look he had seen on the face of the country boy as the students had taunted him in Notre Dame square. Étienne gestured to him to come to his side, and pointed out toward the water.

Abel looked out at the sea. The waters surrounding the ship were dotted with the wreckage of the storm: masts, topsails, planks torn and splintered. There were other objects bobbing in the water that at first Abel couldn't identify. He felt his stomach turn over as the realization hit him.

The objects were bodies. The bodies of dead pilgrims.

The hermit of San Pietro could not make them join his madness. Instead he had claimed their souls.

"How could Saint Nicholas let this happen?" Étienne cried. "How could he not save them?"

Abel could only shake his head helplessly, as the words of the prophet Isaiah filled his mind. *"Hayn, lo katsrah Yad Adonai mihoshiya, velo cavdah Ozno mishmo'a." Behold, God's hand is not shortened, that it cannot save, neither is His ear heavy, that it cannot hear.*

It was all he could do to keep from shouting his own anguished cries to God. *Was Your arm too short to save them? Was Your ear too dull to hear their cries?*

༄

Abel tried everything he could think of to restore Etienne's spirits.

"Don't lose heart, Étienne. How many times have you told me that? That everything that happens is the Lord's will, that we must embrace even what we don't understand? We still have five ships full of pilgrims. The Lord means for us to go on to the Holy Land. He means for you to lead us there."

Étienne looked at him with a faint smile, and Abel could tell only part of him was listening. Something in him had broken. There was a hollow look in his eyes, even at prayers, and he seemed only to be going through the motions of being alive.

The atmosphere on the ship was like a blanket of gloom. At times Abel felt that he too was falling into a deep pit of despair, and it was only by focusing all his attention on Étienne that he was able to keep going. He tried to summon up the exultation he'd experienced that night on the deck as he gazed up at the stars. Now it felt as distant as his home in Troyes.

A day passed. Abel decided he had to do something to shake Étienne out of his gloom.

"Étienne, you yourself are always telling us that it's in times of trial and suffering that our faith must be strongest. The pilgrims who drowned are now looking down upon us from heaven. We should rejoice for them."

"You don't understand!" he cried, covering his face with his hands. "God's wrath has come down upon me. He wrecked those ships to punish me for my sins."

"What are you talking about? What sins?"

Étienne turned to him with a tortured look in his eyes.

"Desires, Abel. Longings that are an affront to Almighty God."

"What do you mean, Étienne?"

"As I watched all the pilgrims leaving , I wanted to leave myself. I felt like just going back home. I wished God had never chosen me to lead the crusade."

"That doesn't make you a sinner, Étienne. You're only human. Everyone feels that way —"

"No!" Etienne broke in sharply. "There's worse, much

worse. The reason I want to abandon the crusade is my longing for Blanche. It was all I could think about back in Marseille. It consumes me even now. I didn't want to go to the Holy Land, I wanted to go back to Cloyes and marry Blanche. I was ready to turn my back on the cross, to put human love above my love for God."

So that was his terrible secret? Didn't he realize his longing for Blanche was obvious to everyone who saw them together?

"Of course I had to be punished for my sin," Étienne went on. "So God sent the shipwreck and took my love from me forever."

Abel realized that this was the true source of Étienne's despondency. He believed that Blanche was dead. It was her loss he was mourning.

"Étienne, you don't know whether Blanche was on one of the ships that sank," he said. "There are still four others besides ours. She could be on any one of them."

"No, Abel. I feel it in my soul. She has been taken by the wrath of God, a punishment I deserve. And so many others also perished on account of my selfishness. For that I can never be forgiven."

Abel realized the time had come. The truth had to come out.

"You're wrong, Étienne. Blanche didn't drown with the others."

"You're only saying that to make me feel better."

"No. She's alive. I know she is."

"How could you know that?"

"I should have told you earlier, but I knew the pain it would cause you. She didn't get on any of the ships."

Étienne looked stunned, uncomprehending.

"What are you saying?"

"She stayed behind in Marseille, Étienne."

"Stayed behind? Why?"

Abel wasn't sure Étienne was ready for too much truth. He thought fast.

"She didn't mean to. When we were getting ready to board she remembered she'd left her *vielle* back at the count's, so she ran back to get it. When she returned to the wharf, she couldn't fight her way through the crush of people. I saw her from the deck of the ship. She was calling your name and desperately trying to push her way through."

"You saw this and said nothing? You should have told me! We could have gone back for her!"

"No, Étienne. All the ships had pulled anchor by then. It was too late."

"No it wasn't!" Now Étienne's face was twisted in fury. "One of the skiffs could have gone back for her! Why didn't you say something?"

"I'm sorry, Étienne. I should have, but everything was happening so fast. I didn't know what to do."

"She's lost to me forever."

"No she isn't. When the crusade is over you can go back and find her …"

"You didn't want her along — I could tell from the day she arrived. That's why you didn't tell me. You deliberately kept her off the ship."

"No, Étienne. That's not true."

Suddenly Abel felt Étienne's fists pounding into his chest. The force of the blows knocked him off his feet. Étienne leaped on top of him, screaming, and continued to pummel him all over. The pilgrims watched, aghast. Never had they seen anything like this burst of savage anger from their beloved leader.

Abel tried to push him off, but he was no match for the robust and powerful country boy.

"Please stop, Étienne," he pleaded. "I'd never do something like that to you. You've got to believe me."

Finally several of the seamen heard the commotion and came running over.

"What's going on?"

"Break it up!"

It took three of them to pull Étienne off and restrain him while Abel staggered to his feet. Tears ran down Abel's face as he struggled for breath.

"I'm sorry, Étienne. Please forgive me."

The sailors loosened their grip on Étienne and waited to see what he would do. One stepped in his way as he seemed to be lunging toward Abel again. Instead he turned and stomped off. Then, abruptly, he turned and glowered back at Abel with a look of fierce, undiluted hatred.

"There's no forgiveness for treachery. Burn in hell!"

∽

For hours he sat below deck, covering his face with his hands, his body curled into a ball.

It was true. He didn't deserve forgiveness. Étienne had seen into the dark heart of his unworthiness, and now their friendship was forever torn asunder, like the ships on the rocks of San Pietro.

"Abel?"

He looked up and saw Étienne standing over him. He shrank back, covering his face again, bracing himself. To his amazement, the blows did not come. Étienne laid a gentle hand on his shoulder.

"It's all right, Abel. I understand now."

"What?"

"I'm the one who's the fool, not you. I was so shocked by what you told me that I couldn't see that it was all part of God's plan, that in His mercy He gathers even the worst sinner to His breast."

Abel could barely speak.

"So … you don't hate me?"

"No, Abel. I see now that it was God's will that Blanche should stay behind. He wanted to be sure I wouldn't be swayed from the great work of the crusade. I was so sure she was dead. I thought it was my punishment for wanting her. But you see, Abel? If she had gotten on one of the other ships, she might have drowned in the storm along with all the others. By leaving her behind, God spared her life. He spared us both. And to know for certain that she's still alive — this changes everything! It's just as you said. Once I've fulfilled my mission, once we've been to the Holy Land and reclaimed the Holy Sepulchre, I'll go back and find Blanche."

"Yes, Étienne. Everything will be all right."

"I know I'll find her. That's why God saved her. It's part of His plan that we should love each other and marry."

Étienne reached over and tightly gripped his hand.

"You're part of His plan, too, Abel. I see that now. There would be no crusade without you. It's because of you that I found the courage to go to Saint Denis. You have been with me from the beginning. God wills that you should be at my side as I walk into the holy city of Jerusalem."

"Yes, Étienne, yes!"

They threw their arms around each other and wept. Abel was flooded with a transporting sense of relief and joy. He and Étienne were reconciled. Once again they were like brothers.

♥

They stayed up long into the night, talking about what they would do when they finally arrived in Jerusalem. They would march straight to the Holy Sepulchre, as the Muslims gaped in amazement at the hundreds of Christian children streaming through the gates of the city, their tunics bearing crosses, the *oriflamme* raised over their heads.

"I must find a way to reach deep into the hearts of the Infidels," said Étienne. "I must make them see the light of the Gospels and embrace the one true faith. Abel, this will be the culmination of everything we've worked for."

Though Étienne spoke with the same heartfelt fervor of those early days in Saint Denis, Abel realized he was no longer listening with the same ears. Too much had befallen them since leaving Marseille. Not that Abel had turned away from God. No, not at all. But what he had experienced that night on the deck of the ship, alone under the heavens, had deeply changed him, and he found he could no longer partake of the childlike faith that seemed to come so naturally to Étienne. Étienne did not understand, as he now did, that the totality of God's mystery was too vast for any person, any religion, to grasp. But he still loved Étienne and still clung to the belief that the *Olam Ha-Ba* was at hand.

"Don't worry about whether or not the Saracens embrace Christianity," Abel said reassuringly. "All you need to do is tell them that the Crusade of New Innocents is a crusade of peace, not war, that the Lord loves all His creatures, that He charges us to love one another as He loves us. That is the message Saint Nicholas called you to bring to the people, the reason why so many have followed you this far."

They finally fell into an exhausted sleep. Not long after dawn, they were wakened by a commotion. The sailors were gathered at one end of the deck, hollering and pointing at an approaching ship. There was always the worry that they might encounter pirates, but Abel saw with relief that Will was hailing the vessel in a friendly fashion. The two ships came near to each other, and a plank was placed between them.

Pilgrims streamed up on deck to see what was going on. They watched several men from the other ship come bounding over the plank. As they boarded the ship, Abel could see that they were Saracens. The sight of them made him uneasy. They weren't far from the coast of Africa, and he knew that shipowners like Will Porcus did frequent trade with Saracen vessels. But this ship was loaded only with pilgrims. There was no cargo to trade. Why would Saracens be coming aboard?

More and more of the Saracens came bounding over the plank and onto the ship. Will was talking to the one who appeared to be their captain, pointing to various of the pilgrims as he spoke.

"That one's strong. He'll be a good worker," Abel heard Will say.

The Saracens began to grab the pilgrims one by one. Fear and confusion swept through the group. Some of the children began to cry. Others tried to evade the sailors' grasp.

Étienne ran over to Will.

"What's going on? What's all this about?"

Will ignored him and went on talking to the Saracen captain.

"Didn't I tell you? All light-skinned children. Well worth the price."

"Who are these men?" Étienne cried insistently. "What are they doing here?"

Abel saw all too clearly what was happening. Blanche had been right. They should never have trusted Hugh Ferrous and Will Porcus. The treacherous shipowners had transported them not to Palestine but into the waiting arms of Saracen slave traders.

For a price.

"Where's the girl?" the Saracen captain was saying.

Will shrugged.

"She didn't come."

The captain lashed out at him angrily.

"You promised me a well-born girl!"

"She got away! What could I do about it?"

"Got away?" the Saracen sneered. "I'll bet you've got her tucked away somewhere for yourself."

"No!" Will objected.

They were interrupted by one of the Saracen sailors calling over to the captain.

"Sir? What do we do with this one?"

He held up Little Guinefort, frozen in fear except for his legs, which twisted and kicked helplessly in the air.

The captain grunted in disgust at the sight of the growth on the child's neck.

"We'd have to pay someone to take one as ugly as that," he shouted back, then turned away coldly.

"Get rid of it."

For a moment Abel wasn't sure what the Saracen captain meant. Then he saw the sailor reach for the dagger on his belt, and heard a scream from behind him.

"No!"

Abel turned to see Étienne lunging toward the sailor. There was a fierce struggle and for a moment he managed to wrest Little Guinefort from the sailor's grasp. Then another sailor tried to grab him from behind, knocking both Étienne and the child against the bulwark. There was a strange, uncomprehending look on Little Guinefort's face as he made one last, desperate attempt to grab on to Étienne.

Abel could only look on helplessly as the child tumbled over the side. As terrible as it was, he knew it was a more merciful fate than Little Guinefort would have suffered at the hands of the slave merchants.

❧

CHAPTER 12
The Wanderer
September 1212

NEVER HAD SHE FELT SO ALONE in the world.

As she stood on the wharf, surrounded by crowds of cheering Massillians watching the seven ships sail out of the harbor, the finality of her decision weighed on her like a stone lodged in her heart.

For the first time since that terrible day in Béziers, she'd found people with whom she felt a kinship. After the coldness and cruelty of the nuns, she'd experienced a sense of belonging that she thought she'd never have again. And now she had left behind her beautiful Étienne, her beloved Little Guinefort …

She had willfully cast it all away. How could she have been so foolish?

Where was she to go now? Christian charity would require the nuns to take her back, and there, at least, she'd have food and a bed. But oh, how Sister Saint Delphin would enjoy making her pay for her willfulness. No, she'd rather die than put herself at the mercy of that woman again.

She had put all her trust in that wisp of a dream, which now struck her as the height of folly. She wanted to cry out to her mother in frustration, *Now what? Tell me what to do!* The only thing she could think of was to head back to Languedoc. Perhaps there, somehow, the true nature of her mother's message would be revealed to her. She had nothing else to go on.

The thought of making several days' journey on her own was daunting. The roads were unsafe for a girl traveling alone. She took out Abel's knife. Quickly, before she had a chance to change her mind, she gathered her hair at the back of her neck and cropped it as short as a boy's. She watched the long strands fall to the ground. It felt as if she was divesting herself of the last vestiges of her old life, the person she had been. She took the knife and cut her tunic shorter, so it looked more like a boy's. Then she packed the *vielle* into her satchel, strapped it on her back and set off through the city gates.

She looked at the countryside surrounding Marseille, covered with scrubs of *garrigue* and wild thyme. It was a beautiful day, and there wasn't a living soul in sight. It occurred to her that she had never in her life been completely alone. In Béziers she was always surrounded by family and neighbors. Even in the convent, she'd slept in a room with three novices. At that moment, the world seemed unutterably large to Blanche, and she herself unspeakably small.

❧

Hour by hour she walked through the rolling Provençal hills dotted with lavender, olive groves and vineyards. Yet she was barely aware of her surroundings. To keep walking was the only reality.

After many hours, she realized she needed to rest and found a spot near a stream. She pulled the cloak up to her neck, wrapping it tightly around her shoulders and torso like a swaddled baby, and lay down on the ground. The rumbles in her stomach reminded her she'd had nothing to eat since leaving Marseille.

She dropped off to sleep, clutching Abel's knife.

She awoke the next morning to a gray, overcast sky and set off immediately. Her stomach was still gnawing with hunger. She picked some lamb's-quarter, but it was late in the season and the bitterness of the leaves was overpowering. She noticed some travelers off in the distance and considered asking them for a bite of something to eat. Then she decided it would be best to keep her distance, especially if they were all men. So far she'd had no chance to test how effective her boy's disguise was.

How was she going to get food? She hadn't seen any fruit trees, and with the small yields after the drought, the vineyards had already been picked clean. She hadn't a *denier* to her name. Of course, she'd been constantly hungry the past few weeks, but at least she'd had the company of the other pilgrims to take her mind off the pangs in her stomach.

She couldn't afford to think about it now. She had to conserve what strength she had left to keep going.

She walked and walked. As the hours went by, her only company was the dragonflies that danced around her in abundance. She was grateful for the presence of at least some other living creatures. She noticed one of the dragonflies landing on a leaf just in front of her. To her amazement, its head grew enormous and its eyes shifted from the side of its head to the centre so it could look right at her, which it did, flashing a wide grin. This didn't strike her as the least strange, and she was about to speak to the dragonfly, to ask how it was able to pull off this fine trick, when its head suddenly shrank back to normal size.

Blanche closed her eyes and and shook her head. When she opened them the dragonfly was gone. She realized that her mind was playing tricks on her in her feverish state of hunger.

She resolved to look at nothing but the path ahead.

ॐ

The next day, she saw a tall spire far off in the distance, which she decided had to be the cathedral of Arles. Since yesterday she'd passed a couple of orchards and had managed to scrounge a few shriveled apples that had fallen to the ground. Her belly still burned with hunger. She had to get to Arles before nightfall and find an abbey where she could beg some food.

Dusk was coming on when she approached the outskirts of Arles. The city was ringed with what looked to be a large burial ground. She passed numerous sarcophagi, which lent the place an air of desolation. In fact, the whole town seemed deserted. She thought she heard music, and she could see the glow of torches in the distance. She set off in that direction, passing a large pond, at the edge of which were the vast remains of an ancient stone arena. In a large plaza in the centre of the arena, a fair was going on, and groups of people were dancing to the music of a troupe playing lute, pipe and tabor. Blanche, seeing banners draped around a statue in the square, realized it must have been the feast day of Saint Genesius, the patron of actors, who hailed from Arles.

Usually on feast days, the priests put out food to be freely shared, but it was late in the day and all Blanche saw were scattered crusts of bread and drained jugs of beer. Exhausted, she sat down at the edge of the plaza and took her satchel off her back.

Just then the musicians stopped playing and began packing up to leave. Seeing the dancers' disappointment when the music stopped, she took the *vielle* out of the satchel and began to turn the crank. As the rich drone spread through the square, the Arlesiens turned to see where the curious sound was coming from. She summoned up the energy to play a tune on the melody strings. The dancers quickly moved back into formation and began the vigorous high steps of an *estampie*.

Blanche found that even in her state of extreme hunger and fatigue, she felt energized by the music of the *vielle* and the dancers' joy in it. She played on and on, one tune after another, and when she finally stopped, the dancers turned to her, giddy with exhaustion, and burst into applause. To her surprise, other bystanders joined in, and several in the crowd began to make their way toward her. She wondered if they were going to tell her to stop, because she was a stranger in town, and she feared that someone might see through her disguise.

To her utter amazement, the first man to approach dropped a *denier* in her satchel, which she'd set on the ground in front of her.

"Fine playing, young fellow," he said. "A wonderful end to the feast of Saint Genesius."

She almost said thank-you, then stopped herself and nodded, realizing her girlish voice would give her away.

Several others followed suit. When it was all done, Blanche counted seven *deniers* in her satchel. She was overjoyed. Not only did her disguise fool the Arlesiens, but they thought she was a traveling minstrel. She wouldn't have to beg. She could earn her keep!

She found an inn at the edge of the plaza and greedily consumed a bowl of stew and a glass of beer. The innkeeper told her all the rooms were taken for the fair but said she could sleep out in the barn with the donkeys. Tonight, at least, she wouldn't be sleeping under the stars.

Later, as she fell asleep, the feeling of her full belly was comforting beyond measure. Still, she took care to keep the knife close at hand.

৯

The next morning she woke up refreshed from her night on the soft hay. She took the *deniers* she had left and purchased a loaf of bread and slab of cheese, along with a bowl of milk, which seemed a great luxury. The meal would be enough to see her through another day's walk.

She set off, heading west toward Montpellier. As she walked, she pondered the fact that so far the things she did without thinking — playing the *vielle*, pretending to be mute — turned out to be the very measures she needed to survive on her own. Perhaps her mother truly was watching over her.

She'd been to Montpellier twice with her family when she was small. At the time, there had been many Good Christians living there. They'd stayed with friends of her parents, but Blanche couldn't recall their names. She might remember the house, though, if she could find it again. She didn't think Montpellier had been subject to attacks by the crusading armies, but she knew that many of the believers had gone into hiding, and she had no idea whether any were left in the city. Still, once in Montpellier she could again earn *deniers* by playing the *vielle*, and she'd have no trouble blending into a city of so many people.

She was heading into the flat terrain of the Camargue region. To the south were salt marshes, coastal lagoons and the ancient port where, according to legend, the three Marys — Mary Magdalene, Mary of Bethany and Mary the Mother of God — had landed nearly a thousand years earlier. Again, she saw a few people on the road, but kept to herself. At nightfall she found a small shelter at the edge of a vineyard to bed down in for the night. She fell asleep, hungry again but nothing like the ravenous ache she'd felt before.

The next day she finally spied the walls of Montpellier and made her way through the winding streets to the open market area. Along one side were stalls selling the red woolen goods for which Montpellier was known, and cooking pots made by the coopersmiths of nearby Dufort. Facing the stalls was a line of shops. She found a bakery and bought a loaf with the *denier* she had left from Arles.

Then she found a spot at the edge of the square, took out her *vielle* and began to play. She played all the carols and *estampies* she knew, but quite a while went by before she heard the thud of a coin falling into her satchel. She realized she probably wouldn't do as well as in Arles, where a festival had been going on, putting people in a celebratory mood. Still, as long as she could make enough to feed herself, she'd be all right.

As the day wore on, she made a couple more *deniers*. One woman asked if she could sing, but Blanche shrugged and shook her head. While she played, she watched and listened, wondering if any of the people in the square might be Good Christians. She didn't have much hope of finding the friends whose house she'd stayed in with her family. Even if she could find some other believers, what would she do? She was a complete stranger here.

She played till the sun was low in the sky. The satchel contained only three *deniers* but it was enough to buy a meal. She packed up the *vielle* and set off to find a place to eat. Soon she found a tavern and went in. A trio of men were having a conversation at one end of a long table. Most of the other benches were full, so Blanche went and sat at the other end of the table from the men.

"Hey, lad. Come on over here. Don't sit by yourself."

Blanche pretended not to hear, but the man rapped loudly on the table, startling her. Involuntarily she looked in his direction.

"Come on, lad, slide on down. Don't be shy."

Awkwardly Blanche moved down the bench. She was still uncomfortable in her boy's disguise, and would rather have sat by herself, but she didn't want to do anything to call attention to herself, or get on the bad side of the locals, especially rough-looking fellows like these. The innkeeper came over to the table and set down a tankard of beer in front of her. He asked if she wanted something to eat. She nodded yes.

"Looks like this lad can't talk," said one of the men.

"But he can hear," said the one who had first spoken to her.

So they thought she was mute! She was relieved she wouldn't have to talk. The innkeeper returned with a bowl of soup, which she eagerly began to eat.

"What's that you got there?" one of the men said, pointing to her satchel.

She took out the *vielle* and showed it to them.

"I've seen one of those things before. A music maker, isn't it? Are you a troubadour?"

Blanche nodded.

The man chuckled and turned to his companions.

"A mute troubadour. That's a good one."

"At least he won't get in trouble for spreading heresy," said one of the others, laughing heartily at his own joke.

Blanche smiled weakly.

"Yep," said the first man. "This town has managed to avoid getting a licking from Simon de Montfort, and we intend to keep it that way."

Blanche had heard the nuns speak with reverent admiration of Simon de Montfort, who was the head of the pope's crusading army.

"He cut a bloody swath through Languedoc. Lately he's gotten more selective — just rounds up the Perfects and roasts 'em on a big spit," one of the men was saying.

"They say Count William offered to surrender all the Perfects in Minerve. They knew what Simon was capable of, from all the stories of the Bitterois who escaped there. They didn't want another bloodbath."

Blanche was stunned. If what this man said was true, there were people who had escaped the carnage at Béziers. This was a possibility she had never considered. All the times Sister Saint Delphin taunted her that her parents were burning in hell, she had never really doubted that they were dead.

She was eager to find out more, but she couldn't afford to break her silence. Still, these men seemed to know what they were talking about. Other Bitterois had survived, as she had, and managed to flee to Minerve. Could her mother have been among them? Her sisters? Her father, who had fought the crusaders on the battlements? Was it possible that some

— even all of them — were still alive?

She was afraid to let herself hope. But she had to find out.

She resolved to set out for Minerve at first light tomorrow.

୬

She walked all day, barely stopping a moment to rest. She found reserves of endurance she didn't know she had. Nothing mattered but getting to Minerve. Even as night fell she kept walking until she couldn't see the ground in front of her feet anymore. She lay down under a tree and pulled Abel's cloak over her.

She rose before dawn and resumed her journey. She found herself walking through blackened vineyards, destroyed by the scorching advance of the crusading army. It was almost midday when, looking down into a valley, she spied the river Orb. A shiver of dread ran through her body. Along its banks, only a few miles to the south, was the city of Béziers, or what was left of it. She felt a sharp pang, a longing to go see it for herself, as if by some miracle of miracles her home would still be there and everything as it was — her mother spinning, Perrine bustling around the kitchen, her sisters playing in the courtyard.

She reminded herself that Minerve was her destination, where she dared to hope she might find some remnants of her shattered world.

The last part of the journey was difficult. The town was in the heart of the uplands, situated on a forbidding cliff, and she found the climb rugged and slow. The bells were ringing for vespers prayers as she walked through the town gate, tense with anticipation.

She made her way to the town square and looked around. There were very few people anywhere. The shops and market stalls were closing up for the day. She kept hoping to catch sight of a familiar face, to have someone come up from behind her and cry out, "Blanche — it's you!" But there was no one.

She sat down and took out the *vielle*, determined to see if she could earn a *denier* or two before the day's end. Far from encountering a friendly — let alone familiar — face, she found the inhabitants of Minerve wary, diffident, reluctant to engage with her or even, it seemed, with one another. It was as if an air of melancholy hung over the town.

After two days of playing in the square, she still had nothing to show for her efforts. Which meant that she was in the grip of hunger again. She'd used her last two *deniers* to buy a meal her first night in Minerve, but since then she'd had nothing. Soon she'd have to find an abbey or resort to outright begging, which would be difficult to do without speaking.

And she was longing to speak, to have human contact with someone, anyone. She now understood the terrible isolation Little Guinefort must have felt every waking moment. How strange, she thought, to have become a kindred spirit to the child after abandoning him. Because that was what she felt she'd done, and every time the image of his trusting face came into her mind it caused her pain.

How long could she keep this up? How long would she have to live this life of a lonely wanderer, belonging nowhere?

It was late in the afternoon of her third day in Minerve. She played the *vielle* now for her own distraction, not from any hope of payment. A woman passed by with her two children, one of whom, a girl of about five or six, stopped to listen to Blanche's playing.

"Come, Blanche," the woman said.

Blanche looked at the girl.

"We have the same name," she said.

She realized she'd let her guard down and spoken, which she immediately regretted.

"Blanche, we mustn't linger," the child's mother called impatiently.

"But, *Maman*," the child said cheerfully, "this boy is called Blanche, too."

"Don't be foolish. Blanche is a girl's name."

To Blanche's acute discomfort, the woman came toward her, followed by the other child. She looked quizzically at Blanche.

"Your name may well be Blanche. You're no boy, are you?"

"No, ma'am." Blanche shook her head sheepishly. "I am not."

"What on earth is a girl doing sitting alone here on the town square?"

"I have no choice," said Blanche. "I have nowhere to go." Tears began streaming down her cheeks. "I've had nothing to eat in three days."

To Blanche's shock, the woman leaned over and gently touched her on the shoulder.

"Don't cry, child." The woman reached into her basket, tore off a chunk of still-warm bread and held it out toward Blanche. "Here."

Blanche breathed deeply to fight back the sobs that were welling up in her throat. She took the bread and bit into it. It tasted like the manna that had fallen from heaven to the Israelites. In no time she devoured the whole piece.

She expected that having done her charitable duty, the woman would walk on with her children. Instead she stood where she was, still looking intently at Blanche.

"Thank you," Blanche finally said shyly.

"You are welcome," said the woman. "But it's clear you need more than a slab of bread. You need a proper meal in you."

Before Blanche could say anything to object, the woman grabbed her by the hand and pulled her to stand.

"Come with me," she commanded. Blanche obeyed.

ớ

Hours later, Blanche was still having difficulty believing her good fortune as she sat at the table surrounded by the members of the Domergue family — the children Blanche and Roger, their father, Olivier, and mother, Constance, the woman who'd marched the stunned girl from the square to their warm, comfortable home. They had just finished a meal of wine, bread and cassoulet. To go from near-starvation to gorging on cassoulet! On this night the Domergue house was, to Blanche, an earthly paradise.

Constance and her husband had guessed that Blanche was one of the young pilgrims who had left the crusade. Others before her had passed through the towns and villages of Languedoc on their way home from Marseille. Now, as she scraped the last morsels of beans and sausage into Blanche's bowl, Constance looked at her with concern.

"So, little vagabond, where will you go now that you've left the crusade?"

Blanche stared back at her, uncomprehending.

"Go?"

"Yes. You're on your way home, too. Aren't you?"

"I …" Blanche lowered her eyes and stammered. "I don't have a home."

"What do you mean? You must come from somewhere."

"I do. From Béziers."

Immediately Blanche wished she'd kept quiet. The Domergues had been remarkably kind to her, but she didn't know them. How would they feel about having a child of heretics under their roof?

"Béziers?" Olivier said. "Béziers was burned to the ground by the soldiers from the north."

"I know," Blanche replied quietly. "I was there."

For a moment there was complete silence in the room. Then Constance spoke in a barely audible whisper.

"You escaped?"

Blanche nodded.

"But how …?"

"I lost my mother and sisters on the way to the cathedral. I hid in some wool bales. A knight found me."

"A knight?"

"Yes. He took me to an abbey near Lyon."

"You are the one!" Constance burst out. "Olivier, she's the one! The story is true!"

She looked intently into Blanche's eyes.

"You are the child who was saved. The one they told about. Some who fled Béziers said that during the siege a knight was seen riding out of the city carrying a child on his horse. Many people dismissed the story, but now we see it's true. You are that child. How precious you must be to God, that He would watch over you like that."

The whole time Constance was talking, Blanche looked up at her with a dazed expression, unable to fully take in the truth that was dawning on her. Finally she spoke.

"Then … you are Good Christians?"

"Yes, child."

As Blanche felt herself enveloped in Constance's arms, great heaving sobs rose up in her chest. The force of will that had kept her going since Marseille, the hardships of the crusade, the pain of leaving Étienne and Abel and Little Guinefort, the desolation of her life at the convent, the terror of watching the soldiers' appalling brutality to the Perfect Aimery — all of it came rushing out in a great flood of tears that would not be held back.

Then, suddenly, she pulled away.

"What about the others?" she said urgently.

"Others, child?"

"You say there were some who fled Béziers. My parents could be among them. My father, Bernard d'Alayrac, my mother and my two sisters. Do you know them? Could they be here in Minerve?"

Constance looked at her husband, then gently took Blanche's hand.

"No, child," she said. "There are only a few men who were outside the walls when the siege began. The women and children were all in the cathedral ..." Her voice trailed off.

Now Blanche knew the truth. The thin thread of hope that had drawn her to Minerve was irrevocably cut. Her family was gone. She would never see them in this world again. Yet as she burrowed into Constance's breast, she knew that her terrible isolation had come to an end. She was a lonely wanderer no longer

Finally, she had come home.

She sat up late into the night, long after the little ones had gone to bed, listening to Constance and Olivier recount the terrible siege of Minerve two years earlier. The town had fought back hard against the fierce bombardment of Simon de Montfort's army. But when their water supply ran out, Count William surrendered. Simon promised to spare the lives of anyone who agreed to renounce heresy and swear an oath of loyalty to the pope. The Perfects, several dozen holy men and women who had fled to Minerve from other besieged cities in Languedoc, advised the believers to swear the oath, which they regarded as meaningless. For themselves, they refused to make any such gesture of submission to Rome.

A year to the day after the massacre at Béziers, the Perfect of Minerve were marched down into the canyon below the town. There they were tied to stakes placed in piles of wood and kindling, which were set alight. Afterwards their burned bodies were buried in the mud and rock.

Now Blanche understood the atmosphere of dread she'd felt when she first entered the town. Unlike Béziers, where Catholics loyal to Rome had stood up for and protected their Good Christian neighbors, the people of Minerve had become fearful and suspicious of one another, constantly wondering who among them could be trusted. And yet other towns had suffered even more at the hands of Simon de Montfort. Constance and Olivier told Blanche of his brutal treatment of the inhabitants of Bram, where he ordered seven of the eight Perfects to be blinded, then sent them on a march to Cabaret — led by the one who could still see — as a warning to the people. A year later he laid siege to the town of Lavaur, where he presided over another mass burning of more than four hundred Perfect and ordered Géralda, the last surviving descendant of Blanche de Laurac, to be stoned to death.

Through all of this the Good Christians and their supporters continued to fight back, and after Lavaur the tide finally seemed to be turning in their favor. Simon mounted several campaigns against Toulouse, the great city of Languedoc, but none had succeeded. The count of Toulouse, enraged by the expansionist designs of this noble from the north, vowed to repulse Simon's army and protect all his subjects, Good Christian and Roman loyalist alike. Toulouse became the centre of resistance, in what was no longer just a religious war but a struggle against northern aggression.

When Blanche went to sleep that night, her head was swimming with all she had learned from the Domergues. Even with all she'd witnessed in Béziers, the barbarity stunned and sickened her. She was acutely aware of the vast gulf between her present comfort and the terrible sufferings of the Perfect in Bram, Lavaur and Minerve, the struggle of the believers in Toulouse. Her mother's words haunted her still: *Never forget that you are named for Blanche de Laurac.* Now that holy woman and all of her lineage were gone forever.

The next day Constance took her down into the canyon, where the Good Christians of Minerve made frequent pilgrimages in secret. When she saw the place, with its piles of rubble and charred wood, Blanche finally understood the air of gloom that hung over the town. Yet, in the centre of the ruins, someone had etched the outline of a dove on a large, smooth rock, to honor the souls of the martyred Perfect.

Constance bowed her head in silent prayer, and Blanche followed suit.

On the way back up the canyon, Blanche posed the question she'd been wanting to ask Constance.

"The knight who saved me — does anyone know who he was?"

Constance shook her head.

"No. None of those who fled saw his face."

That night Blanche dreamed again of the Good Knight, of riding through the darkness encircled in his strong arms. This time, without warning, she suddenly found herself at the bottom of a canyon, like the one below Minerve. She called out again and again to the Good Knight to come and rescue her. All she heard was the fading gallop of his horse as he rode off into the distance.

She woke up with tears streaming down her face. She understood now that there was no hope of ever discovering the identity of the Good Knight. He was never going to come back to take her away from the cruelty of the world. She would have to claw her way out of the dark canyon herself.

She never dreamt of him again.

ও

CHAPTER 13
The Palace of Knowledge
October 1212

As the ship approached the harbor of Alexandria, the white marble of the Pharos lighthouse gleamed in the distance. So thrilled were the young pilgrims by the sight of this fabled wonder of the world that for a few moments they forgot the purpose of their arrival in Alexandria. The true misery of their situation came flooding back soon enough: tomorrow they were to be taken to the city's busy slave market.

A rumor ran through the ship that Maschemuth, the governor of Alexandria, planned to buy a whole slew of new slaves to work the grounds of his vast estate, a prospect that sounded appealing enough, given the circumstances. Whatever their fates, they knew their old lives were gone forever. They would never see their families and home villages again. A position in a good house, doing bearable work, where they could live out their days serving a not-unkind master — this was the best any of them could hope for now.

It had taken a while for them to grasp the nature of their situation. After Will Porcus had handed them over to the slave traders, they were surprised that they were treated reasonably well by the Saracens. The rations they received were generous and tasty: stews of lamb and vegetables, flat Arabian bread, even sweet dates and almonds.

"This won't be so bad," they told one another. "We're better off than we were under Will the Pig!"

Abel didn't have the heart to tell them his suspicions — that the real reason for the Saracens' hospitality was to fatten them up for market, like cattle.

For his part, he spent little time worrying about his own fate. His mind was too consumed with self-recrimination for all that had befallen them. How could he have led them into this trap? In hindsight, it all seemed so clear to him now, why the shipowners had been so eager to offer them passage. Blanche had tried to warn him not to trust them, but he had discounted her fears. And he had failed miserably in his pledge to take care of Little Guinefort. The memory of the child's death haunted him daily. He would be eating or speaking to one of the young ones and suddenly in his mind's eye the image would come, as vivid as if it were happening at that moment, of Little Guinefort's limp body bobbing in the waves next to the ship.

Now they were coming into Alexandria, where they would be sold into lives of bondage. It was all his fault. How could he have been such a fool?

He was realizing he'd been willfully blind in so many other ways, too, ever since that day he'd first laid eyes on

Étienne in the square of Notre Dame. How readily he'd convinced himself that he was only going on the crusade for a short time. How casually he'd put aside his schooling, knowing his father's greatest hopes and dreams rested on it. How willfully he'd tossed aside the sacrifices his family had made for him. Now they had no idea where he was, what had become of him. It was as though he'd dropped off the face of the earth. How could he have done this to them? What kind of person was he?

He was powerless to do anything about all that now. At the very least, he decided, he had to stop dishonoring his heritage by hiding who he really was. He wanted to be truthful with Étienne, especially after last night, when, out of the blue, he began to talk of his mother, the subject he'd always avoided. Abel heard, for the first time, how Étienne's mother had gone to join the community of women called the Beguines and left him behind, to be raised by an uncaring uncle.

"You mother is a holy woman," he told Étienne. "Think of how proud she would be of you now."

Instead of finding Abel's words comforting, Étienne visibly winced and turned away.

Abel saw clearly that the wound of her abandonment was as fresh as if it had happened yesterday.

The time had come. He had to tell Étienne that he was a Jew. With their fate so uncertain, he wanted to finally throw off the terrible burden of secrecy that had weighed him down for so long. He would tell Étienne later that night, when they were alone.

As soon as the decision was made, he felt a lightness in his soul. He wondered if this was the kind of relief Christians felt after receiving the sacrament of confession. He no longer feared bringing the truth out into the open, for he knew in his heart that Étienne would forgive him for keeping it a secret. No matter what became of them, their bond would be stronger than ever.

Now the ship was coming into the harbor, past the Pharos lighthouse, and they could see the massive obelisks rising up in the heart of the city. The grandeur of Alexandria was such that it excited even the sailors, who had come into port here countless times before.

"Look!" The Saracens couldn't help pointing out, in their halting French, all the wonders of the port for the benefit of their human cargo.

"Cleopatra's Needle!"

They pointed to the tallest of the obelisks, then indicated another, with what looked like a statue of a reclining lion beside it.

"Pompey's Pillar!"

The pilgrims were herded into skiffs and rowed to shore. It was the first time they'd touched land since leaving Marseille, Abel thought ruefully. How different from the joyous arrival they'd anticipated in Jerusalem.

They were met by a cluster of turbaned men, one of whom conferred with the Saracen captain. Abel surmised that he was the head trader. He turned to his companions and barked an order, and they began to usher the pilgrims off the boats and into groups. The head trader continued to look around quizzically as he talked with the captain. Finally the captain nodded vigorously and pointed toward Abel. Two of the turbaned men came toward him and grabbed him by the arms.

"What are you doing?" Abel cried, knowing they wouldn't answer him. They began pulling him away from the rest of the pilgrims. Étienne watched what was happening with alarm.

"Abel!"

He struggled against their grip.

"Wait! Let me talk to him! Please!"

As the men pulled Abel away, he called out to Étienne.

"Étienne! There is something I must tell you. I am a Jew, Étienne. I wanted to tell you before but I was afraid."

Étienne stood watching him with a look of utter bewilderment, as though he was hearing Abel's words but could make no sense of their meaning.

"Please forgive me, Étienne. I am a Jew and you are a Christian, but we are brothers! I will carry you always in my heart."

‮੭‬

For a day they traveled by camel, then took a small boat down the river Nile to Cairo. Abel had heard of the city and expected it to be smaller than Alexandria. If anything, it was bigger, sprawling and new where Alexandria was ancient. Everywhere he looked he saw slaves laboring to build walls, mosques and other buildings. The grandest of all was the

Citadel, the massive fortress on a hill, where it was visible from every point in the city. Saladin, the great Muslim leader, had initiated construction of the Citadel more than twenty years earlier, and now it was nearly complete.

Abel wondered if this was why he'd been brought to Cairo — to join this throng of laborers working in the unrelenting heat and sun. He wanted to cry out in terror and loneliness. Why him? He could've endured any hardship as long as he still had the companionship of Étienne and the pilgrims. Why had he been wrenched away from the only ones he knew?

He was mystified, then, when the two guards who brought him to Cairo led him through the streets to a palatial building, more modest than the mosques they'd passed but still imposing. Listening to the guards, he thought he heard the name of Malek al-Adil, the current sultan, one of the sons of Saladin. Was this building the palace of Malek al-Adil? If so, why had he been brought here?

He was taken inside and left alone in a large, light-filled rotunda. He was so absorbed in looking at the intricate tile work on the walls that he didn't notice when someone entered the rotunda.

"Oh!" Abel was startled when he turned to see a young man in a white turban and robe standing behind him. The young man smiled as he bowed his head slightly, and Abel saw that he wasn't much older than Abel himself.

"I bid you welcome to Cairo," he said. "My name is Kamil."

Abel was aghast to hear French spoken by someone in this faraway part of the world.

"Yes, I speak your language a bit," said the young man, reading his thoughts. "And some Latin, too. My father wishes that my mastery of these languages should grow, a task for which he looks to you."

"Me?" Abel blurted out. He was still at a complete loss for words. Who was this Kamil, who so far seemed to be treating him more like a guest than a servant? And who spoke of his father as a person of importance, someone Abel should know? Could his father be the sultan himself? Kamil had to be the son of Malek al-Adil and he, Abel, had been brought to Cairo to serve as his teacher!

"My father wishes me to tell you," Kamil went on, "that while you are in his service, you will be permitted to practice your Christian faith."

By now Abel was so flabbergasted that he spoke without thinking.

"I'm not a Christian."

Kamil looked at him with curiosity.

"We were told you arrived with the children on the ships from Marseille."

"I did," Abel replied. "But I'm not one of them. I am a Jew."

"I do not understand. I thought those children were Christians on a pilgrimage."

Haltingly, Abel began to tell the story of how he had been drawn into Étienne's crusade. Kamil listened with great interest, peppering Abel with questions.

"It will not be necessary to hide your faith here," Kamil said when Abel had finished. "Cairo welcomes Jew and Christian alike. My father the sultan says that Muslims, Jews and Christians are all People of the Book, that to obtain a better understanding of other faiths, a man should read the Gospels and the Torah as well as the Qur'an. Now, come and I will show you your place of work."

Abel followed Kamil out of the rotunda and down a long corridor of cool white stone. Kamil paused at a doorway and turned to Abel.

"Here," he said.

Abel expected to see a modest workroom, but was amazed to step into a large, high-ceilinged room, its walls lined with shelves.

"This is my father's library," said Kamil. "It will be at your disposal."

Abel looked around, so stunned that he could barely speak. From floor to ceiling the shelves were lined with books — some with leather-bound spines, some loosely tied scrolls of parchment. There were hundreds of books, more than Abel had ever seen in one place.

"All these books belong to your father?" he finally said.

Kamil nodded.

"Feel free to look around."

Abel spied the works of Plato, Aristotle, Ptolemy. Books he'd only heard about, like the dramas of Euripides, Aristophanes, Seneca the Roman. He reached out and took down a volume from the nearest shelf. On the cover were the words "Qanun" and "Ibn Sina." He recognized it as Avicenna's

Canon of Medicine, the text his father had studied during his training at Montpellier, that he consulted daily in his practice. Avicenna's *Canon* was the only book in their house in Troyes that was not in Hebrew. Seeing it now, Abel was flooded with emotion.

Sensing his emotional state, Kamil spoke quietly.

"My father looks forward to meeting you in a short while. For now I will leave you alone to look through the books as you wish."

Abel nodded a silent thank-you as Kamil withdrew.

Never in his wildest imaginings had he expected to find himself in a situation like this. He had gone from the well of despair to the Palace of Knowledge.

As he roamed farther along the shelves, his eye fell on another book that seemed familiar. He took it down and looked at the cover, on which was inscribed the name of Solomon ben Isaac.

It was a copy of Rashi's commentary on the Torah.

His eyes filled with tears. He was seized by a fierce longing for his family and for Troyes, and the knowledge that they were lost to him forever stirred a grief that was deep beyond words. He clutched the book tightly to his chest, as if doing so could summon up the physical memory of his father's arms around him, carrying him down to the banks of the Seine.

Now begins your study of the Torah, a task that, like this great rushing river, will never end.

CHAPTER 14
The Eighteenth Martyr
December 1212

FOR DAYS THEY WALKED through the endless desert. There were dozens of them, all tethered to one another and to the donkeys. Since leaving Alexandria, they had crossed the delta of the great river Nile. Now they were in burning heat, and the sun beat down on them relentlessly. Sometimes Étienne thought back with grim humor to their march through drought-ridden Provence. What they wouldn't give now to trade that Provençal heat for this desert inferno.

Every so often, when one of the pilgrims stumbled or looked as though he might succumb to the heat, the guards would allow him to ride on one of the donkeys for a little while. It wasn't out of mercy, though. Étienne was pretty certain of that. For some reason, the slave traders wanted to make sure as many of them as possible survived the journey.

Their destination was Baghdad. He'd overheard the guards talking about it.

Why hadn't they been sold at Alexandria with the others? Why were they being taken all the way to Baghdad?

One of the traders in Alexandria had told them, in fractured French, that the idea was to make an example of them. What did that mean?

They saw nothing for days on end, except for the Bedouin caravans that passed every so often, their camels moving slowly and gracefully across the sand. They had stopped at an oasis the day before, and now Étienne found that the memory of the water filled his mind, the only distraction from the vast emptiness around them.

And he sorely needed distracting, not only from his anxiety about what lay ahead but from the memory of those terrible moments back in Alexandria, and the fierce anger and feelings of betrayal they stirred up.

He played the scene over and over in his mind — the men dragging Abel away, his voice echoing across the wharf.

I am a Jew. I am a Jew.

How could such a thing be true? How could he not have even suspected?

How little he'd learned about Abel's life before that day they met in Paris — that he was a student, that he came from Troyes, that he had five sisters. He'd once mentioned that his father was a physician but nothing else about his family. Now Étienne understood why.

They'd been through so much together. But everything they had shared was now tainted by Abel's deceit.

What made it even more painful was the fact that he was now utterly alone. It had been such a comfort to share the burden of leadership with someone. The pilgrims still looked to him as a pillar of strength, as if they were blind to the real situation and still believed, against all evidence, that he had the power of miracle. They prayed to God to rescue them, but Étienne knew in his heart that no miracle awaited them in Baghdad. He didn't want to crush their spirits, so he said nothing.

More than ever, he told himself, he had to hold fast to the belief that he was an instrument of the Divine Will, that all their suffering was for a purpose.

He had only to wait for God to reveal what that purpose was.

&

Their first sight of the city on the river Tigris was the great circular wall that surrounded it. Looming above the top of the wall were massive domed structures whose surfaces reflected blinding rays from the strong desert sun.

As soon as they passed through the city gate they were surrounded by a crush of people, mostly bearded men with a sprinkling of women with veiled faces, shouting and gesticulating. The pilgrims had no idea what was going on, and were terrified by the intense reaction to their arrival. The guards began leading them through the city. Everywhere they went the streets were lined with more onlookers.

Despite their anxieties they couldn't help being amazed by the sheer opulence of Baghdad, its lush gardens and grand temples. As they were paraded through the city, Étienne saw what appeared to be a vast system of walled canals bringing water from the river into the heart of the city, the scale of which far outstripped anything in Europe. He felt as though he'd been transported to some strange land full of things never even imagined. He'd grown up believing that the Muslims were ignorant, barbaric people, but the grandeur of Baghdad put the lie to all that. For a fleeting moment he wished that Abel were at his side, to help him understand the wonders he was seeing.

Finally they arrived at a large open square before an opulent palace. In his exhaustion and disorientation Étienne imagined that he'd been miraculously transported back to the great square of Notre Dame, where he'd been spurned by King Philip Augustus. He shook his head violently to focus his thoughts, telling himself that he had to keep his wits about him and be strong for the pilgrims.

Gathered in the square were hundreds of men with beards and turbans. Their long robes were simple but finer and more varied than the rabble they'd passed in the streets. An imposing figure came forward, surrounded by several attendants. The crowd parted to make room for him as he moved across the square. All the men bowed their heads as he passed, in what Étienne figured was a gesture of respect and veneration. He had to be a holy man, or possibly even the caliph himself.

As the man approached the pilgrims, the guards began shouting and hitting them on the back with sticks, trying to force them to their knees. The ruler raised his hand and the guards let up. He gestured to one of his attendants, who stepped forward and, to Étienne's amazement, began speaking to the pilgrims in impeccable French.

"Listen to my words. Abbasid An-Nasir, caliph of Baghdad, does not force you to your knees, for he knows that glorious and merciful Allah accepts only the worship of those who freely give it. Therefore you are being given the chance to make the *shahadah*, a public declaration of faith: *La ilaha illa Allah!* There is no God but Allah! Whoever among you makes this declaration, you shall be allowed to live here in Baghdad, in freedom and comfort, for the rest of your days. Whoever refuses must face the wrath of Allah."

The attendant pointed to a long brick wall that ran along one side of the square. A line of soldiers stepped forward, carrying bows and arrows. In perfect unison they turned, raised their bows and stood stock-still, aiming their arrows directly at the wall. Ripples of terror coursed through the pilgrims, and some of the young ones began to cry.

In a flash everything became clear to Étienne. They were to be used as weapons in the Muslims' war against Christendom. If word got back to Rome that the children of the Crusade of New Innocents had publicly renounced their faith and proclaimed allegiance to Allah, what a victory it would be for the Infidels! The realization roused him to a smoldering anger, a fierce determination that they would not have their victory. At that moment all his doubts and regrets fell away. He saw that God's divine plan was unfolding as it should. It was for this that he had been called, that they'd been led here to Baghdad. A deep sense of peace came over him. His faith was, at long last, being rewarded, and for that faith, he was ready to give his life.

"Who will be the first to make *shahadah?*" the attendant called out. "*La ilaha illa Allah!*"

No one moved or spoke.

He nodded to the guards, who pulled a boy out of the crowd of pilgrims and brought him before the caliph. Étienne recognized him as Basile, the boy who had abandoned his plow to join the crusade, who had wept over the body of his little brother Léolo in the fields of Provence. The attendant began to badger Basile, urging him to renounce his God. The boy was so frozen with fear that he could barely speak.

After a few moments the caliph made a gesture, and the guards dragged Basile toward the wall. They left him, quivering and sobbing, kneeling at the base of the wall. Without warning, the archers released a volley of arrows, and Basile fell to the ground in a crumpled heap.

There was shocked silence. Then the caliph's attendant spoke up.

"Behold the fate that awaits those who refuse to honor Allah!"

For a long time there was no sound. Then a voice rose up from among the pilgrims, the sweet tones they as recognized as Étienne's, singing the hymn of hope they'd sung countless times before.

> *Veni, Creator Spiritus,*
> *mentes tuorum visita,*
> *imple superna gratia*
> *quae tu creasti pectora.*

Hesitantly, they began joining in. Another boy was pulled from the line and led to stand before the caliph.

> O comforter, to Thee we cry,
> O heavenly gift of God Most High,
> O fount of life and fire of love,
> and sweet anointing from above

A great calm seemed to settle over them as the notes of the hymn wafted through the air. Unlike Basile, the second boy did not quake or cry.

"Repeat after me," the attendant ordered him. "*La ilaha illa Allah!*"

The boy just shook his head firmly. He was led away to the wall, where he stood facing at the archers.

> Far from us drive the foe we dread,
> and grant us Thy peace instead;
> so shall we not, with Thee for guide,
> turn from the path of life aside

As the arrows struck his body, he slumped to the ground. The pilgrims kept on singing. One after another they were brought before the caliph, and one after another they remained steadfast, barely acknowledging the attendant's questions and exhortations and calmly allowed themselves to be led to the wall to face the archers.

Sixteen had been felled by the arrows when a boy was brought forward, quaking even more violently than Basile had. He wept and begged the caliph to spare his life.

"Then embrace glorious and merciful Allah."

"I will, I will!" cried the boy, by now nearly hysterical with fear.

Aghast, the pilgrims abruptly stopped singing.

"*La ilaha illa Allah!*" said the attendant. "Repeat after me in your own tongue, 'There is no God but Allah.'"

"There is no —" began the boy, but he was cut off by a shout from within the pilgrims.

"No!"

The voice was Étienne's. Every head in the square turned to look at him.

"Don't say it or you'll damn your soul to Hell for all eternity!"

"Ignore him!" the attendant commanded. "Speak the words!"

The boy stammered in confusion as Étienne spoke up again.

"Do we want the Infidels to be able to say that even one of the children of the Crusade of New Innocents renounced his faith in Almighty God? Not a single one of us must allow our will to be broken. We must stand together in glorious martyrdom!"

He resumed singing as the boy lowered his head in shame.

"I command you one last time," said the caliph's attendant. "Speak the words, 'There is no God but Allah!'"

The boy shook his head and the guards dragged him over to the wall. Tears streamed down his cheeks, but he was silent as the arrows struck his body and he fell to the ground.

The caliph conferred animatedly with his attendant, then gestured to have Étienne brought before him.

"Caliph An-Nasir sees that you are a young man of great courage. He wishes to make you this offer: if you proclaim your faith in Allah he will not only spare your life but grant you freedom to return to your homeland."

"My freedom? Why?"

"The caliph does not wish to deprive the world of your exceptional qualities. And he knows that you will spread word of his mercy among your fellow Christians."

Étienne was so taken aback that he could hardly speak. For a few fleeting moments, all he could see in his mind's eye was the image of Blanche, the light of the Midsummer Night fire reflected in her eyes. He was gripped by a fierce longing to see her again, and felt the sharp arrows of desire he'd almost forgotten in the terrible hardships of the past few weeks.

He let the impulse pass through him like wind through a reed. Then a thought came to him, the kind of idea that Abel might have come up with. There might be a way, he realized, to turn things around, to play on the caliph's desire to present a good face to Christendom.

"Well?" said the attendant. "What do you say to the caliph's offer?"

"Since the caliph has such high regard for me, I wish to offer him a challenge of my own."

When the attendant translated what Étienne said, ripples of laughter at his arrogance went through the men standing around the caliph. But the ruler himself silenced them, and conferred again with the attendant, who turned back to Étienne.

"Caliph An-Nasir wishes to know the nature of your proposal."

"I will never renounce my beliefs," said Étienne decisively. "So I offer my life in exchange for all the others assembled here. You have seen that our resolve cannot be broken. Our faith in God is as strong as your faith in Allah. So I ask that no more blood be spilled this day. Let my death be the last. Then truly shall word of the caliph's mercy resound throughout Christendom."

As the attendant translated, the caliph regarded Étienne with a penetrating stare. There was silence throughout the square as he deliberated. Finally he turned back to the attendant and conferred briefly. Then he nodded to Étienne.

"The caliph accepts your proposal. After you, the rest live. No more deaths."

"And no more trying to force them to renounce their faith?"

"Agreed."

A cry went up among the pilgrims.

"No, Étienne!"

"Don't do it!"

"We want to be with you in heaven!"

Étienne shook his head firmly.

"It's God's will that you live out your lives among the Infidels, and by your example try to teach them the love and grace of Almighty God."

His plan worked. He was filled with joy. Now he was ready. He offered no resistance as he was led to the wall and turned to face the archers.

The caliph summoned the attendant again. They conferred briefly, after which the attendant told Étienne that in recognition of his bravery, the caliph was allowing him a few moments of prayer. Then he signaled the archers to lower their bows for a moment.

As Étienne closed his eyes, all the faces of his life seemed to scroll past — his father, his infant brother, Uncle Gaston, Brother Ignace, Little Guinefort, Blanche. He saw his mother, smiling and touching his cheek as she did when he was a small boy, before his memory of her was clouded by the pain of her abandonment.

The last face he saw was Abel's, racked with anguish as he begged Étienne's forgiveness back in Alexandria.

We are all the beloved children of God.

As the words of Francis of Assisi echoed through his mind, Étienne felt himself wrapped in a cloak of Divine Love, and all the anger and bitterness he'd been holding in his heart flowed out of him.

Abel, my brother.

He opened his eyes, raised them toward heaven, and began to sing.

Deo Patri sit gloria,
et Filio, qui a mortuis
surrexit, ac Paraclito,
in saeculorum saecula.

He was still singing when the arrow pierced his heart.

CHAPTER 15
The Miracle Child
July 1218

As Blanche looked up at the siege machine towering over her, shivers of anxiety coursed through her body.

The trebuchet, with its twin upright beams and outstretched wooden legs, its tangle of ropes and lumbering sling, looked like some kind of gigantic spider poised to pounce on anything in its path. Until now she'd only seen the trebuchet from a distance, when she delivered food to the men on the battlements. She watched them pull the ropes to lift the weights, load the sling with rocks the size of cabbage heads, then release the weights. She watched the sling shoot out and send the rocks zinging through the air and over the city wall where, with luck, they would strike the bodies of the northern invaders.

Now the sight of the trebuchet brought back that horrific memory, of the time she had been hauling jugs of water up the stairway of one of the corner towers when something came streaking over the wall onto the landing just below her. She assumed, of course, that it was a rock catapulted by one of the enemy's trebuchets. She was shaken by the rough, croaking screams of the men on the battlements, and when she leaned down to get a better look, she realized the object on the landing was a human head, that of a butchered Toulousain soldier.

Her stomach began to churn. She dropped the water jug, smashing it to pieces, and vomited on the stairs.

She'd heard the stories of the terrible burnings at Minerve and Lavaur, of the savagery at Bram, but at that moment on the landing, Blanche saw for herself the true monstrousness of Simon de Montfort. The fierce hatred she'd observed all around her in Toulouse — for a man she herself had never laid eyes on — now took root in her own heart.

Truly, she had become a Toulousaine.

She'd resisted Constance and Olivier when they announced their intention to move to Toulouse. Of course she was infinitely grateful to them for taking her in and making her one of the family. Her days were once again filled with the normal rhythms of life — cooking, marketing, spinning. She took long, solitary walks where she looked down from the wild mountaintop of Minerve at the surrounding valley, secure in the knowledge that a warm, welcoming hearth awaited her at the Domergues'. To be uprooted again after all her wanderings was more than Blanche thought she could bear.

Constance and Olivier were convinced that Minerve was no longer safe for Good Christians. The town was riddled with informers eager to curry favor with Simon's men by exposing neighbors as heretics. In Toulouse, they told her,

Good Christians could walk freely and practice their religion openly, under the protection of their steadfast patron, Count Raymond. Reluctantly, Blanche helped them strip the cozy house, load a wagon and make the trek to Toulouse.

From the very first, she disliked the city intensely. Their new house was cramped and dark, much smaller than the house in Minerve. The sheer size and sprawl of the city overwhelmed her. There was no sense of the countryside nearby, just narrow lanes full of shops, carts, animals and people — anonymous crowds of strangers. The textile district was especially crowded with visitors looking to buy the deep blue woad-dyed woolens for which the city was known.

It was another world from the shrouded, fearful atmosphere of Minerve. Here in Toulouse everything was out in the open. The Perfects freely walked the streets in their black robes giving their blessing, the *melioramentum*, to the believers. Even the Jews of Toulouse defiantly refused to wear the yellow star decreed by the pope three years earlier. Blanche knew she should embrace the openness of spirit that prevailed in the city, but in the early days there she felt morose, inclined to find fault with all kinds of things. These Toulousains even made their cassoulet with mutton, which she regarded as an abomination.

Often at night she was racked with thoughts of Étienne. Every time she walked past the cathedral of Saint Étienne she felt painful reminders of him. What had become of him, of Abel and Little Guinefort and the rest of the pilgrims who had sailed from Marseille that day? What would her life be like now if she'd gone with them?

She had no regrets. She had chosen instead to heed the warning of her mother and found her way to life with a new, loving family. Still, she couldn't stay with the Domergues forever. She was nearly grown up. She still didn't feel she belonged anywhere, certainly not in this city teeming with strangers.

Not long after the move, something happened that, to her consternation, brought her to the attention of the Toulousains. The Domergue children bragged to their new playmates that their adopted older sister was the same child rescued from the Béziers massacre by a knight. The story of the miracle child of Béziers was well known throughout Languedoc, and the rumor that the child might have been living right in their midst spread through the city like wildfire. Blanche began to notice people pointing at her on the street, whispering to their companions. Small children came up to her and asked in wide-eyed wonder, "Is it true? Are you the miracle child of Béziers?" Some of the older people even approached her, asking for strands of hair and nail clippings, as the pilgrims had done for Étienne. At first she shrank away angrily from these requests, which never came from other Good Christians who, of course, gave no importance to relics of the carnal body. Constance urged her to be more understanding and tolerant.

"You can decline their requests, but do it kindly. Their faith is misguided in many ways, but these people mean no insult to you. They honor and respect the Good Christians in their midst, and we must do the same for them."

She tried to follow Constance's advice, but all the attention continued to weigh heavily on her. Being singled out made her feel more alone and apart than ever. Sometimes she wished she could disappear into the great, anonymous mass of humanity that filled the streets of Toulouse. Sometimes she wondered if she should just retire from life altogether, take the *consolamentum* and become a Perfect herself.

Finally, at Constance's urging, she sought the counsel of Rixende Donat, regarded as one of the wisest of the Perfects.

"It's true that you carry a great burden," the holy woman told her. "But it has been given to you and you must not turn away from it. You *are* a miracle child. You were saved for a reason."

"But what?" she asked. "How can I find out what the reason is?"

"You must wait until your purpose is revealed to you. Whatever it is, it is not time for you to turn away from the world. You must go on living fully in it."

After her talk with Rixende, Blanche felt a weight slowly lifting from her heart. Finally, she began to feel a sense of peace, even deeper than that first night in Minerve when she fell, sobbing, into Constance's arms. Her attitude toward the Toulousains slowly changed. She began to see their attention as a special form of acceptance.

She continued to ponder the Perfect's words, especially whether living fully in the world included marrying, having a family. For so long she'd felt she could never love anyone after Étienne, but the pain of losing him was receding. Pierre

Maury, one of the young Toulousains, was showing an interest in her, and more and more she found herself returning his affection.

Of course there was no time to think about such things now, with the city under siege by the crusading army. For several years Toulouse had managed to avoid the crusaders' assaults, due mostly to the skilled machinations of Count Raymond, the lord of Toulouse. But in 1215 Pope Innocent III had formally given Simon de Montfort control over the whole of Languedoc, which enraged the people of Toulouse. It was bad enough their neighboring towns and villages had been besieged and devastated under the guise of combating heresy. This latest move was a land grab, pure and simple. Never would they surrender their sovereignty to the control of the pope and his henchman Simon. Innocent's action had the effect of uniting Toulousains — Good Christians and those loyal to Rome alike — in their mutual hatred of Simon de Montfort, the Wolf of Normandy.

Now Simon's army had set up an encampment, calling it, with his massive arrogance, "New Toulouse," from where he intended to rule, once he'd burned the old city to the ground. The Toulousains had stocked up on arms and provisions. The city walls were fortified, moats dug deeper. The entire population was mobilized — men and women, rich and poor, everyone down to the smallest children joined in the work, wielding picks and shovels. Toulouse was determined, and well prepared for a long siege. The Garonne River ensured an inexhaustible supply of water, and the sheer size of the city made it difficult to surround. After several long and frustrating months, Simon de Montfort's army had made no headway in subduing Toulouse.

In fact, the crusaders' fortunes fell so low that Simon himself narrowly escaped death when his horse drowned in the river. The Toulousains told the story with great relish, but they had no illusions that a retreat was at hand. They well understood that this was a fight to the death, that their own resolve was matched by Simon's grim determination to assert once and for all his domination over the southern kingdom.

The evidence of that came soon enough, though the Toulousains had trouble believing it at first. Their spies brought reports of a massive siege engine that Simon was having constructed, the likes of which had never been seen before. It was a platform carrying hundreds of archers, which would tower over the tallest parapets on the city walls. The structure was supported from underneath and pulled by hundreds more men, sweating and groaning under curtains of animal hides. The spies said it looked like an entire town on the move, like a bad neighbor, and dubbed it the Malvoisine. It was clear from their reports that if Simon managed to move it close enough to the city walls, it would rain arrows down on the city like thunderbolts.

People flocked to the cathedral square to hear Count Raymond's plans. He tried to calm the near-hysteria, proposing that his men launch a secret attack on the Malvoisine and burn it before Simon had a chance to use it. The plan generated heated debate. So many soldiers had been lost already, and most of the remaining men would be needed to carry out the count's plan. The battlements would be left undefended in the meantime. The risk was too great.

Fear spread through the crowd. Arguments broke out, and for the first time since the siege had begun more than a year ago, there was talk of surrender.

A woman's voice cut through the hubbub.

"Let us ask the miracle child what we should do!"

Other voices shouted their agreement.

"Yes! Only a miracle can save us now."

As Blanche reluctantly rose to her feet, there were more murmurs of "miracle child." She had never spoken at a town gathering before, and she nervously cleared her throat before she began.

"I have no miracles to offer you. No miracle came for my mother and sisters and all the others butchered in the cathedral of Saint Mary Magdalene. I don't know why God saw fit to spare my life at Béziers. I refuse to believe that it was only so that I would be slaughtered in Toulouse. I don't want to listen to all this talk of miracles and surrender. We've stood up to the Wolf until now."

"If the men go after Malvoisine and fail, there'll be no one on the battlements. Simon will charge the walls," a man called out.

"We'll be crushed like ants under his heel."

Blanche felt her voice rising in anger.

"What's the matter with all of you? The battlements will not be left undefended. Who has worked tirelessly all these months side by side with the men, rebuilding the walls, stockpiling weapons and supplies? While the men are out attacking the Malvoisine, the women of Toulouse will defend the city!"

She looked around the hall. For a few moments there was a stunned silence. Then a man spoke out.

"Women aren't strong enough to pull the weights on the trebuchets!"

A woman's hand shot up in the midst of the crowd. It was a woman whose husband had been killed in a skirmish only a few days earlier.

"Oh, really? We shall see about that. I, Guillaumette Saint-Cyr, will take my husband's place on the ramparts!"

There was a volley of cries, as more women's hands shot up.

"Count me in!"

"Me too!"

And now, a day later, she found herself on the ramparts with a small corps of Toulousaines, including Guillaumette, her daughters and her aunt, old Esclarmonde, all ready to work the trebuchet under Blanche's command. As she looked at the machine up close for the first time, she wondered how in the world this tiny crew of women could possibly manage to hoist those weights. What had she gotten herself into?

Somehow, they were going to have to make this great spider pounce.

∞

The women hovered on the ramparts in the moonless night. Just before nightfall, young Blanche Domergue showed up, eager to do her part in defending the city. Blanche let her stay awhile but later, toward midnight, she tried to send the girl home.

"Why?" young Blanche objected.

"Because it's late and you're not strong enough to lift these rocks."

"I am, too!"

Huffing and puffing, young Blanche made a show of lifting a huge rock.

"Don't treat me like a baby. You said everyone had to do her part."

Blanche relented, smiling at her obstinacy, but she insisted the girl get some rest, and after a while she drifted off alongside the other women. Now as Blanche listened to the measured breathing of the sleeping women, she felt herself starting to nod off too. Then after a few moments, the flicker of distant torches far out on the plain snapped her awake.

In the predawn light, she could make out what looked like an enormous moving platform draped with animal hides. Even after all the talk, the actual sight of the Malvoisine struck terror in her breast. How was it possible to build something so huge? What use would it be to catapult rocks against it? Burning it to rubble was the only hope. She knew the men wouldn't ambush the Malvoisine until it got closer to the ramparts, where the enemy soldiers would be within striking distance of the trebuchets.

Her heart raced as she watched the great lumbering beast inching its way toward the walls of Toulouse.

She was glad the other women were asleep. She couldn't afford to let them see her fear. She had to fight a powerful instinct to run away, as far as she could get. The worst part was the waiting, not knowing when the battle would begin in earnest, which only gave time for her fear to feed on itself and grow stronger.

For the first time in ages, she thought about her father. She wondered if he'd felt like this during his long wait on the battlements, waiting for the pope's army to strike Béziers. His determination to protect his family and defend his city must have steeled his resolve. And yet his bravery had been in vain. Béziers had fallen, and all its inhabitants had been slaughtered. What use to stay and fight? The naysayers at the town meeting had been right. They were doomed.

She struggled mightily to push these thoughts from her mind. She was joining the company of her father and mother and all the other Good Christians who had fought and died for the survival of the faith. Even if she was to die this day, she would not dishonor their memory.

She heard the women stirring awake. They looked out on the plain.

"There it is!"

"The Malvoisine."

Blanche turned to them with a look of fierce resolve.

"Get more rocks, the heaviest ones you can find."

One of Guillaumette's daughters begin to whimper in fear.

"What's the point? We're helpless against that thing!"

Blanche cut her off sharply.

"Stop crying and do as I say!"

She was shocked at the harshness of her own voice, but it

snapped the girl out of her hysteria. The women moved with swift, quiet resolve, hauling rocks from the nearby stash and piling them at the foot of the trebuchet, while Blanche kept watch out on the plain. After a while she noticed that nothing seemed to be happening. The Malvoisine had become strangely immobile. Then she saw one of the Toulousains appear out of the dim light.

"What's going on?" she whispered.

"Simon and his officers are at mass," he replied. "They won't leave until after the host is consecrated. We'll make our move anytime now. They'll try to breach the walls, so be ready."

"We are."

The soldier headed back into the darkness, and Blanche felt somewhat relieved. If the men succeeded in destroying the Malvoisine, the enemy would pull back without storming the walls. The trebuchets wouldn't be called into service, and the women's mettle wouldn't even be tested.

Suddenly there were shouts. From every direction Toulousains raced out from behind trees and bushes, carrying spears and flaming torches. Within moments, they had set one whole side of the Malvoisine on fire. Archers scrambled down from the platform, and soldiers raced out from underneath the burning hides. Even engulfed in flames the great siege engine continued its inexorable march toward the walls of Toulouse.

Blanche watched the men engaged in fierce hand-to-hand combat at the base of the burning structure, and after a few minutes it appeared as though the Toulousains had managed to bring the Malvoisine to a halt. The relief she felt was short-lived when she saw the crush of enemy soldiers surge toward the walls.

Now it was the women's turn. She shouted at them to hoist the weights.

"Heave!"

The women groaned with the effort of pulling on the ropes.

"Higher!" Blanche shouted. "Higher!"

Finally the sling was ready. "Hold!" she ordered the women as she loaded a large rock.

"Now!"

The women let go, and the rock whipped through the air, landing on the ground just short of the enemy line. Blanche quickly mobilized the women for another attack. This time the rock sent a few of the northern soldiers scurrying but still made no impact. Realizing the big rocks were ineffective, Blanche got a handful of smaller rocks and loaded the sling again. This time the women let out a triumphal whoop as the rocks rained down, felling almost a dozen enemy soldiers. They kept on firing volley after volley, and many of the crusaders began to retreat in panic.

Blanche heard the thunder of galloping horses and saw a line of knights in full armor riding into the melee, carrying banners with crosses and the standard of the French king. One knight led the contingent, barking fierce orders at the fleeing soldiers to turn back and storm the walls. Many of the fleeing soldiers obeyed his command, Blanche saw with dismay. The rout they'd begun was starting to turn around.

If the women were going to keep the enemy away from the city walls, this knight and his contingent would somehow have to be stopped.

In the short time she'd been operating the trebuchet, Blanche had discovered that she could aim her shots with reasonable accuracy by releasing the sling at different angles. She decided to try to aim the missiles at the knights' horses. Even a strike on a hoof would throw the animals off balance and make them pitch their riders. She waited until the knights had ridden almost to the base of the ramparts, just below her. Then she ordered the women to release another volley.

A shower of rocks rained down and struck the flank of one knight's horse. The animal reared up in pain and pitched its rider, trampling him underfoot. As the women hoisted the weights again, Blanche saw that the lead knight had dismounted and was running to the fallen comrade. He knelt down and pulled off the mangled helmet, and the stricken knight's head fell limp in his confrère's arms. He was dead.

The lead knight let out an anguished groan and then, to Blanche's astonishment, he took off his own helmet and planted a tender kiss on the fallen comrade's forehead. Then he raised his eyes toward heaven, moving his lips in prayer.

Blanche looked into the lead knight's face, no longer hidden by his helmet. Even from up on the battlements, she could make out his features, and what she saw stunned her. It was the face of the one she had seen when she was hiding in the wool bale that day in Béziers. The knight who had pulled off his helmet and bade Aimery Golairan to take one last look at a human face.

The face she had vowed never to forget.

I think I hear a bell, said the False Knight on the road
It's ringing you to Hell, said the child as she stood.

There, below her, was the False Knight himself, the devil in disguise, who had brutalized Aimery and ordered the deaths of all in the cathedral of Saint Mary Magdalene. She could see his face etched with anguish. Who was the dead comrade? His son? Brother? Cousin? He had lost a loved one, but that day she had lost everyone in the world who was dear to her.

Now was the time for her to make her move. With his helmet off, his eyes closed in prayer for the soul of his dead comrade, the False Knight was vulnerable. His fellow feeling for another human being would be his downfall. The words she'd said to Abel flashed through her mind: "All religion does is give people an excuse to kill one another." Now the task had fallen to her to kill another human being, in the name of religion.

Calmly, without anger, she loaded a single large rock into the trebuchet, feeling nothing but the sense of a large, impersonal destiny unfolding, beyond all human intent or feeling. The women released the weights, and the rock flew from the sling. Blanche watched it sail through the air in slow motion, as if time itself had slowed down.

She had no doubt where it would land.

The stone struck the False Knight on the temple with tremendous force, shattering his skull. His body crumpled like a sheet of parchment, falling in a heap on top of the body of his friend.

"He's down!"

There was a moment of utter silence as the other knights, the soldiers at the base of the Malvoisine, all froze. Then they dropped their weapons and ran.

"You got him!"

Blanche looked around in bewilderment.

"Who?" she said.

"Simon de Montfort! You got him!"

She could barely make sense of the flood of words uttered by the Toulousain soldiers as they rushed toward her. Bit by bit, she was able to comprehend what they were telling her: The last rock she released from the trebuchet had struck Simon de Montfort, who had dismounted to assist his fallen brother, Guy.

The False Knight, Simon de Montfort himself, had been felled by a blow from a single stone. The battle of Toulouse was over.

A wave of jubilation swept through the city. The sound of bells and drums went on into the night as the people cheered.

"The Wolf is dead!"

Simon de Montfort had met his own avenging angel.

ꙮ

CHAPTER 16

The People of the Book
March 1219

ABEL POKED HIS HEAD OUTSIDE and felt the searing heat of the sun beat down on him. He quickly closed the flap and went back to his reading. He hated living here, in a tent, on the plain outside Damietta, so far from the comforts of the palace and his beloved study. But he had no choice — the sultan needed him at this difficult time, and of course he wanted to be at his friend's side.

Sometimes he felt a tinge of guilt at how accustomed he'd become to palace life, given the lamentable fate of the other crusaders, the hardships and privations they'd endured together. Now he felt thoroughly at home here, and memories of his family and his life back in Troyes were becoming hazier. When he first came to Cairo, he sometimes saw his parents in his mind's eye, their faces etched with sorrow. He imagined the agony they must have felt, wondering what had become of him. Given his position in the sultan's household, it might have been possible for him to send a letter to Troyes, and several times he sat down to compose one. His sense of guilt and shame always got the better of him, and he abandoned the effort.

What use would it be, anyway? Maybe it would be better for his family to believe him dead, for he would never see them again. He could not leave Cairo. As comfortable as his life was now, he was not a free man and never would be.

Yet the life he was living was nothing like the slaves who did humble service in the palace or the backbreaking labor of building the magnificent structures of Cairo. Almost from the first day of his arrival, he'd spent nearly every waking moment in the company of Malek al-Kamil. Officially Abel was Kamil's tutor, but they were so close in age that their relationship was more that of friends than teacher and pupil. They read aloud to each other and spent endless hours talking about philosophy and the sciences.

The only difficulty that arose was Kamil's insistence that Abel stay at his side and perform *salah* with him five times a day. It was his father, Adil, who pointed out the absurdity of expecting a Jew to follow the practices of Islam.

"Judaism has its own prayers," he told his son. "How would you feel reciting the *shema* with your tutor?"

"That would feel very strange," Kamil replied.

"Then you can understand why he is uncomfortable when you ask him to face Mecca and recite prayers in Arabic."

From then on Abel was free to pray and keep *Shabbat* in his own fashion. He recalled how he always had to pray in secret on the crusade. How different these people were from the Christians, how unlike the barbaric "Infidels" they spoke of with such contempt. He remembered the sick feeling in the pit of his stomach when he listened to some of Étienne's sermons, with their unsettling mixture of love and hatred, peace and war. At those times all the contradictory feelings he had never been able to admit to himself, much less to Étienne, came flooding back.

He wondered about Étienne. Was he still alive? Was he a slave toiling in Alexandria? Or was he one of those taken to Baghdad, who had sacrificed their lives rather than declare allegiance to Allah? The story of the eighteen Christian martyrs had traveled throughout the Muslim world. Abel had heard the story from Sultan Malek al-Adil himself.

"What folly of Nasir. The prophet Mohammed, peace be upon him, was very clear that true *shahadah* cannot be extracted by force."

As Abel listened to the account of the youth whose unshakable faith and proud bearing had so impressed Caliph An-Nasir, he found some comfort in the thought that the last of the Baghdad martyrs might well have been Étienne himself.

Still, there was still an ache in his heart, one he thought would never really disappear. As close as he was to Kamil, as much as they shared a communion of minds and interests, he did not love him the way he had loved Étienne.

And things had changed greatly in the year since his father had died and Kamil had become sultan. Abel was still his friend and confidant, but there were no more games or leisurely discussions lasting long into the night. Kamil now had two wives and three children, so he was constantly surrounded by family, attendants, advisers of all sorts. There was a great weight on Kamil's young shoulders, but his upbringing had prepared him for it, and Abel was impressed with how well he bore the mantle of responsibility. Especially now that his army was in the thick of a war to hold back the advance of the Christian crusaders.

That was why they were now camped here, outside the port of Damietta, fighting to wrest back control of the city. Damietta had been captured by the crusaders in a surprise attack the year before. Their plan was to use the city to launch a campaign to conquer Egypt and ultimately regain control of the Holy Land. Abel was appalled by this turn of events. Earlier crusades had at least confined their target to the Holy Land itself. He saw more clearly than ever how different the Crusade of New Innocents was from these thugs occupying Damietta, who seemed far more interested in killing Muslims and conquering their lands than in reclaiming their sacred shrine in Jerusalem.

Still, in many ways the Muslims were no better. Many had the same fierce hatred of Christians, especially after the brutal massacre perpetrated by Richard Coeur-de-Lion during his siege of Acre, to which Saladin's troops had responded with an equally bloody retaliation. Abel tried to convince them of the folly of meeting violence with violence, but his arguments fell on deaf ears, even with Kamil, who was becoming hardened by the prolonged war over Damietta.

With resignation, Abel came to accept that peace between Christians and Muslims was little more than a distant hope. Crusade would be met with *jihad*. The Holy Wars would play themselves out for years to come. But for how long?

The flap of the tent flew open, and Kamil entered, accompanied by several of his officers. Abel sprang to his feet and bowed in greeting. It was something they both accepted, the fact that their relationship was now a more formal one. Kamil almost always broke the tension with a grin and a teasing comment about Abel's endless reading.

Not today, though. Deep in discussion with his soldiers, Kamil only nodded and barely met Abel's gaze. They were conversing in Arabic, which Abel had learned to read, but he still had difficulty with the spoken language. He could see from the anxiety and fatigue etched on the sultan's face that things were not going well.

There was a commotion outside the tent. Fearful of a sneak attack on the camp, Kamil and the officers rushed out to see what was going on, followed by Abel. They were relieved to see the sentries' agitation came only from the sight of a lone figure making his way on foot across the wide stretch of plain between the walls of Damietta and the encampment. As he moved closer, Abel could see the man was a slight figure in a rough brown woolen robe, his head bare but for a ring of hair in the tonsure of a Christian monk.

"What does he think he's doing?" one of the soldiers called out.

"He must be a madman!" said another.

For a time the sentries stood motionless, gaping as the curious figure approached the camp. Finally they sprang into action and raced toward the man, grabbing him by the arms. He made no resistance and allowed his body to go limp, a look of almost preternatural calm on his face. To the sentries' astonishment, he began to speak to them in what sounded at first like sheer babble.

"I come … preach … Sultan al-Kamil."

All the soldiers in earshot exploded in laughter at his mangled Arabic.

"What shall we do with him?" a sentry called out.

One of the officers standing with the sultan began to make a sharp downward motion with his arm, but Kamil swiftly raised his hand to halt the officer's gesture.

"Bring him to me," the sultan said.

The lucky fool had barely escaped having his head cut off, Abel thought. It was likely no more than a temporary reprieve. No Christian foolish enough to walk into the enemy camp would make it out alive.

The sentries dragged the man along the ground and tossed him at the sultan's feet.

"Here's the sultan," said one, to more laughter. "Start preaching!"

The man seemed to have no reaction to the jeers of the soldiers. He lifted his head off the ground but remained on his knees as he opened his mouth to speak again.

"I bow before the great ruler of Cairo," he said, this time in Latin, which elicited more scornful laughter from the soldiers, to whom the words sounded like more gibberish. The sultan eyed the man with curiosity.

"I accept your homage," he said. "But how did you know that the great ruler of Cairo understands the language of the Christians?"

"Latin is not only the tongue of Christians but of all learned people," the man replied. "And it is known everywhere that Sultan Malek al-Kamil is a learned man."

The soldiers continued laughing, but the sultan raised his hand to silence them.

"Since you know me to be a learned man, why preach to me? Surely the great ruler of Cairo has nothing to learn from a Christian cleric, especially one foolish enough to walk into the arms of his enemy."

"Even the mightiest must learn from the lowly," the man said calmly. "That is the teaching of our Lord, Jesus Christ."

Abel watched Kamil's eyes flash with anger. He pulled his sword out of its sheath and raised it over the man's head.

"You dare speak to me of your Jesus, infidel? Tell me why I shouldn't kill you right now."

The man didn't flinch at the sight of the sword but simply lowered his head further.

"I come armed with nothing but words. The wise man does not fear words but listens to discover what knowledge can be gleaned from them."

The sultan was taken aback by the man's response. For a few more moments he held his sword aloft, then put it back in its sheath.

"Fine, Christian," he finally said, to break the tense silence. "I will hear your words. But I warn you: You better be a good talker if you're going to convince me not to kill you."

Kamil gestured to the sentries to bring the man into the tent. Then he turned to Abel.

"Stay by my side," he said. "My Latin may not be up to the job."

As they entered the tent, Abel looked more closely at the Christian. He still saw no sign of fear in the man's eyes. Either he was indeed a madman, or his faith was exceedingly strong.

The officers began to come inside, but Kamil waved them away.

"Leave us alone."

"But sir, what if …" one of the officers started to object but Kamil shook his head.

"We are in no danger from this man," he said firmly. Then he turned to the Christian.

"Who are you? Where do you come from?"

"My name is Francis," the man replied. "I come from the region of Italy called Umbria."

The sultan was about to ask another question, but Abel suddenly broke in. "Which city in Umbria?" he found himself blurting out. Kamil looked at him, annoyed at being interrupted for such a minor detail.

The man turned to Abel.

"Assisi," he said.

Abel gasped out loud.

"You're the one they speak of!"

Kamil looked at him, now more perplexed than annoyed.

"What are you talking about, my friend?"

"This man," said Abel, "is well known among the Christians. They speak of him with great admiration."

"Oh?" said the sultan. "Tell me more."

Abel recounted what he could recall of what Étienne had told him — that Francis was the son of a wealthy merchant, that as a young man he had given away all his possessions and taken a vow of holy poverty. That he had thousands of followers, but refused all their efforts to exalt him, and maintained his humility and simple way of life. That he traveled throughout the Christian world, preaching love and forgiveness, extolling peace rather than the sword.

As he spoke, he watched Francis, who looked slightly embarrassed and a bit impatient, as though he'd listened to similar descriptions of himself many times before, but gave them little importance.

"Francis of Assisi," Abel went on, "is regarded as a great holy man by the Christians, some say the greatest since Jesus Himself."

The sultan turned to Francis, wide-eyed with curiosity.

"So it's true what my learned friend says? That you are a great imam to the Christians?"

"Only God is great," Francis replied. "I am His humble servant."

Kamil nodded thoughtfully.

"Why have you come to me?"

"To bring you the word of God," said Francis.

"I already have the word of Allah," Kamil rejoined. "*La ilaha illa Allah.*"

"And to ask that you put an end to this terrible war," Francis added.

"Your fellow Christians are the ones who started this war, by invading my kingdom. What possible reason would I have to embrace the Christian God, who permits greed and murder in His name?"

Francis nodded solemnly.

"It is true that some Christians are evil. But the Christian faith is not evil."

"So you admit that a person can be Christian and evil at the same time?"

Francis shook his head.

"One may call himself a Christian in this life, but if he does not follow the teachings of Jesus Christ, God will call him to account in the next life."

Kamil posed more questions, trying to break through his visitor's calm demeanor, but at every turn Francis responded in ways that caught the sultan off guard. At times Francis's manner seemed to Abel to border on arrogance. It reminded him of the self-assured bearing of the wealthy boys he'd known back at the University of Paris. He could see that it was that very quality that had allowed Francis to venture into the enemy camp and dare to speak to the sultan as an equal. Abel knew that when he first began preaching, Francis had nearly been declared a heretic by the pope. Now, watching and listening to the friar, Abel could well understand how he could have won over even the likes of the hard-nosed Innocent III.

After a while Kamil relaxed his combative stance a bit.

"Great imam to the Christians that you are, Francis, I think you know that you cannot persuade me to adopt your faith. Nor do I expect you would have much success with my learned Jewish friend," he said, nodding in Abel's direction. "But we are all People of the Book gathered here in this tent. How good it is that Allah has brought us together so that we may talk and listen to one another."

He sent a servant for tea and called musicians into the tent. Three men came in carrying a bent-necked stringed instrument called an *oud*, a *tabla* drum and the wooden reed *ney*, whose sweet sound Abel had become particularly fond of. They played several pieces, after which Francis leaned over and ask to borrow the *oud*.

"You play?" asked the sultan.

"A little," Francis replied. "When I was a boy I learned to play the lute, which is very similar to this. For a time I wanted to become a troubadour. But God had different plans for me."

The musician handed the instrument to him, and Francis began to play, a bit awkwardly at first, but soon his playing became smoother and more melodic. Then, to everyone's surprise, he began to sing in a strong, clear voice.

*Lauderis, domine deus meus, propter omnes
creaturas tuas
et specialiter propter honorabilem fratrem
nostrum solem,
qui diescere facit et nos illuminat per lucem;*

*pulcher est et radians et magni splendoris
et tui, domine, symbolum praefert.*

*Laudetur dominus meus propter sorore
m lunam et stellas,
quas in caelo creavit claras et bellas.*

Francis's song was a hymn of praise for the beauty of all creation, giving thanks to God for Brother Sun and Sister Moon. He went on to sing several more verses, paeans to Brother Fire, Sister Water, Mother Earth, Brother Wind and even Sister Death, who should be embraced without fear because she opens to door to Paradise.

"That is a beautiful prayer," said Kamil when he finished. "Where does it come from?"

"I composed it myself," said Francis, then quickly corrected himself. "I mean, of course, that it was given to me by Almighty God."

Abel was charmed to get this small glimpse of the holy man's ordinary humanity.

"Then it truly can be said that you are God's troubadour," he said.

Francis beamed with delight.

The three men stayed in the tent long into the night, talking of Islam, Christianity and Judaism. At times they debated fiercely, refusing to shy away from their differences. Always they returned to their commonalities, especially their shared belief in the sacred Word. They agreed that there was no reason why the People of the Book should not be able to find a way to live together in peace and mutual understanding.

Toward dawn Francis rose to leave. Kamil tried to give him a bag of gold coins as a parting gift, but he shook his head firmly.

"Coins are to me as pebbles in the road."

"Well, you're the first Christian I've met who wasn't interested in gold," said the sultan. "But if you won't take coins, I have something even better."

Kamil took his sickle-shaped sword from its sheath and held it out to Francis.

"Take this, the sword with which I threatened to kill Francis, the Christian imam. The all-merciful and compassionate Allah willed that we should meet and try to understand one another. Let this sword be a sign of our desire for peace between our people, our hope that no sword is raised in the name of religion again."

Francis took the sword and bowed to Kamil.

"I accept your gift as a memento of our meeting. Thank you, my friend. Go with God."

Than he turned and began the long walk back to Damietta.

As he watched the small brown figure disappear in the haze over the plain, Abel noted ruefully that for all their protestations of peace, neither Francis nor Kamil had made any further mention of the current conflict over Damietta. Perhaps they both sensed that things were already far beyond their control. The Christian commander, Cardinal Pelagius, had steadfastly refused to withdraw, despite Francis's own entreaties. And the sultan would not consider surrendering any part of his realm to the crusaders. This war, at least, would be left to play itself out to its natural end.

Still, Abel felt exhilarated by the events of the past day and night. In Francis of Assisi, he had seen for himself what had inspired Étienne's unshakeable belief in peace and love, and now he felt a renewed sense of hope, a return of the youthful optimism they both felt when they met those years ago in Paris.

A Jew, a Muslim and a Christian had passed the hours speaking of their faiths as equals, without fear or rancor. It was a small glimpse, at least, of the *Olam Ha-Ba*.

Perhaps the only one he would ever have in this life.

৩

CHAPTER 17
The Last Cassoulet
April 1233

Blanche emerged from the kitchen carrying a large pot of cassoulet, its top crust still sizzling from the heat of the fire. She set it down on the table, spooned some into two waiting bowls and held one of them out to the visitor from across the sea.

"I prepared this specially for you," she said. "You can be sure that it contains no pork."

He nodded his thanks, and for a few moments their eyes fixed on each other, as if words were inadequate to express the emotions that passed between them.

They ate a few bites in silence, then Blanche spoke again.

"People were fearful when word came that a man had been spied making his way up the mountain. We get very few visitors here at Montségur, and of course we are wary of strangers. When we went out to look I saw immediately that you were no stranger."

"You recognized me after all these years, even at that distance?"

She nodded.

"Every moment of that summer is as vivid in my mind as if it happened yesterday. How did you know where to find me?"

"I didn't. I asked all around Toulouse, but whenever I mentioned your name, people would clam up, as if I were some kind of spy. I could tell that you were well known to them, that you were a person of considerable importance. One night I was sitting in a tavern when I suddenly heard a voice behind me, whispering in my ear. 'You will find one you seek on Montségur,' the voice said. I turned around quickly but the tavern was crowded and I couldn't tell who had spoken. That was all I had to go on, but it turned out to be enough."

"I'm very glad you found me, old friend. Here. I have something of yours to return."

She reached down and picked up an old, weathered cloak that lay on the bench beside her.

Abel laughed when he saw it.

"You've taken care of it all these years?"

"Yes, very good care," she replied. "There was a time when it was my only companion. And this, too," she said, taking out the knife and handing it to him.

Abel ran his finger along the blade, struggling to compose himself as a flood of emotion welled up in him. What would he find when he finally returned to Troyes? His parents would be well along in age now, if indeed they were still alive. His sisters had all likely married and had children. How could he possibly explain to his family, to the Elders, what he had done all those years ago? How could he convey the full import of all that he'd been through? Would they even want to hear it? Would they welcome him with open arms? Or turn away from him?

For the moment, he needed to put all those fears out of his mind.

"What did you do after we left Marseille?" he asked Blanche.

She told him of her long, lonely journey, how she was taken in by the Domergue family and moved with them to Toulouse, how she fought on the battlements in the great siege, which ended with the defeat of the northern invaders and the death of Simon de Montfort.

"But as you can see, our victory proved to be short-lived. Terrible times have fallen on Languedoc. Our olive groves have been hacked to shreds, our vineyards uprooted. Toulouse lies in ruins, and merchants have been threatened with excommunication if they carry on any trade with the Toulousains. There are still Good Christians holding out in Foix and Albi, but none can afford to practice their faith openly anymore. So more and more of us have retreated here to Montségur. I came here when my children were small. Now they are both nearly grown."

She watched to see his reaction to the revelation that she had a family now.

"So you married a Toulousain, then?"

"Yes, my husband's name is Pierre Maury. He is a Good Christian and a good man. I will take you to meet him, and my son and daughter, in a little while. Now you must tell me of yourself, and how you've spent the years since we last saw each other."

Of course, he knew the question that was uppermost in her mind. He couldn't answer it yet, not until he'd recounted what had happened to the ships that had sailed out of the harbor of Marseille that day. He told her of the terrible shipwreck on the Isle of San Pietro, of the treachery of Will Porcus and Hugh Ferrous, of the slave market at Alexandria, of the pain of being parted from Étienne.

"At least you had no choice," she said. "He must have regarded what I did as a betrayal as great as those shipowners."

Abel shook his head.

"No. I told Étienne that it wasn't your fault, that you tried to get on the ship but got stuck in the crowd on the wharf. So no, he bore no ill feeling toward you. He loved you. You know that."

"Thank you," she said, "for telling a lie that was a mercy for us both. And what of Little Guinefort? Was he taken into slavery too?"

Abel paused a moment.

"No," he said. "Fortunately for Little Guinefort, he took ill early in the voyage and was buried at sea."

Another lie of mercy.

They sat in silence, both keenly aware of the unasked question hanging in the air between them. After a few moments Blanche spoke up.

"And Étienne?"

"I wish I could tell you with certainty of his fate. We never saw each other again after Alexandria. But there is something …"

"What?"

Abel told her the story that had made its way back to Cairo, of the young Christian slaves who had been taken before the caliph of Baghdad, and of the one who, after the slaughter of the seventeen, had challenged the leader to spare the lives of all the rest in exchange for his own.

"They say that the caliph has held to his promise, that to this day, whatever tasks they are engaged in, the Christian slaves of Baghdad are allowed to stop work at noonday, drop to their knees and recite the *Pater Noster*.

"Of course, I have no way of knowing for sure," Abel went on. "But from the time I first heard the story, I believed that the eighteenth martyr was Étienne."

They sat without speaking for a long time. Finally Blanche broke the silence.

"What became of you?"

"I wish I could report a life of heroism, like yours or Étienne's. In truth I have led an embarrassingly comfortable life."

He told her of his studies in the library in Cairo, his friendship with the sultan, of their visit with Francis of Assisi, who had since died and been declared a saint by the Church of Rome.

"Yes," said Blanche with a tinge of bitterness. "Francis, once regarded as a heretic, like the Good Christians, now embraced by the pope and venerated as a saint! Tell me this: if you were a slave, how you were able to return to Europe?"

"The sultan released me from his service because of a dream."

"A dream?"

Abel told her about the recurring dream that had been haunting him for some time.

"I am climbing a mountain. There is a mist at the top, and out of it emerges a woman. I can't see her face, but I feel I know her. I try to scramble the rest of the way up the mountain, but I always wake up before I reach her. When I told Kamil about the dream, all he said was, 'There is no mountain in Cairo.' The next day he informed me that he was freeing me from his service so that I could return to my homeland. At first I refused to leave. For so long I had known no other home but Cairo. I was happy there, Kamil was my friend. But he insisted, saying that I must go seek out the mountain in my dream."

"So, it seems you've learned that dreams sometimes bear messages of importance." She looked him mischievously as she said this, remembering his dismissal of her dream back in Marseille.

"Yes, as you can see."

"Have you been back to Troyes?"

He shook his head.

"Not yet. I long to see my family again, but I'm a bit afraid to go home to Troyes. I don't know what I'll find there. In the Jewish quarter of Toulouse people were wearing yellow stars on their tunics. And I heard that in Paris, the writings of Maimonides were burned in a great public bonfire."

"I'm afraid the times are no kinder to your people than they are to mine."

There was a somber silence between them for a time. Then Blanche spoke up again.

"Have you heard the stories people tell about the summer of 1212? How the flocks of birds and animals followed us as we walked? How clouds of butterflies hovered over our heads?"

Abel shook his head, laughing.

"That's not the half of it," she went on. "Pope Gregory is planning to build a shrine to the crusade of 1212. The *Ecclesia Novorum Innocentium*, they're going to call it. The hypocrisy! After Innocent tried to ban the crusade and fought it tooth and nail!"

"The Church of Rome is nothing if not endlessly resourceful in finding tools to achieve its ends," said Abel.

"Yes," Blanche agreed. "Like the new weapon they're using against us."

"Weapon?"

"An order of priests, the followers of Dominic of Castile. They wear brown robes like Francis's followers, but there the resemblance ends. These Dominicans travel from town to town through Languedoc. They set up quarters in each church and call the townspeople to come and submit to questioning. That's why they're called Inquisitors: supposedly all they do is ask questions."

"What kind of questions?" Abel asked.

"They ask them to give the names of Good Christians hiding out in their town."

Abel shrugged.

"People can just refuse."

Blanche shook her head.

"It's not that simple. The Inquisitors offer people money to name names — using our own tax money to pay for it, of course! If that doesn't work, they threaten them with death — which of course would lead straight to Hell and eternal damnation. So what choice do people have? They give the names of Good Christians to ensure their own survival. These Inquisitors are far more effective opponents than the pope's soldiers ever were. They are an enemy I fear we won't be able to defeat."

She looked at Abel and paused a moment before she resumed speaking.

"Your people are spread throughout the world. Mine are holed up here on this mountaintop halfway between heaven and earth. Yours will prevail. Mine will not. Our way of life will disappear from the face of the earth."

As she said this, a shiver went through Abel's body. He wanted to argue with her, to tell her not to be so pessimistic, but she spoke with such fierce conviction that he knew there was nothing he could say.

She offered him some more cassoulet, but he declined, saying the hearty dish had more than filled him up. She spooned some more into her own bowl. He was fascinated with the way she seemed to have completely turned her attention from the grim subjects of their discussion and was now utterly absorbed in savoring each bite. Soon there was only a single piece of duck left in her bowl.

"This is my last, and I'm glad to be enjoying it with you, my friend."

"What do you mean? Your last what?"

She scooped up the duck into her spoon and looked at him mischievously.

"My last cassoulet."

This was the last bite of animal flesh she would ever consume, she explained. At dawn the next morning, she would receive the *consolamentum* and become a Perfect, a holy woman of the Good Christians.

She put the spoon in her mouth and chewed slowly, with delight, till it was gone.

༄

EPILOGUE
April 1233

HERE ENDS MY CHRONICLE, written here on Montségur, before the events recounted herein begin to fade from my memory. I believe that it was for the purpose of recording this chronicle that God kept me alive through all the travails that befell those who journeyed with me in the summer of 1212.

I have set down these events as truthfully as I am able, drawing from my own experience and, where necessary, from accounts told to me by others.

I do not know what the rest of life holds for me. The one thing I do know is this: there is no hatred in the heart of God.

To whosoever might, in a future time, come across this chronicle and read it, I say this: go, love one another. Do what you can to bring about *Olam Ha-Ba*, the world to come.

As I prepare to begin my journey down the safe mountain, I vow to do the same.

And now, to Troyes …

1212 France

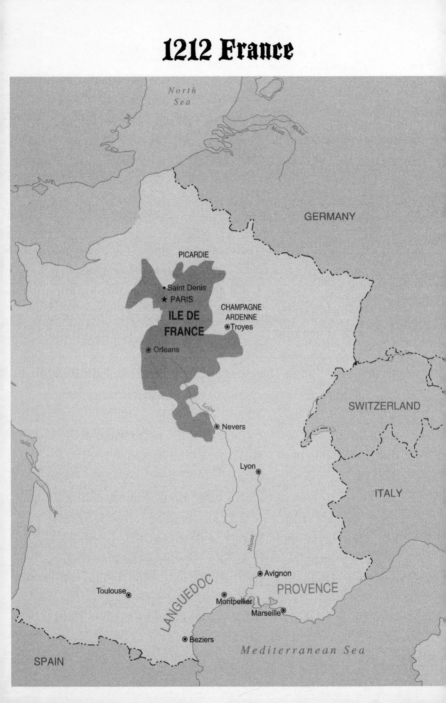

Present-day France

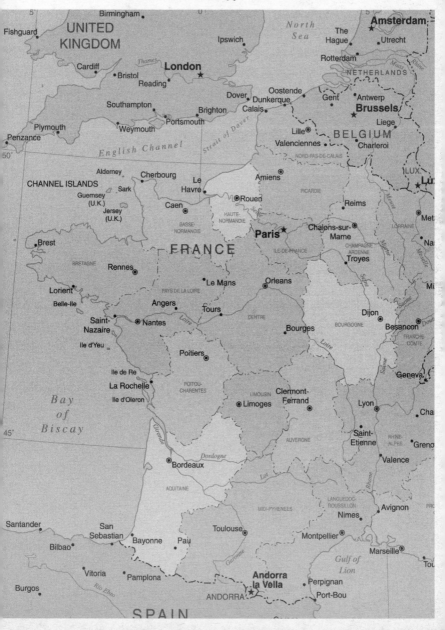

1212 in History

THOUGH MANY OF THE CHARACTERS in this book are my own fictional creations, the story is drawn from real historical events.

The Children's Crusade

In the summer of 1212 a charismatic shepherd boy from Cloyes, a village about seventy miles southwest of Paris, led a march of several thousand children through the countryside south to the port of Marseille. The youth's name was Étienne (Stephen), and he claimed to have received a message from God to mount a crusade to free the Holy Land from Muslim rule. Around the same time, a separate gathering of children departed from Cologne in Germany and trekked over the Alps with the intention of meeting up with the French children. When Pope Innocent III sent word ordering them to disband, most of the German contingent abandoned the quest and returned home. The French group continued on, suffering terrible hardships from a scorching heat wave and drought that destroyed most of that year's crops. They finally reached Marseille, where they were offered free passage to Palestine by two shipping merchants named Will Porcus and Hugh Ferrous.

Nothing was heard of the French children until eighteen years later, when a priest arrived in Europe, claiming to have accompanied the young crusaders on their voyage out of Marseille. He reported that many of the children had died in a shipwreck off the island of Sardinia. Most of the rest had been taken to Egypt, where they were sold into slavery and prostitution. A smaller group had been moved to the city of Baghdad, where eighteen of them were publicly executed for refusing to convert to Islam. Sometime later, at the behest of Pope Gregory IX, a shrine called the Church of the New Innocents was erected on the small Mediterranean island of San Pietro, where bodies from the wrecked ships had washed ashore and been buried. For a couple of centuries the shrine served as a well-used destination for pilgrimages, but in time it was abandoned and left to ruin.

These are the broad outlines of the phenomenon that has come to be known as the Children's Crusade. From a distance of nearly eight centuries, it is difficult to know for certain what actually took place. There are no firsthand accounts of the events of 1212, and the few chronicles that refer to the Children's Crusade were written many years later. Some historians believe that what occurred in 1212 was not really a "crusade" but a mass movement of impoverished, homeless youth, and that later chroniclers put a religious spin on the phenomenon, with the blessing of Church authorities.

The crusading ideal was a powerful force in thirteenth-century life, one that provided the people of the medieval world with a unifying belief system. The freeing of the Holy

Land from Muslim rule was regarded as the great imperative, and participating in a crusade was the highest calling a Christian could aspire to. Beginning in the year 1095, when Pope Urban II proclaimed the First Crusade, a series of military expeditions over the next two centuries attempted to win back control of the holy city of Jerusalem, which had been taken over by Muslim forces. Though the First Crusade was victorious, Jerusalem again fell to the Muslims, and all the subsequent crusades were unsuccessful in winning it back. During the Fifth Crusade in 1219, Christian forces attacked the port city of Damietta in Egypt. During the prolonged siege, Francis of Assisi journeyed alone into the camp of Sultan Malek al-Kamil, where they discussed their respective faiths and shared their hopes for peace and reconciliation.

The Cathars

By the early thirteenth century, the Church had become an institution of great wealth and political power. There was a tremendous gap between the comfortable lives led by the clergy and the vast majority of the population, who lived in acute poverty. A number of groups and movements emerged that were critical of the wealth and earthly power of the Church. Some, like the followers of Francis of Assisi, embraced a life of voluntary poverty.

One of these movements, Catharism, grew particularly strong in the cities and towns of the southern region known as Languedoc. Also known as Albigensians (after Albi, a town near Toulouse), the Cathars were among the sternest critics of the Church's wealth and power. They did not consider themselves a breakaway sect of Christianity, however. They referred to themselves as "Good Christians" and believed they were remaining true to the original message of Jesus Christ. The Cathars had their own equivalent of priests, known as Perfects, so called because they took vows of chastity, abstained from eating meat and, like the followers of Francis, lived lives of voluntary poverty. Women had positions of respect and influence in the Cathar movement and also served as Perfects.

The Church of Rome regarded the Albigensians as heretics. In 1207, Pope Innocent III called for a crusade against them, and prevailed on the French king, Philip Augustus, to use whatever force was necessary to crush the movement. Philip readily agreed, as he was eager to expand his kingdom, and defeating the southern nobles would give him control of their lands. (In the early thirteenth century, France was not a unified country but a collection of independent fiefdoms. Philip Augustus's domain included Paris and the surrounding region known as Île-de-France.)

On July 22, 1209, the king's forces launched a siege of the southern city of Béziers. When the soldiers asked the pope's legate, "How shall we be able to tell the faithful from the heretics?" he is famously reported to have replied, *"Caedite eos. Novit enim Dominus qui sunt eius."* ("Kill them all. God will know his own.") By the end of the day, thousands of men, women and children had been slaughtered and their bodies burned in a mass funeral pyre. The Albigensian crusade continued for more than a decade, with attacks on other southern cities and towns. The Perfects and those who refused to renounce Cathar beliefs were rounded up, tortured and executed in public burnings. The last great resistance of the Cathars took place at the battle of Toulouse in 1218.

According to an eyewitness account of the battle, Simon of Montfort, the leader of the papal forces, was struck and killed by a rock from a trebuchet operated by women. The Cathars' victory at Toulouse was short-lived. Over the next few decades many Cathar believers retreated to the mountain fortress on Montségur, while others continued to practice the faith in secret. In 1233 Pope Gregory IX established the Inquisition for the express purpose of rooting out and eliminating what remained of the Albigensian heresy.

The Cathars were not the only group to suffer religious oppression in Europe. The early years of the thirteenth century also saw a sharp rise in anti-Jewish hatred.

The Jews of Medieval Europe

In the year 70, the Jewish people mounted a revolt against their Roman overlords. When this uprising was crushed and the Temple in Jerusalem destroyed, the Jews were driven from Israel and spread out all over the world, a phenomenon known as the Jewish Diaspora. In the ensuing centuries, many Jews kept alive the idea of one day returning to their homeland, and in the year 1211 a group of three hundred rabbis set out from Europe with their families to help re-establish the Jewish presence in Palestine. For the most part, however, the Jewish people laid down permanent roots in the various countries to which they had migrated. Though there were periods of tension and unease, Jews lived in relative harmony with their Christian and Muslim neighbors.

In Europe, this period of peaceful co-existence came to an abrupt end in the eleventh century, ushering in a period of brutal persecution. During the First Crusade in 1096, there were vicious attacks on Jewish communities in the Rhineland. In 1144 the death of an English youth, William of Norwich, was blamed on the Jews. It was the first in a long line of "blood libels," in which Jews were accused of murdering non-Jews in order to extract blood or body parts for religious, magical or medicinal purposes. From the thirteenth century on, public burnings of the Talmud, one of the principal Jewish texts, became a frequent occurrence throughout Europe. In 1215 Pope Innocent III decreed that all Jews had to wear a yellow star or other identifying marker, a practice that continued until the nineteenth century and was revived by the Nazis in Germany in the years leading up to World War II.

Acknowledgements

Thanks to my loving partner Alec Farquhar, and to my good friends Ellen Murray, Jon Caulfield and Susan Roy, for reading the manuscript at various stages and giving me their honest reactions. I'm grateful to Michel Lefebvre of Youtheatre for his support of the story in its earliest stages. Working with Anne Millyard on this book was a joy. I thank her for her enthusiasm, her support, and her insistence that I keep trying to make it better. I also want to thank Carolyn Wood, Alison Reid and the staff at Second Story Press for their professionalism and hard work. I'm especially grateful for the steadfast support and encouragement that I've received over the years from Margie Wolfe.